HORNET RÍ

Volume 1

STEPHEN JOHNSTON

Happy
Reading!

SRJ

ABOUT THE AUTHOR

Stephen Johnston is the co-owner of SonDad Enterprises LLC, Tabhair Records and Music Publishing LLC, and SonDad Studios. In addition to authoring both the "VR Nana" and "Hornet Rí" series, he has co-produced six music albums along with his father, singer/songwriter Thomas Johnston. Furthermore, Stephen has other literary projects in the works, including a soon-to-be-published graphic novel based on a cartoon series he is creating. Stephen is a graduate of Rider University.

HORNET Rí, VOLUME 1

Cover Art by Stephen Johnston

First published in the United States of America in 2024 by SonDad Enterprises LLC, Whitehouse Station NJ.

Proofreader, Editor: Thomas Johnston

ISBN: 979-8-35096-536-0

Printed by BookBaby, Pennsauken, New Jersey, United States
First Printing: 2024

10 9 8 7 6 5 4 3 2 1

PROLOGUE

It just didn't look right that the grass was so plentiful here. Not just plentiful, but the perfect height. Long enough to show its green but short enough to not be a launch point for any biting pests who might seek opportunity should they spy a gaping pants leg. The young soldier had the ends of his uniform's leggings in order but was keeping his eyes on the grass. He wasn't watching for pests. He was watching the green of the blades, and when one or two of them bent low from a lick of breeze.

All this soldier could do for now was watch. Watch and breathe. The encampment was in an open meadow. Slopes and hills of green all around, with a few clusters of pines here and there. Any flowers were among the higher grasses by those trees. A space like this made this encampment very much exposed. No one, not higher up in the ranks at least, was worried about that; this land was still part of their territory, and where they were heading to was still miles away. The soldier breathed in the air again, then winced and sniffed. Something in this refreshing air made his stomach disagree a bit. Something from the flowers or trees. Or this grass. It smelled sweet.

It had been early in the morning when this battalion had set off from their base. The sun was barely up and there was an awful lot of damp mist lingering above the ground. Around dawn was the most appropriate time to inspect if the enemy line had come any closer. The general had made it a point for the battalion to mount up in both silence and speed when the time came. Weeks of training later and that day was here.

The soldier, Private Liam Pairc, had trained for three whole months at Cliar Base, the army's primary training camp and the sole outpost that protected the city state of Fort Lightwing up north. Endless drills and lectures day by day, learning to use rifle, pistol, cannon, and bayonet on dummies

1

representing the enemy. There was nothing left out about what they were fighting, as the dummies were varied in appearance. Most of the time they were plain scarecrows dressed in the enemy's fearsome burgundy. But at other times, the special non-scarecrow dummies were hung from custom wooden rigs present on the training ground. It was on those days that there was no cannon practice, for the enemies being faced in this scenario could easily fly away from the blast. It would also be foolish to damage these rigs in the process.

These special dummies represented no ordinary soldier, not at all. They represented the enemy's greatest asset; a menacing plague upon the known civilized world. The kind of plague that flew and stung and devastated without mercy. Private Pairc had yet to see this menace, and he figured that day would come soon. Despite his reasonable endurance for the training and basic will in following orders without question, he still felt a twinge of nervousness. And that nervousness was making him sniff the air more, sniff more sweetness, and furthermore make his stomach queasy.

It was midday as he sat outside his tent in the campsite. The cavalry scouts had left more than an hour ago, after they did their part in setting up. Now there was just waiting for them to come back. If the enemy was still far away, they would all keep where they were. But if the enemy was marching forward, they'd all mount up again. They'd also probably leave their sacks and tents where they were, as trying to stop the enemy's further encroachment was priority. But for now, Private Pairc was just facing the tedious lull of a waiting war with his army brothers and sisters (women had an equal stance in this military). He tried to get his mind off his stomach and the sweet air by scanning his eyes across the camp. Far left of him were some of his fellow common soldiers. Three or four of them were staring off in their own directions, not one of them looking right at him. This didn't mean they had any quarrel with him. One of them was already in his tent and napping. Off to the right was one of the battalion's two corporals showing a blonde private how to whittle a piece of branch. The other corporal was part of the

2

scouting party. In the camp's center were three sergeants, the artillerymen, and the archers, all leisurely guarding the supplies. They made sure to keep their tents close to those wagons. The munitions wagon was behind Liam's sitting position on the other end of the campsite. Two more sergeants were guarding that. Further right was the general's tent; it was taller than all the rest and the only one with door flaps. All of the horses were hitched up to posts feet from behind there. The general and his cavalrymen were all inside the tent no doubt discussing the battle to come. The only guard posted was the bugler, and he was occupied with polishing his trumpet. The distinct gold-yellow stripes on his emerald uniform made him look brighter than anyone else outside.

Private Pairc smirked a little, noticing that his queasiness had subsided a bit now. Everyone looked so damn calm! Why shouldn't he? With luck, the scouts would be back and there'd be nothing to worry about. No sooner did he think this that hoofbeats came from the left. The rumbling and trotting of the scouts' horses were slowly bringing everyone else to attention, and within moments the party in the office tent emerged just as the bugler was putting down his rag and readying to sound the arrival. A lieutenant raised a passive hand to stop him. Liam carefully rose to his feet as the head of the scouting party came into his field of vision, breaking off from the other six riders behind him. The corporal checked his horse and brought it to a canter just feet away from the officers. When the camp had been set up, there had been strict instruction to keep a wide path in the center for any rider.

General Reeth, a clean-cut man with a thin drooping mustache, stepped forward as soon as the horse ceased prancing.

"Corporal, report on the enemy's position?" he asked.

"Sir, a hive base has been established fifteen miles from here, west of the entrance to Hornwhite Forest," the corporal answered. "Double Nest. More swarm than troops. Fiabhraceal and Eaglaceal."

"Any of the Ginearals in sight?"

"When we surveyed, none were present, sir."

General Reeth lowered his head and put his finger and thumb to his chin, pondering for a moment.

"That's a strategic position," he muttered aloud. And if it's those swarms, there's a chance *he's* in the field today..." Reeth swung around to his officers.

"No time to fortify our camp, everyone. We need to mount up and fast. They're closer than we expected. Get everyone up and ready!"

"YES SIR!" replied the officers.

It didn't take long for everyone else to get the message (though that one sleeping rifleman needed prodding). Liam checked that his sacks were safe in the tent and retrieved his rifle, bayonet, and canteen. He then ran up to join the others in preparation for flanking. A sergeant was shouting for assistance in hitching up the munitions wagon. Reeth was directing two lieutenants and the bugler to stay behind and watch the camp. Other cavalry men were already prepping their horses. Liam kept an ear out for any superior orders directed at him as he walked. Doing that lessened his stomach trouble even more. No order came to him as he settled in line between an archer and the blonde private. He took a glance at her face to check if she was nervous. She didn't appear to be.

Both rifle and bow infantry were in the center of the marching party, with the munitions wagon following behind them. Reeth rode in front alongside the scouting corporal. The scout force rejoined the rest of the cavalry in bringing up the rear. This march was slower than the morning one, as it would be unwise to alert the enemy as they came close. Subtracting those watching the camp, the battalion comprised of sixteen archers, thirty-two riflemen, twenty cavalrymen including the general and the corporal, and a ten-person munitions crew. They traversed the fields in straight fashion for about the first nine miles. At mile eleven, Reeth signaled a halt. All units stopped in proper fashion. Reeth surveyed the terrain before him and noticed the dirt road off to his left. He silently signaled to the corporal if this led to their destination. The corporal nodded with swift, somber confirmation. Reeth then wheeled his horse around to the others.

"All cavalry, hold this position until signaled. Archers, spilt in two; one with cavalry, the other as infantry rearguard. Infantry, munitions, you're with us. We find a position quick and quiet and draw them out. Let's move!"

Now Liam was feeling the queasiness returning. This was it. They were going right into the thick of it, fighting the bigger enemy. He would have been calmer if they were facing more, as many soldiers called them, wine-coats. But they were facing more stings instead.

Reeth, the infantry, and the munitions slowly made it down the ridge. They went alongside to the right of the road instead of on it. A healthy cluster of tree and bush was just up ahead. The idea was that they'd find a clearing in it and traverse through there. Once Reeth saw the enemy's position for himself, they would all be given the idea of how to set up. The munitions wagon would take the path but they would keep traveling behind until everyone else was ready. The corporal surveyed the foliage ahead with his field scopes. He then found the gap they needed. Reeth directed munitions to stop until infantry went in. He and the corporal took the path themselves while the infantry sergeant led the troops into the wooded opening. Liam and the other riflemen jogged at steady but silent pace.

A minute or two later the whole infantry was through the entrance and in the thick of the woods. Trees were all around them, but there was still plenty of room to move about. It was shady, but beams of sunlight shone all through the canopy. Also, it was impossible to take a step without brushing the ankle high plants on the ground; none of these were fatally harmful but there was still the risk of tripping on the odd branch or creeper.

The infantry sergeant, name of Norv, signaled all units to fall in. He then silently directed one half to find the edge of the woods that ran along the path and follow it while the other half followed him. Liam was in the first half. Four archers and sixteen riflemen resumed their jog. They moved in cluster formation at first, then took on more of a line as they found the path's track. Liam didn't bother to watch the second flank make their own way. Once he saw the path he joined up in the line, third one on the end. This flank then ceased the jog and moved more slowly. All of them were now looking to keep the general in sight. Seconds later, they saw him and the corporal trot past. Their pace quickened a little when he was out of sight. The idea was not to catch up but to keep moving until further orders.

Liam followed the others in front of him for what seemed to be a few more minutes. Then suddenly his fellow private made an abrupt halt. He braked himself and almost collided into her, but his unit's drill sessions at Cliar kept him from doing so. He righted himself just as he was inches from her back. She gave the upward clenched fist signal for silence, still facing forward. Liam mimicked her motion and the two behind him followed suit. One rifleman and one archer. They all kept their fists up for about a minute, no noise around them, save for the clicking of an unseen insect among the brush. Then, the blonde private made a darting motion toward the right. *Regroup and fall in.*

The flanks reassembled at a thicker group of trees that stood at the end of the central path. Reeth and the corporal were positioned on either side of the woods' exit. Both of them were looking to what lay beyond. Norv stepped forward.

"Sir, what is it?"

"Quiet, Sergeant!" Reeth snapped under strained breath. "Take a look but don't stick your head out." Norv carefully walked up to where the corporal's horse was positioned; Reeth was on the left of the forest path's lip. He leaned his face towards the opening and held his breath from what he saw beyond.

6

Down the hill, yards away from their position, was the enemy's camp. Two enormous, round structures were sitting on the grassland below. The buildings were made of thick, grey pulp, and both had a single doorway with no door in the front. Above the doorways and going around the whole of the structures were large, circular holes, and flying and crawling out of those holes were the dreaded true enemies. Hornets, about the size of a full-grown cow but made taller by their own legs, were moving about the nests like a respectable colony. Some were red, while others were the lighter shade of vermillion. Their colors were similar but, as the corporal reported, they were two different types.

Reeth handed Sergeant Norv his field glasses and instructed him to look. Norv started looking for wine-coats moving around the camp. He leaned back as he spotted one, then turned back to the general.

"He's armed, sir. No one in fixed position; mobile perimeter defense. The gun's changed, though."

"What?" Reeth snatched the glasses from Norv and looked for himself. He looked further to the right, as the soldier had gone a further pace by now. Reeth eyed him making his round past the second nest. This was a typical enemy soldier; purple skin instead of earthy tan or something lighter, wine-red uniform instead of green, and pointed ears that were shaped like small axe heads instead of saber tips. A common Shade Elf soldier. Then Reeth noticed the gun. The Shade Elves had long used special firearms that used energy ammunition, as well as their own proficiency for archery. The ammo was provided by special red crystals that were fit into the weapon, and it fired multiple rounds without delay. However, the gunfire only lasted until the crystal's red was completely drained. Then the soldier had to remove the gray crystal, discard it, and load a new one from their ammo bag. In short, it was an effective weapon but it had an enormous drawback in reloading.

The gun this soldier had was different. The rifles that Reeth had seen before had a bulbous stock to them, with the trigger in the back and another handle in the front, as well as a short butt. The crystal was loaded on the top. Reeth saw that this new gun had a longer, curved butt and a thinner stock. The crystal was still in its designated position, but a new component was taking up the space between the handle and the trigger: a round vertical drum of some sort. Its metal was a lighter shade than the rest of the weapon and it had some kind of tiny window on the front of it.

"Orders, sir?" the corporal asked. Reeth lowered his field glasses and turned immediately to him.

"Unload munitions. Wheel one cannon out the edge of the wood and prepare for a warning shot. Find some sturdy ground in the woods for the other two." He then turned to Norv. "Get infantry into position on both sides of this path. Absolute silence."

"Yes, sir!" they said in whispered unison. Sergeant Norv set off back into the foliage. The corporal urged his horse to head up the path.

"And Corporal," said Reeth.

"Yes, sir?"

"Inform the cavalry that they are to file and charge at my signal."

"Very good, sir. I'll inform them right away."

Minutes passed as the corporal gave the order to unload the cannons. The wagon was only about half a yard up the path when he informed them. There were three cannons in stock, with six balls and a barrel of powder for each. The wagon was also large enough to accommodate three small trolleys to carry the ammo and powder. The munitions crew divided into threes, with the lieutenant serving as wagon driver staying put. He watched the left and right teams as they scoped out a position. The middle team had already set off to link up with the general; two men pushing the cannon and the third pulling the trolley. The leader of the right team was the first to scope out an unobstructed path. He got the lieutenant's approval and immediately set off to find the troops up ahead. The trolley bearer went next, while the cannon bearer waited for his partner. The left team found there path soon after, but their cannon bearer was strong enough to push by himself.

Another hour had passed before the other two cannons were wheeled into place. The left and right teams were to wait on firing their shots until the fighting started. The middle cannon, level on the path but still hidden in the trees was already being loaded. General Reeth had backed away, still keeping a visual on the nests' activity below. Nothing unusual, and no sign of the one he was looking for. He then turned back to inspect the cannon's status. All was set and the cannon was aimed straight out toward the clearing. The loaders had backed off, while the third member had his torch ready to light the fuse.

"Fire the warning," Reeth whispered. The fuse was lit and the torchbearer stepped away to the side, looking out to the space between the nests where the ball would fly. The fuse sizzled away for seconds until

POW!

The cannon fired off and the ball shot straight out into the valley. It soared forward with no sign of dropping. There was no silence as it flew; the moment that boom sounded a flurry of buzzing went off down below. Reeth urged his horse forward and looked down at the camp. The hornets were already crawling out of the holes in the nests and taking flight. More shade elves were coming into view and gathering between the two bases. Reeth put away his field glasses and drew his saber.

"Both flanks, prepare for attack!" he called to both sides of the path.

***

Liam's flank had been readying their weapons a little before the warning shot was fired, but only after they hurriedly broken off again and headed back to the left. The archers stepped further back to ready their bows and to let the riflemen get into place. The cannon was in position and so were most of the other soldiers, eight to opposite sides of it. Liam was one of them. He had loaded his standard rifle with no problem, with its five rounds and powder capsule. However, the four in his flank that had longer rifles had taken longer to stuff their rounds in. Norv was commanding the right flank; the left flank's stand-in commander, an archer woman named Xanthe, was looking displeased at their lapse in readiness.

Liam and the other three with short rifles were all crouched on one knee, peeking over the bushes and aiming their guns at the nests. The long-rifles joined them as the boom went off. They all saw for themselves how that noise stirred the hornets out of rhythm and into frenzy. Liam kept his eyes trained on below, the focus subsiding his queasiness. No one dared to say aloud that the enemy was "here and coming". They didn't want to hear it and wouldn't hear it anyway. All of them watched as the hornets were rising into the air, their antennae twitching to pick up the soldiers' scent. Once they picked it up, they would dart right at them, and it'd be imperative to fire before those stingers could make any contact. Liam's flank aimed their rifles up as they minded the twitching.

As anticipated, the hornets picked up the scent. The first to do so were five of the red ones and four of the vermillion. As soon as they were flying over the hill and in range, they pointed their abdomens forward and dove fast. Xanthe had no need to say "fire." The rifles went off, almost in unison. The long ones fired on the tail end of the noise. Two shots hit a vermillion in a front leg, right at the joint. The hornet squealed as it flinched away. That proved a mistake as another bullet went flying into its eye; it spun and dropped to the ground, only feet away from the soldiers' position. Another one, a red, was grazed in the thorax. One of its comrades saw it hit and went to assist moving it away from

10

further bullets. The short rifles had already drawn their hammers back and fired again. At least one more of both colors was shot down. The rest, however, were skilled at dodging, and they pressed their charge. And as they did more were coming over the ridge.

POW! The cannon fired and hit the closest hornet, another red. The ball blew it to pieces, legs and head flying in all directions. The blast galvanized the others into fury. Soon the newer ones were flying straight to the tree line. They didn't even notice the other pow from the right flank's cannon.

"Back away, they're on top of us!" Xanthe called. Liam and the others moved as quickly as they could, though not so easy when crouched on a single knee for a duration. The short rifles faltered back just before the first three or so hornets came into the clearing. Liam's one comrade, the blonde, managed to fire her last round as she moved back. It clipped an antenna. The long rifles had fixed on their bayonets before loading, and now one of them got the chance to use it. He meant to thrust but ended up slashing the injured hornet's wing. It tipped down. Moments later, another flew in and got the soldier in the arm. The stinger was a foot long, retractable, and sported a fierce sheen along its dark brown color. The soldier screamed in pain as it went in.

He wrenched himself off it immediately, but in vain. The hornet's venom would affect him in an instant. Each one had venom of a different power. The one that stung him was a vermillion. He staggered as his vision began to cloud and flit. Shadows began to flash before his eyes, and a deafening assortment of chirps and shrieks filled his hearing. What he saw next, no one could say, but whatever it was made he scream and stiffen in place. The vermillion ones had venom of fear. He stayed in place for a second more, then dropped his gun and began to flee. But given what he was seeing he couldn't know that he was running the wrong way; out of the woods and towards the enemy! He only winced as he was met with the burning shots that hit his chest.

The shots came from the laser blasts fired by a wine-coat's gun. The same one who had been marching the front perimeter. Now he was joined by ten comrades, all armed with the new, queer weapons. Their job was to bring down any green-belly that was making their way down the hill. Didn't matter if that was by initiative or by panic (like that unfortunate one just now).

"Keep ready. More will be coming." Behind these eleven was their commander. This Shade Elf was a female whose hat reflected her rank; like the enemy general, her hat was long brimmed, as opposed to the lower soldiers' kepis. Emblazoned on its front was a unique, immaculate patch; a stylized hornet, that same pale red as the FearStings (Eaglaceal). Only a Ginearal sported this patch. Her name was Fite.

"We hold this line until reinforcements arrive," she ordered. "Let our swarms do their jobs."

As soon as she said that, a cannon ball shot out of the woods and smashed into the top side of the nest to her left. One of Fite's troops then lent his ear to the hill as the others recovered. He heard distant hoofbeats amongst the swarms' buzzing. "Cavalry approaching," he said.

1

Fite was brushing off bits of pulp from the nest as her soldier said those words. She looked to where the cannonball had hit. A good portion of the nest's roof had been blasted away. Some vermillion who evaded the hit were flying out now, angrier than ever. No time to look for casualties. Fite turned her attention back to the hill. The gunfire from the woods had lessened and was replaced with arrows. The hornets could avoid those no problem. Fite looked further up and saw two horsemen emerging from the trees.

"They won't charge yet," she said. "But when they do, be ready." Another Shade Elf came up to Fite's left. He likely had emerged from the damaged nest, as he was shaking a few pulp flecks off himself as he ran up. He wore a uniform similar to hers, only the stylized hornet patch on his hat was a darker red, and this was reflected by the two Fiabhraceal flanking him. His face was hairless but for a pair of muttonchops that matched his long, silver-white hair. He carried a sturdy, single bladed axe on his back. Fite's soldiers saw him and gave a quick salute.

"Ginearal Hurch, are you alright?" one asked.

"No problem," Ginearal Hurch replied casually. "At ease."

"Brother," Fite interjected. "You have to be careful. If you were on that nest's level, you could have been killed."

"You worry too much, sister," Hurch replied. "We're in war. Worry's got no place in war." Fite sighed. Her brother had a point, and his enthusiasm helped drive it home.

"Did you lose a lot up there?" she asked, voice still with a note of concern.

"Just a half dozen. Poor bastards weren't quick enough to deploy or ready at ground level. Still got plenty on hand, though." Hurch then turned to the two hornets beside him. He unslung his axe and used it to point to the battle lines, all while looking them straight in their big dark eyes.

"Position in the center and fly at my signal," he commanded. Both hornets gave a tiny nod and flew off in that direction.

"And our troops in that nest?" Fite was leaving no stone unturned. Hurch swung around and directed her attention to the nest's base, again using his axe as the pointer. Half a dozen Shade Elves, all armed with the laser guns, were forming a firing line.

"Better get yours into place. We'll need them ready. Still no message from his Majesty?"

"Not yet. And we can't get a message in so easy when we're under attack. You know that!"

"Just asked." Fite scowled at her brother. "We know Vez, sis. He's coming soon, and he's gonna bring the hammer down on these fools." Fite sighed again as Hurch walked off to stand with his troops. She then turned to her own and ordered them to link up with the others. Seventeen soldiers readied their weapons. They were all looking up to the hill. Any minute now that cavalry would find a way to assemble and make the charge down. About three each of both Eaglaceal and Fiabhraceal were hovering above them, adding to the watch. Fite took a spot behind her troops. Hurch was feet away to her left, now holding his axe in both hands as if he was ready for a fight right here and now. She took a quick glance at him before turning her attention back to the hill. Another cannon blast came from the right; it flew high and hit nothing. The twangs of the bows and the pops of the rifles were dying down. Mounted figures were emerging from the shade in the trees. They looked to be lining up three at a time. Fite's brows furrowed. Moment of truth on seeing these new guns in action.

General Reeth was keeping off to the side as the cavalry assembled. He looked both forward and back as the bows and gunfire died down. The flank commanders had given their ceasefire order. They'd keep on standby until further notice. No time to check on anyone who'd been stung. Plenty of hornets were over the trees now, looking to hit the infantry when they least expected it, and there were even more out in the field. The corporal was on the other side of the path, monitoring the cavalry as they got into place. The order had been previously given: three at a time. They would spread out once the charge was made. The hill was steep, but their horses were strong enough to handle the descent. All that was needed was patience and coordination. Soon all eighteen cavalrymen were formed in a line of six groups of three. The last four of them had a rearguard archer riding with them. The cannon had been moved away beforehand.

The objective was wiping out the soldiers, and trying not to get stung by the fifty or so hornets that were fortifying the defense. Reeth acknowledged that they were grossly outnumbered. Probably even more so now. But they still had the high ground and mounted forces. The hornets may be the enemy's pride but he had never seen a Shade Elf ever riding one. Had to be the bugs' aggression forbidding it. He allowed himself a brief smile. As frightening as the enemy was, they still had a flaw or two that could be countered.

"The soldiers are lining up, sir," said the corporal. "Only seventeen of them, plus their two commanders. Neither of them has bows or firearms."

"Ride fast and surround them," Reeth ordered. "Anyone who's got an arrow or bullet at the ready shoots to kill."

"YES, SIR!" The cavalry's reply was in unison and in good volume, but a note of hesitation brought on by the environment could not be hidden. Reeth bristled at the uncertainty but didn't make it known. Instead, he promptly mounted his horse and trotted out to the edge of the hill. The hornets saw him emerge and angled their collective sight towards him. Their buzzing's tone became more ominous but they dared not attack. Not yet. Reeth's horse snorted discomfort at the sight of those wretched things. The general checked his reins with both hands, then carefully drew his saber. He spurred his horse to turn slight so he was looking at the force in waiting.

"Forward…CHARGE!" he cried. No sooner did he say that that the reins of the cavalry cracked one by one, and the first row of three began sprinting to the edge and down the hill. In milliseconds, the next row followed. The corporal had already drawn his own sword and was pointing the direction. The latter rows followed suit, and the riding archers were already nocking their arrows.

"Hold!" Fite and Hurch called in unison to their fellow soldiers. They would wait until the horsemen were in range, then open fire. Of course, their flying comrades would certainly do their part beforehand. The hornets above the hill began to dive as soon as all the cavalry's rows were in sight. The archers were the first to notice and aimed their bows at the nearest ones. No need for a firing order here; they let their arrows fly and set to nocking the next one. Three of the shots almost hit their targets. The fourth one flew wild and skewed off to the archer's right, no doubt from being too hasty on the shot.

The hornets' dives made lining up an arrow even harder, as the riders worked to steer their mounts away from them without colliding into each other. The middle rows were already breaking up halfway along the slope, two going left and one going right. Now the corporal, saber still in hand, was making his move. He spurred his horse forward and set down the hill. There was enough room for him to gain speed.

16

General Reeth, on the other hand, sheathed his saber but urged forward to begin his own descent.

Fite and Hurch anticipated that their hornets would cause the lines to waver, even fully break, but neither of them imagined a cavalry force would keep to this much discipline in this rising chaos. Now the riders were beginning to break off formation and as soon as they hit the hill's base, they'd start going around.

"They'll try to encircle us," Fite shouted. "Keep to here but start moving!"

"And fire at will!" added Hurch.

Their troops obeyed and began to form their own ring around the Ginearals, all while moving their feet in place. Their guns were at the ready. By this point, the four enemy archers were still targeting the attacking hornets. All of them were down to less than half a quiver. One of them managed to nick an Eagla's leg, but that hardly phased it. The archer's partner made the better move and shot an antenna with his pistol. All of the cavalrymen had standard issue revolvers, and they were expected to have six bullets in the chamber for a quickdraw situation, especially when riding. The archer took this as a sign to hold his arrows; the others were given verbal instruction over the din of hooves.

Two of the riders with archers turned left, following six other riders. The other pairs kept to center charge, behind two more. The remaining six riders went wide right. By now, hornets were backing towards the Shade Elves to provide defense. They were now beginning to fly over the developing ring.

The left-side riders were moving fast, and the first three or so ignored that they were in enemy range. Sensing to heed Gineral Hurch's words right now, a wine-coat opened fire at the second close horseman. The gun let off a string of red blasts, and those hit the horse right in the foreleg! The horse's scream of pain drowned out the searing and scorching from the impact. It veered back and collided with the horse and rider that were feet behind it. That other rider jumped clear, but the first one wasn't so lucky. He tried to escape but his left foot was caught in the stirrup, and as his horse was tumbling down his free leg was swinging wildly. Another wine-coat saw his chance and fired at the green-belly's leg. Four red-hot blasts hit home, making the rider shout. He made an even louder shout as his other leg was violently sandwiched between the fallen horses. Even at that distance the two wine-coats could hear the resulting crunch of bone. They both fired again on the trapped rider and silenced him in an instant.

The other green-belly had only been in the air for seconds before returning to the ground. He tucked-and-rolled away from the gunfire that took his comrade. But now he was looking to fight back; fully out of the safety position, he had drawn his own pistol and was charging in a rage.

"Filthy corcras!" he screamed as he fired off two shots. He got their attention, but not with the bullets. Corcra was the common slur that the Earth Elves called the Shades. Those two furrowed their brows right away as he said it. Shades didn't mind the wine-coat term because it plainly described their uniforms' color. However, that other word always made them bristle because it had long been a disparaging reference to their purple skin. They saw the shots he fired and dodged, then aimed their guns at him. He thought fast and tumbled off to his left as the blasts came his way. He braked from rolling as soon as the blasts stopped. Unfolding and now on his knees, he aimed his pistol back in the wine-coats' direction. They were now feet away from him, with guns still pointed. He looked at the weapons and was surprised to notice that the crystals were no longer red. The ammo was depleted. He gave a thin smile.

"Tch… stupid corcras," he sneered under his breath as he cocked his pistol.

SCHICK! SCHICK! The two Shades had cocked their machine guns. This was then followed by a quick rattling. The green-belly looked at the guns and noticed the rattling was coming from the strange drums. He then looked up in surprise as the crystals suddenly refilled with glowing red. A quick rove of his eye and he noticed other shades cocking their weapons as they fired on the cavalry. Their guns' crystals made a similar re-red. The noise of hornets and horses made it impossible to hear more rattling, not that it needed to be heard after that first time. Whatever it was, it was the solution to the enemy's reloading problem.

Now it was the Shades' turn to sneer. They refined their aim and were just about to pull the trigger when more buzzing, separate from the hornets in the field, came from the south. All three soldiers turned to see what it was, and they were not alone. The cavalry, other wine-coats, hornets, and both Ginearals turned to the coming sound. The reactions were different, as one could anticipate. The Shades looked relieved. The hornets looked attentive. Fite seemed neutral and Hurch was grinning. The cavalry was horrified.

Approaching from the south were another swarm of hornets. There seemed to be just as many as those present, maybe more. And there were people riding them! That was shocking enough, but what made the battlefield even more silent was the one leading the flight. Instead of a hornet mount, this leader was standing straight, hands behind his back, on top of an unusual contraption. It was a circular deck draped with metallic vulture wings that did not flap. A machine designed for flight, and more so for a leader's flight. Its rider was a Shade Elf, and a tall one at that, but he did not wear the same outfit as his brethren and he had no hair. He wore a full-body suit, the same color as his soldiers' uniforms, but the arms and legs were covered with green, oval-shaped pads. The feet of his suit were both studded with three curved blades; one on the heel and two on the toes. The enameled chest armor he wore was a pale orange with some green inlay. A mask of those same colors was upon the lower half of his face, with a matching horned crown atop his bald head. The mask also had a large, peculiar ornament on it; a carving of a hornet, made from an indeterminate blue material.

The newcomer was now straight above them all, the pink swarm with riders flanking behind him. He looked down on the battlefield with fierce golden irises within the black sclera that all his people shared. He said nothing, but his eyebrows were frowning.

The battlefield was now in a total hush. No one dared to say anything. They didn't need to. Not with him here. With this one present, there was only one thing that could be said in silence.

The Hornet King… name of Vez… had arrived.

2

That green-belly was still on his knees, but now his head was to the sky, his pistol was lowered, and his mouth was agape. He had completely forgotten about the two he was fighting and was staring right up at the imposing figure above. Then he winced for a moment. He thought the dread king up there was looking right back at him, straight in the eye.

Vez was, in truth, looking at the entire terrain rather than one spot. The forces accompanying him, both kinsmen and hornet, were surveying as well. They all looked upon the nests and more closely at the one that was missing a piece of its top. They all looked at the enemy cavalry, what remained of it. All but one of the four archers present were dead, along with their riders and horses. They had all taken hits from the laser guns. Five more men and eight more horses were scattered on the ground. A closer look revealed that only two each were still alive but suffering from the effects of hornet sting. Those had been done by the ones Hurch commanded. The Fiabhraceal, or FeverStings as these dark red ones were called, inflicted a sting that began with searing pain in the impact that quickly turned to a high and insufferable fever. Curable, but only with the right timing. A victim who was too far away from relief could die within three hours.

A group of five FearStings were hovering over the remaining archer and his cavalry partner. Three Shades were four feet to the left, their guns poised. The other riders present were still horsed, but very much outgunned at this point; the one who led the charge was nowhere in sight. One more had actually been unhorsed, as a FearSting took his mount and made it frenzy away in terror. He himself had landed on his knee and was clutching it now. Not one Shade present was a casualty.

Ginearal Fite stepped forward now; she had drawn one of her sabers during the fighting. As she made her way to the king, she half-turned back for a moment and pointed a hold signal to those five units, then resumed looking forward as she approached him. She made no smile, but her eyes were wide enough to suggest that the hope of his arrival had been restored. King Vez noticed her approach. He gave a subtle tap to the platform with both his heels and the wings of his deck made a clicking noise as they lifted up. More rattling emanated from the deck as well as a few hissing puffs of steam from sets of tiny exhausts beneath the wings. The king touched down about three feet from his commander. The deck's wings were pointed up now, making it look like a stylized dais. King Vez stepped off the deck and he walked towards Fite, hands still behind his back. His walk was very much an imposing, regal one, and it kept the silence across the field, save for the flitting of the hornets' wings.

Vez stopped a foot away from Fite. Standing face-to-face made it even more evident that he was taller than her, by about two or three feet. Hurch was standing by about a yard away behind his sister. Despite his preference for wild melee, evidenced by his axe and the tears and stitches on his uniform, he took care to stand to attention in the presence of his ruler. Vez looked out to the battlefield once more, glimpsing Hurch and the other soldiers, then turned back to Fite.

"I see the new guns appear to be a success, Ginearal," he said in a low, firm voice that hinted no weakness.

"Yes, my king," Fite replied. She lowered her head and went to sheath her saber as she began to kneel. The king raised his left hand.

"Belay that knee," he said, a little louder than before. Fite returned to standing but sheathed her saber anyway. "I do not need to always have a physical demonstration of your loyalty, my friend. The results that you and your brother have produced before me now are demonstration enough."

"If you say so, my king." Fite's voice was genuine with duty.

Vez lowered his hand now but did not return it to his back. He wore a large, round gardbrace on his left shoulder. Its inner layer was the same enamel as his chest armor, but the outer layer was burnished steel. The inlay on this was the same blue as his mask's ornament, but it did not gleam the same as that. The gardbrace had a stylized insectoid face embossed on it. The king wore gauntlets on both hands. His left was bronze while his right was that same steel. A pair of curved bronze blades, facing inward and upward, protruded from the right one.

"Are there more enemy forces in the woods?" he asked, looking at the hornets above the trees.

"Yes, your Majesty," Fite answered. "They had rifles and cannons but they've used them up. We are looking for movement, be it retaliation or retreat, and will respond to it accordingly."

"Both of your swarms have done their part. Let Turnie's take it from here."

"As you wish, my ki…" Fite's response was interrupted by a shrill neigh that broke the field's silence. An enemy horse, minus a rider, thundered into view. It was the horse that was stung with fear, and now it had rounded back and was charging towards Hurch. There was another riderless horse following close behind. It was not frazzled like the other one, rather it was determined to catch up to that one. Hurch saw both coming his way and stepped aside. Those two Shades shifted their guns from that one enemy soldier, turned them on the horses and fired immediately at the frightened one. Its terror throes were even louder as the lasers hit its legs and body. The other horse saw its tortured compatriot crash to the ground and turned away, taking a graze in the flank; it saw Fite and Vez in its sights and gave a snort, now making the charge towards them.

The king and his Ginearal saw the horse run at them. Fite wasted no time and ran at it, drawing both her sabers now. She came straight at the beast at first, but then sidestepped just before it could be on top of her. Vez had backed away at the moment Fite began running. He watched unblinking as she slashed at the horse. The sabers made contact one after the other, both somewhere between the foreleg and the neck. They were not deep cuts but blood still spurted from the horse as it fell. Another laser shot met its head for good measure before it hit the ground dead. With his mask on, it was impossible to tell if Vez's expression was either neutral or astonished. Fite was standing bent and bowlegged, catching her breath, arms out wide and sabers pointing in opposite directions. She had succeeded in keeping on her feet and sliding to a resting position after she made the kill.

"RAAHH!" Fite was given no chance to turn around to the shout behind her. The missing corporal had reappeared and managed to surprise her from behind. He gave her a hard kick in the back, making her stumble forward. She dropped one saber while the other was flung out of her hand. Fite then swung around as soon as she heard a blade unsheathing, reflexes kicking in. In a half-kneeling recovery position, she saw the corporal right in front of her, his saber drawn and overhead. Fite snatched up her nearby sword and blocked his swing. The blades were locked for the moment. Fite was at a disadvantage because she was not standing at full height, and if she moved her feet while crouched, he'd have an opening and likely knock her on her back. She eyeballed his footwork. He was keeping steady, no sign of shifting as he leaned forward now, pressing his weight down.

That other green-belly shouted something to the corporal, but he was too fixated on breaking the Ginearal's guard to hear. It sounded like a warning, but it was tuned out.

SCHIIZZZZZZZPOWWWWW!

Something else hit the corporal in the midsection from the side. It was like the laser blasts, but this was just one concentrated hit. Fite witnessed that it also came from her left, and that it was green, not red. The blast was in her view for an instant. It stopped short of exiting the corporal's left hip. His sword pressure faltered and Fite seized the moment, rolling out of the way so he didn't fall on top of her. She planted her saber in a soft part of the ground to keep her balance. She looked at the corporal; he was already dead before his face met his now-upward saber. Fite then noticed the half-cauterized exit wound in the side of his waist. His legs were limp and almost detached from the rest of his body. She turned her head up again to see Vez walking closer to the fallen attacker. His left arm was out and pointed, and his hand appeared to have morphed into a three-prong claw. In truth, he had crossed his middle finger over the index, and the ring finger over the little one. A wisp of green energy sparked from his palm. Fite's face went from surprise to confirmation. *His power*, she thought.

Fite got to her feet and sheathed her saber once more, after wiping the dirt off the blade. She clasped her empty right scabbard and remembered the other one was missing. Before she could say anything, Vez had already bent down and picked it up. He walked around the impaled corporal and presented the sword to her with his other hand. She took it and nodded thanks to him, still at a loss from words in the excitement.

"Even in open space, we should look to mind our surroundings," he said. His tone was firm but guiding.

"Yes, my king."

Vez's ornament gleamed brighter than before, and in no time at all one of the pink hornets broke off from the waiting swarm. It flew over to where the king stood and descended a little. Its rider was firmly standing on its back. The hornet made no sign of protest. This rider was no Shade. She was, in fact, an Earth, and a very tall one as well. Slightly taller than the king. She was barefoot, and her terracotta-hued skin was slightly darker than that of an average Earth. This hue did not conceal her lean but profound muscles. Her uniform was comprised of only a stylized leather corset that was a mix of purple, green, and orange, a tan wool loincloth held up by a light purple belt, and a purple and orange headband that was somehow successfully wrapped around her large, spiked mane of crimson hair. The corset exposed her toned abdominals. In her left hand was a spear that was completely made out of the most refined steel possible. Her name was Turnie Mave.

"Orders, my king?" she asked in a husky brogue. Vez turned and looked up at her to respond.

"Take the SlaveStings into the woods and capture any stragglers that attempt to retreat. Feel free to look for one you might like to take under your wing."

"Thank you, my king. It will be done."

The giant Earth turned back to the pink swarm, still standing. Her mount rose to meet at the others' level without a prompt from her. The Shades under her command looked straight at her as she raised her massive spear.

"Prepare to begin the hunt!" she ordered.

***

The forest line back up the hill was quiet, outside of the hornets buzzing above. Those that made it into the forest line had done their work and regrouped in the sky. The entire right

26

flank had been devastated. Norv had been stung by two hornets, possibly one FearSting and one FeverSting. He was out of sight on the ground. Only four were untouched in the left flank: Liam, Sergeant Xanthe, one long rifle named Gert, and the blonde soldier named Irelan. They were all crouched low and had their backs against the trees, hardly daring to move. They were also spread out. Xanthe was furthest away, leaning on a tree that was more into the woods and away from any gaps in the canopy where the hornets could easily spot her. Gert was more exposed but he was still keeping to the shade. He had no more ammo but his bayonet was on his rifle, and he was prepared to use it. Liam and Irelan were still by the tree line, and they were about seven feet apart from each other. Both of them had managed to reload. Their fallen comrades were scattered all about. Some were already dead because they tripped on something and broke their necks while running in sting-induced fear. One of them was crushed by a weak branch that he didn't see overhead. Others were taking on fever. The fever venom wasn't contagious, so anyone who wasn't stung could carry a victim without protective measures. But given the current situation, no one would be able to move them without being spotted and attacked.

There was no word or sign of General Reeth. It was possible he followed the cavalry down the hill and was killed by either hornets or gunfire. None of the four knew what had transpired down there. The near-silence was palpable, and the survivors' uncertainty was surely growing.

Liam felt his stomach becoming queasy again, even more so than earlier. Try as he might, he couldn't keep his face from mugging discomfort. He uttered a small grunt under his breath. Irelan heard it and signaled him to be quiet. Liam was too focused on the ache to notice her put her finger to her lips.

"Is he stung?" Gert called in a muted tone.

"SHUSH!" Irelan answered through clenched teeth. She then shook her head to further answer his question. Liam grunted again, a notch louder. This time Irelan took a better look at him before responding to his noise. She saw him clutching his stomach hard. An ache like that would prompt vomiting as its only relief, and he looked to be on the verge of doing so. No way would he be able to keep that quiet. She also noticed there was no mark or wound whatsoever, further confirming that he hadn't been stung. The buzzing was in earshot for a moment as another hornet passed over the canopy break. Irelan looked up to watch it. The red hornet didn't even stop to look below. It just flew off back in the direction of the nests. Three more, actually two reds and a vermillion, followed the one that passed. As they flew off, Irelan had managed to inch closer to Liam. Now they were only about three feet from each other. He was still focused on his stomach but he was avoiding making any further noise.

Gert saw his chance to regroup with the other two. He dashed from his hiding position, keeping light on his feet and holding his rifle like a spear with one hand. Sergeant Xanthe kept to her position. She was too focused on the canopy to order Gert to remain in place. He was near those bushes where the other privates sat when a horse's thunder caught all of their attention. It was only one horse, the dark brown steed belonging to their general, but Reeth was not riding it. The horse itself was restless and looked terrified. It bolted up the path and did not stop. The flap of a saddlebag was wide open and something was bouncing inside. A few more gallops and the item finally flung out. Reeth's field glasses dropped to the edge of the path and hit an embedded stone lens first, breaking the right eye lens in an instant. An agitated groan sounded from where the horse emerged. Gert and Irelan then saw General Reeth half-crouched on the path. He appeared to have been limping this way, and the sight of his valuable field tool being cast aside by the horse was enough for him to stop in frustration.

"Lousy scared beast!" he growled at the exiting horse. Gert instantly sprang away from the others and ran up to him.

"Sir, are you alrigh…agh!" The general shoved him away.

"Don't come runnin' up to me out of your position, idiot!" he snapped. Reeth winced from his twisted ankle. He bent down again and clutched it to subside the pain. Gert stumbled back but turned himself quickly and broke his fall by landing his free arm's shoulder on a tree.

"General, what happened?" asked Xanthe.

"Damn horse of mine was a coward all along. Didn't even need a FearSting to poke it. Moment the corporal went down, she started rearing… ngh… got tossed off the seat and my ankle got knotted in the stirrup. Hanging upside down, nearly got dragged. Lost my pistol, too."

Xanthe noticed that Reeth's holster was empty. His saber was still on his person. She then saw a small, fresh cut in the space between his temple and his cheek. Didn't look too serious. It seems that he got that nick upon sheathing his sword when the horse started jumping. Reeth was panting loud as he removed his hands from his ankle and started to look up again.

"We… gotta move. Get back to camp. Maybe take someone or two back with us for treatment. Can't take more."

"Was he there, sir?" The *Rí*… was he in the nests?" Reeth winced. He hated that term for Vez. Saying that gave him authority. Reeth was grimacing more from the pain than from the word, though. And he was afraid. He was not showing so, but it would rise in his voice as he spoke again.

"He came during the fight, like he was waiting for us. And he brought the Wheel."

Now it was Xanthe's turn to wince in speechlessness. Any mention of the Wheel brought instant dread to anyone in the ranks. There were other names for this one (the Slaver, the Brawn, Red Mane, the Traitor), but none of those made anyone pause quite like when the Wheel was uttered. Officer and soldier alike, whether they'd seen her or not, feared the Wheel.

"She's coming. All with Pinks. All *mounted*. And they've all got those new guns." That news even got Liam's attention away from his stomach, but hearing it made him feel another pang and he groaned again.

"What's with him?" Reeth asked. No concern in his voice.

"Don't know, sir," answered Irelan. "Just started having this."

"Had a little ache before we moved out, sir," added Liam. "Wasn't as bad then."

"Never mind when you got it, Private. Can you walk unaided?"

"Not sure, sir."

"I've got him, sir," said Irelan.

"Well make sure you both hustle. Sergeant, you and the other Private pick up whomever you can, but make sure you're certain you can carry them. I don't want to leave anyone behind but I don't want anyone getting sliced by the Wheel either. With her power she'd mow down this whole wood to get to us!"

A new chorus of buzzing was beginning to rise from beyond the trees. It was distant, but Reeth sensed it would not be for long.

"Get moving! Sooner we're on foot, the less chance we get caught by them!" He started to move again but could barely bend his right leg to make the correct motion. Gert got up and went to assist him but the general pushed him back again, not as hard this time. Reeth cast a look of command to Xanthe; to him only a lower officer should help him move and the foot troops look out for each other.

Irelan was getting Liam to his feet and helped sling his rifle over his back. She had already slung hers beforehand. Gert, now feeling indignant from the general's shoving, began trotting ahead of the others. Reeth or Xanthe would normally reprimand such a maneuver, but time was short as the buzzing of the pink swarm sounded closer. Gert didn't bother to check any survivors he passed. One of them was getting to his feet, even though he looked nauseous and his face was red and sweating. Two more were helping each other up, then checked each other for stings. Nothing but a few scratches. They were right by the dead one under the branch. They shuffled a few paces before they faced another foot soldier on the ground. He was hunched to his side and shaking, but his face was neither red nor heated, and they could see that he was biting his lip hard. Both of them reached down to help him up but he flinched. The fear venom had rooted him to that spot.

Only these eight were moving now. With each step they took the swarm sounded closer behind them. How close was different for each of them, relative to their speed and pace. Gert was way ahead of everyone else. The fevered one linked up with the other two. Feet behind them were the general and the sergeant. Liam and Irelan trudged last. Liam had let go of his stomach and was looking ahead, focusing on the returning path. Then the commanders started to quicken their pace. Irelan noticed this and nudged Liam a bit to tell him to move a little faster. Liam grimaced from another pang but did so. The buzzing behind them was even closer now.

They all soon reached the halfway point of the path and Reeth called for a fall in. Gert braked from his jog ahead and pivoted himself back to the group. Reeth then motioned for silence and directed the others to listen carefully to the buzzing. It was still pretty close, but it hadn't sounded any closer.

"They stopped," said one of the three.

"They're waiting for the Wheel to make her move," said Reeth. "And her power makes little noise when it charges up." Liam and the one fevered soldier couldn't look up to react, but everyone else was at attention and dreading that fact.

"We have to get back to camp, get an urgent message to Cliar and Lightwing. Get reinforcements, maybe a Laoch or two." Laochs were the Earths' elite, the heroes of their people. However, there were only fourteen official ones in the entire military; there were supposed to be fifteen. The Wheel was once one of them, which was why she was also called the Traitor.

"You really think they'd waste a Laoch on a small group like us?" Gert remarked. Reeth bristled; this infantryman needed to mind his tone.

"They will!" he barked. "Bringing the Wheel down is priority. Both they and the Fortchiefs all agree on that! Now stop questioning command, boy!" Gert furrowed at the general but somehow thought better than to talk back. Everyone was worn and frightened and needed to get further away. Infighting would make things slower.

"We'll get that one there treated and see what's wrong with this private here once we're in safety," Reeth continued, pointing toward Liam. He then noticed that Irelan was holding up Liam's hand, her thumb running over his left palm and stopping at the base of his pinky finger.

"What is it, Private?"

"Sir, you should look at this."

32

"Wait, wha…?" Liam was becoming more fatigued by his ache. Reeth took a closer look as Irelan turned Liam's hand toward his line of sight. She removed her thumb to reveal a prominent wart on Liam's pinky. The tiny area of skin that it made up formed a bald, elevated, slightly angled shape, surrounded by curved, horizontal lining. That piece of fingerprint was warped.

"How long have you had that, Pri…"

FZZZZZZZZAOOOOOOWWWWW!

An ugly buzzing of a different note tore through the trees, almost directly above the soldiers' heads. Someone shouted for cover and everyone but Irelan and Liam scattered in confusion. The two other soldiers dropped their fevered comrade. He landed flat on his face in the path's dirt. Reeth had almost wrenched Liam's finger off when he sprung for cover. As he was diving off the path, he saw the rapidly spinning, razor-edged disc of blue energy slicing off the treetops. Branches and splinters flew in all directions. Irelan pulled Liam down into a crouch to shield both of their faces from the debris.

The disc lopped through about six more rows of trees before finally dissipating, each strikethrough lessening its force and form. The tops of all those trunks cracking apart echoed through the wood as dust and needles finished settling. The noise of the tops drowned out the audible snap and accompanying shout from Reeth. He had forced himself onto his bad ankle when evading the disc, and now his sprain had become a break. He was doubled up on his side, clutching the broken ankle and gritting his teeth in an attempt to stifle screaming in pain. Xanthe had dived behind a tree that was near him during the evasion and was the first to spot where he lay. She spotted those two other privates and beckoned them over. Gert emerged from a bush but held back for a moment.

Then he decided to help the unconscious private instead. Still armed with his empty rifle he made his way back to the path.

He stopped dead when the foot soldier began to rise from the ground, being lifted up by nothing.

3

The soldier, Private Skylark Reoite, was still completely knocked out. His nose was quite bloody from when the others dropped him, and the blotched streams on his face were dripping as he hung in the air like a rag doll. He was only a few feet off the ground now but was slowly rising. Irelan and Liam were now seeing this and looking just as frozen as Gert. Liam jumped a bit as he saw Skylark going up. Another pang occurred, and the resulting groan was rising in pitch. Before anyone could address it, the buzzing had finally caught up to them. The pink hornet riders, now flying lower in the space that the disc had cleared for them, passed over the survivors below. Many of them, both hornet and Shade, had eyes locked on the group. About a dozen of this air cavalry turned around to face them as they landed to cut of their retreat. Despite these eight being under-armed, the riders were giving an unusual amount of space. Half a dozen more came lower behind the eight but did not land. They too spread themselves out. A few Shades in both groups dismounted from their hornets and fixed their guns on these captives. The crystals in the guns were all at full red.

The wine-coats stepped forward and stopped within reasonable firing range. Nobody in this group was going to escape with a barrage of lasers through their body. Unlike Fite and Hurch, these were all foot soldiers; they had less buttons on their coats and they all wore kepis just like the Earth privates. But since they somehow mastered riding the hornets, it was doubtful that all present were privates themselves, even though none of them wore any embroidered stripe or symbol to indicate this.

They began stepping closer and closer to the Earths. None of them moved, but nearly all looked like they were about to pounce. Private Reoite was still out cold and dangling, only now he was beginning to float off to the right with every step from the soldiers closing in. And with each of those steps followed a louder groan from Private Pairc. After the third one, the Shade that was closest stopped moving and signaled a halt to the two behind him. He looked at Liam, who was very buckled in now.

"What's wrong with him?" the Shade asked. "Shot? Stung?" Irelan looked straight at him but didn't answer. She just gave a hard glare at him, her lips pressing tight.

"Secure their commander!" somebody else shouted. And with that two more Shades jogged towards the spot where Reeth lay. Another one secured the sergeant. Gert and the other two privates now suddenly stiffened, as if something unseen was right behind them. Liam groaned again.

"Answer me!" the first Shade spoke again. "What's wrong with him?!" Irelan kept her glare but spat at him. The spit didn't reach at all. The Shade was still offended by the response and aimed his gun right at her. Irelan gripped Liam tight.

"Ngh…" A bit of static came into view as Liam uttered pain once more. The Shade noticed it and leaned in.

"What was that?!" he demanded louder. Irelan didn't spit again but gripped Liam even tighter.

"Ngggh!" More static.

"Last chance!" the rider shouted. "Tell me what's wrong with him or I shoot you both!"

"NGGGGGGGHHHH!!"

With that loudest grimace of pain came more than just static. A whole branching surge of electricity gathered around the cringing private. He curled up more and fast, trying to pull himself free of Irelan's grip. The gritting turned to a scream, and with his "GGGHHHAAAAA" the statics transformed into a bubble. A wide, fast-expanding bubble that knocked Irelan's hold right off of him. It did even more than that. The bubble expanded even further, and it knocked down all Earths, Shades, and hornets in its reach on both sides of the forest path. In truth, it wasn't a bubble at all but a field. An electrical force field.

The field's static and expanse sent everyone else sprawling. Its charges clipped many leaves and branches and even ripped out a sapling that was feet away. The field also exposed the enemy's forces that were present but unseen. More hornets -two dozen of them- not pink but clear of any color, as if they were made of the purest sea glass. They were present this whole time but invisible. And now the field had unveiled them as it blasted them aside.

The field expanded quite wide but dissipated faster than the disk. It finished trimming off the splinters on the broken trees but did not move farther than that. Liam had stopped screaming and now felt a moment of relief. He swayed his head a little as he began to feel dizzy again. He gulped and without further warning, vomited off to the side. There was ringing in his ears now and everything seemed a little blurry; he was in such a haze now that he didn't notice another hornet rider slowly land far behind him. He teetered in a sitting position a little more before passing out altogether.

***

Back out in the meadow, a baggage train had arrived. This had traveled slowly behind Turnie Mave's reinforcements and remained out of sight until the battle was truly finished. Vez had returned to his platform and was overseeing his troops and swarms taking the spoils to it. There were five different wagons in the train, four of which were pulled by horse teams. The fifth one was actually a wheelless litter, carried by its handles by four pink hornets and by ropes held by four clear hornets. The litter itself was made of the same pulp material as the nests, only it had windows and coach doors installed. It kept a good distance behind the others as they circled and stopped on the crest of the hill.

The FearStings were busy lifting the dead cavalry horses to the third wagon, a caged munitions cart much like the one the enemy brought but much older looking. They piled them up one at a time. The wagon bounced as the carcasses were dropped in. In minutes it was loaded and then Fite gave the driver an order. Soon the wagon started on its way while the others stayed put.

Next to load up was the fourth wagon, a large wooden crop cart reserved for the wounded and fevered prisoners. Both FearStings and FeverStings went about collecting these. A Shade medic was present. The driver here was assisting him in unloading three tubs of ice water and a crate of laundered rags. The hornets gently placed the Earth soldiers by the wagon rather than dropping them in. Hurch directed a FeverSting to place one soldier to the closest tub.

For now, it seemed this cleanup was in working order. Vez turned away to look back at the forest route the enemy came from. What happened back there was too far away for him to have witnessed, but he did hear the muffled commotion, discharge, and some snapping of the trees before all then went silent. He hoped nothing had happened to his hunter Ginearal. He then noticed movement from the trees and looked closer. A team of about six hornets (two of one red hue, four of another), and nine Shades were carefully maneuvering the enemy's empty cannon wagon. They were trying to bring it down the hill slowly, and they were supervised by two mounted Shades hovering low on either side. Vez watched as the team began to

38

sidle down the hill with their prize, the kinsmen checking their steps as they moved. It was a long, ponderous progression but one still necessary to monitor. Once they hit the base of the slope, Vez assured himself that he could look up again and did so.

His timing was spot on as he noticed some clear hornets emerging from the trees, followed by some pink ones without riders. The pink ones were carrying what appeared to be more prisoners instead. Vez looked back at the train for a moment, then he shrugged. Fite and Hurch had this covered. He looked forward again and tapped his foot. The deck responded with a hiss and lifted off the ground. This time it kept low and kept its current shape, giving Vez the appearance of a floating peacock. He gently flew over to meet with the clear hornets. He looked straight at them, his ornament gleaming again. The hornets looked back and clicked their jaws, as if responding. The king nodded understanding and sent them on their way.

Another clear hornet then emerged from the woods, but this one had a rider. A sturdy young woman, taller than Fite but shorter than Turnie, was a-hornet. She was wearing a dull orange tunic and olive-green pants. Her cap was bright blue-green and looked like it was more suited for colder weather. Her boots were made of felt and hide. Hooked into her blue belt was a small, thin axe with a head made of a mix of bronze and iron. It looked more like a one-handed scythe. The spike that served as the axe head was covered by a safety device made of stuffed cloth. This rider was neither Earth nor Shade; she was a dwarf.

"Runke," called Vez. She noticed him and immediately bid her mount to touch down. The hornet landed at the slope's base just before the deck stopped in the same spot. Runke dismounted and kneeled to her king. He stepped off the deck once more and bid her to rise. They were almost equal height.

"Report," he commanded.

"Lot of dead, fevered, and scared still to pick up. We chased the last eight, including their general to almost the whole path. He's injured and one of the other survivors was out by the time we caught them. They're all subdued now."

"And the covert outnumbering, was it a success?" Runke frowned at that. Something in her expression told Vez that this had failed.

"It would have if it wasn't for one of the *ogs* having a tummy-ache." Her voice was much coarser than Turnie's.

"What does a youth's stomachache have to do with anything?"

"Perhaps it's better if Turnie explains. Looks like she managed to get a prize as you suggested."

Vez was now curious but he knew that the cleanup and getting the prisoners ready for transport came first. "I'll ask her when she returns. In the meantime, have the Dofheiceal retrieve the enemies' cannons and get them back onto their wagon. After that, regroup and prepare to take flight ahead of us. All but the one you're riding are to conceal themselves during transit, as before." The Dofheiceal, or InvisiStings, were Runke's swarm. Their name, abilities, and venom were just as clear as their exoskeletons.

"Yes, my king." Runke paused. "Do you wish to have any of them assist in moving it once we head out."

"That'd be good. Couple it to the medic's wagon. Those horses are strong on their own but they'll need assistance."

"My king!" Vez and Runke turned around and looked up to see Turnie approach from the woods on foot. Her mount was flying beside her, carrying her spear. She herself was carrying a young, unconscious Earth soldier in her arms. Seven of her troops followed behind her. They were also

40

dismounted but their hornets were each carrying a prisoner. Vez nodded a dismissal to Runke and she left to carry out her orders. He then stepped back a little and waited for Turnie and the others to come down the hill. When Turnie arrived he stepped forward again to get a look at who she was carrying. This soldier was young (very much a private) and had reddish brown hair and glasses. One of the lenses was chipped. There also appeared to be some stains on his uniform. He looked closer and recognized that the stains were vomit.

"A rather small, sickly prize there, don't you think?" he said.

"It was from his stomachache, my king. But there is more to it." Turnie gently grabbed the boy's limp arm and held out his palm. Vez looked closer and almost jumped when he saw the wart on his pinky.

"A Wart of the Power!" he exclaimed under his breath.

Turnie nodded. "And you've noticed the placement, my king? Laoch Tier, like us." Vez tried to get a better glance at Turnie's right hand. He was looking for her own Wart, even though he'd seen it before. It was in the middle of her index finger. He then raised his own left hand (the very hand that fired his green lightning) and stared at it.

"Like me," he whispered. "What sort of power does he have."

"Some sort of protective, electrical field. It knocked down my men and his comrades pretty hard. I was far from it and high enough to avoid it. It also blew Runke's swarm out of hiding."

"And the vomiting was…"

"Because it was likely his first time using his power," Turnie finished.

"Yes, an uncommon side effect of early power use, but still known to happen. Very well, Turnie. You may keep him. He's young so we may have a chance to persuade him to see the truth. And I think you'd be more than qualified to convince him. We'll have to keep the other seven separate from him for now. Tell your men to bring the others to the medic wagon. Have any who are stung treated with the rest, then chain these seven apart from the other prisoners. They held out the longest, we'll at least give them the honor of that distinguishment. We have manacles to spare. Take this one back to your litter."

"Yes, my king. It will be done."

4

Liam's sleep of unconsciousness had changed from silent to fitful within a moderate time. When he passed out, there had been only dark silence before his closed eyes, but then there was a rapid shift into white, speeding flashes and indecipherable shouts piercing his hearing. He could not determine whether those shouts were in the waking world or just in his head, and the sickness he had just felt kept him from wanting to ascertain this. He slowly opened his eyes to find himself laying on his side. No longer on the ground in the woods, he was laying on an elongated felt cushion attached to a pulp bench. He winced and realized he had his right arm pinned between the cushion and his body. He shifted to lay on his back only to find he couldn't move his arms much. Liam raised them to his line of sight and noticed the manacles on his wrists. He could only spread his arms for half a foot, indicated by when the small chain between his cuffs became taught.

"If you sit up too fast, you'll get dizzy again," a low voice said to him. Liam jumped at the sound and looked across from him. He wasn't wearing his glasses now so things were a little blurry, but he could see the one speaking to him very clear; sitting opposite of him was the feared Wheel herself. The space they were both in was wide, but even sitting her height made her seem to fill the room. Liam noticed she was holding something green in her hands.

"Hey, that's my ha…!" He forced himself up as he exclaimed, and just as she pointed out, he became disoriented. A sudden weight filled his head and made him lay it back on the cushion. He then noticed his stomachache was gone; an instant fear then crept up in him that it would come back. Turnie Mave had shifted her gaze back to Liam's hat. A standard Earth Elf soldier's kepi. Emerald green. Those in

43

certain divisions had an embroidery to indicate their unit. On Liam's kepi were two circling curves of bright yellow-green- a stylized "C".

"You are from Cliar, aren't you?" she asked. She looked up at Liam again. His brows were furrowed and his mouth was well pressed into a frown.

"Hmph... either you're not willing to talk to the enemy before you or you're concentrating so as not to feel sick again." Liam didn't answer. He was looking up at the pulp ceiling.

"You don't strike me as someone who wanted to be a soldier," she continued. "I've heard Cliar's the best place to train the grunts. Didn't have that luxury when I was recruited as a Laoch." Liam kept staring at the ceiling, face contorted, not saying a word.

"I understand you don't wish to speak, but you'll have to talk sometime. I'll expect you to speak when asked to when I start training you." That made Liam sit up.

"Training me?!" He tried to respond out loud but it came out in a weak volume.

Turnie smirked. "So, you do speak. Yes, once you recover, I'll be training you to use your power so that you'll serve as a great asset to our king. Your Wart is now vital to us and is marked as so." Liam, now more puzzled, looked at his hands again. His left pinky had cloth wrapped around it. He didn't notice that earlier because it was wrapped firm but not tight.

"That's also to keep you from picking at it. With the confusion and damage your field did who knows what could happen if its source is disturbed. For now, just enjoy the ride." Liam was far from enjoying it. He was now more awake and rolled himself off the bench, landing hard on the floor; instead of this ever-present pulp, the floor was hard, varnished wood. The room lurched a little. Liam had landed on his elbow and

44

knee. He gritted in pain from the impact. Turnie remained seated, not even attempting to put him back in place. Hurting and now going into a little panic, Liam inched his bound self over to the closest window as fast as he could manage. He peeked through and jumped again. The two of them were high above the land below. Still in shock, he looked at Turnie again. She had put his hat to the side and was giving him a fainter smirk.

"I also doubt you're the suicidal type." She carefully leaned forward, only leaving her seat in a crouch, and reached to prop him back up. He flinched away. Turnie resumed her seat and frowned.

"Lay there if you wish," she said, her tone low and unfriendly. "You'll be getting up when I tell you to once we land, which shouldn't be long. You were out for at least a couple of hours." A bell gave a muffled ring outside. Turnie smirked again. "How about that? We're here."

Turnie's litter was soaring above and in time with the rest of the caravan, flanked by the pink hornets and their riders. Only the baggage train below was lagging behind. The king was flying in the space between sky and ground, with Fite and her Eaglaceal as his own guard. They had all long left that forest area and traveled the whole lip of the border of the Green West. Awaiting Vez only a few yards now was his home and seat of power, the city village of NightPeace.

The king was eyes forward the whole time, looking upon the familiar sight of his capital. Closer and closer the procession was approaching the single arched bridge that lay over the deep ravine that outlined the wild river Díog. The bridge itself was made of a mix of granite and imported red stone, and it was long well-constructed. At both ends of the bridge were a cluster of three small nests accompanied by a larger one in the center. These nests had wooden lean-tos and framing on them. The structures served as both the city's garrison and department for the bridge's maintenance. Vez tapped his foot again and brought his platform down to the centermost nest, all while signaling the air troupe behind him to stand by. A Shade sentry, wearing a suit of light armor instead of the ubiquitous wine uniform, emerged from the post and bowed.

"Welcome back, my king. Ginearal Crosta is waiting across the bridge to escort you back to the Last Cloch."

Vez frowned. "I did not give him such an order to wait for me."

"It was the queen's order, my king." Vez relaxed his face a little at that response.

"Hmph… yes, she always worries about me. Never shows it out loud, mind you, but she did tell me once that a queen will always fear for her king's safety." The sentry raised his head, puzzled by this casual response. Vez noticed and cleared his throat. "Inform the Ginearal to meet me here to begin the escort. I need a moment to inform Ginearal Fite and the rest of my guard to fly low alongside me."

"Yes, my king." And with that Vez took up slowly into the sky again to issue the new orders. The sentry waited until the platform actually lifted before getting to his feet and dashing across the bridge to the waiting horseman on the other side. Minutes later, Vez, Fite, and her troops all descended to the bridge's entrance just in time to meet with the returning sentry commander. Ginearal Crosta was also a dwarf. His tunic and pants were a reddish salmon with blue spot accents, and he wore bronze scaled chest armor and a matching helm. He carried a cavalry saber with an orange tassel tied to the handguard. A red recurve bow in a canvas pouch and a quiver of arrows with salmon fletchlings were tethered to his saddle. Instead of dismounting to bow, he simply lowered his head and kept it low for a few seconds.

"We will proceed across and to the castle first, Ginearal," Vez stated. "The prisoners and baggage will follow once we're off the bridge."

"Very good, my king," Crosta replied in a voice like broken shell.

"The sentry tells me that Smazeph ordered you to meet us here when we returned. Is that true?"

Crosta raised his head and looked Vez in the eye. "Yes, my king. To the queen your safety is paramount. As strong as the swarms are there is always the danger that the enemy will find a way to get to you."

"True. But it's a minimal chance all the same. Shall we proceed?" Crosta nodded and turned his horse around and back across the bridge, galloping at first, then a slow trot as the procession followed feet behind him.

***

NightPeace's limits were serene and quiet. The outskirts within were marked by modest fields tended to by a total of eight Shade farming families, whose lands were spread out into fair sections that formed a downward spear point, with the road serving as the tip. Their properties each consisted of the tended field, a small thatched house (round as the Shades' tradition), and a grain silo of imported steel.

As Vez and his guard passed the farms closest to the road, the occupants paused from their work and bent their knees in the progress' direction. The king and the two Ginearals sideways glanced at the subjects, not that they needed to check; the loyalty of Vez's people was absolute and genuine, and the farmers that were farther off would always kneel in turn as their neighbors took care to signal them to with the indigo pennants atop their huts.

Upon leaving the farms, the royal procession made way to the bulk of the city. This was set on the flat, jutting base of an enormous three-layer hill. The huts here were just like the ones on the farms, only these were larger and reinforced with stone as opposed to wood. The thatch roofs were plated with rainproof canvas. The fields below this base were reserved for livestock, and the granaries and other buildings of process were nestled within and towered among the huts, as they were built of a different design. More pennants rose up, and soon the procession was greeted by Shade citizens of all ages and soldiers on police duty who had all put aside their work to kneel on both sides of the road. Vez looked to them all and raised his hand.

"All is well, my people. Return to your activity." No one moved or looked at him.

"You heard your king's command!" shouted Fite, almost too forceful. Vez looked at her, with a face that said that was unnecessary. Fite lowered her head in apology, not noticing that the people were returning as they were.

The procession passed across the middle layer without incident. Here were the barracks, all of which were bigger and not made like the Shades' huts. All of these buildings had an adjoining nest for protection. Hornets of all seven colors were present in these. No one here dropped everything to kneel by the road. Their collective duty was priority. At last, in what seemed an hour later they came to the top layer of the hill. Past the front edge of the ring of nests that protected it was Vez's castle, a rough but imposing stone construction with an inner perimeter wall. The Last Cloch.

The main entrance was off to the left. A dozen Shades, half with bows and half with guns, were at attention but standing on the grass instead of the walkway. The three that stood between them were the ones who, at present, had the right to stand on these cobbles. An interesting factor to note was that they were not natives to the Continent but long-present foreigners. Standing front in center was Queen Smazeph. She was tall and statuesque. Her deep blue dress, adorned with pale green trimming and spots, was an import itself but magnified her station when combined with the bracelets of burnished gold she wore on both wrists. Her large, striped brown tail, darker than the fur on her body but matching her long hair, was on display thanks to the accommodating space in her dress' back. Her crown was a strap of fine leather with a plate of the same gold in the middle, and the round ears on top of her head both had a single teardrop-cut emerald in them. Her lipstick matched the blue of her dress.

Flanking her were the last two of the Seven Ginearals. They were Gavis, also known as Longcrocs; large, fearsome beastmen of crocodile form who originated from a country that sat southwest to the queen's homeland, both of which were far out east. Aamjunta, at Smazeph's right, wore fine garb of his home. His pants, turban, and saree were a bright mix of reds and oranges and displayed uneven patterns. His long, thin snout with a prominent knob on the end illustrated the common name of his kind. He was the only one present who was barefoot, as the soldiers had their boots and the queen wore sandals. The one at Smazeph's left, Kavanchi, was taller and larger than their kinsman and was clad head to toe in bronze-and-iron armor. They carried a two-handed sword that looked more like a spear. The varnished handle sections were separated by three large brass orbs. Not even Aamjunta knew if the one behind this armor was a man or a woman. Dark green scales and bloodred eyes were shown behind Kavanchi's pangolin helmet.

Vez's platform stopped on the dirt part of the walkway, just before the borderline of the cobblestones. He was about five feet away from his queen. Vez moved his right foot closer to the platform's edge, his toe pressing down on a bolt. It was actually a cleverly disguised shutoff button. The platform's humming died down as a long trail of steam was let out of the exhausts. Fite and Crosta had followed the king from behind and dismounted feet away from the evaporated warm water. Once Vez stepped off the platform, they both drew up to his sides as he walked up to the entrance. Smazeph and the Longcrocs stepped forward as well, keeping very neutral expressions. In moments both king and queen were face to face, with their respective escorts filing in behind them. Smazeph was about a foot taller than her husband, and the Gavis were biggest of all of them. The queen looked Vez in the eyes. Both of them had bright golden eyes, the only difference being Smazeph's white sclera and visible pupils. The thin fur around her eyes was tan and looked like a bandit's mask. She stared at him for a further moment, then gave a light smile.

"Welcome home, my king. I trust you all fared well."

"Yes, my dear. All was well. Turnie and the prisoners shall be here soon."

"That will still be some time. Would you be so kind as to remove your mask, so I may look upon your returning face in full?"

"In front of our Ginearals is hardly an appropriate time, dear." Vez paused. "But then again, since you were so concerned for my well-being, how could I deny you here and now?" He began to reach for his mask but Smazeph stopped him.

"Oh, don't do it yourself, my king. Let Aamjunta's orderly do it for you."

"I'm much more comfortable with sparing him the burden. Besides, it's more special when I present my face to you on my own."

"Hmm, that is true."

Vez brought his hands to his head and undid the clasp in the back. The ornament made it heavier than it actually was, but the king could manage. He lowered the mask from his face to reveal the trimmed dark beard that surrounded his thin mouth. Looking closer, there were a few small hairs of blond and copper present. Overall, his face was handsome in its own way. Smazeph's smile widened into a casual grin. She took a step toward him, leaned forward, and gently kissed his forehead. She left a blue lip mark that somewhat blended into his purple skin. Neither of them noticed Fite gritting her teeth. Smazeph then brushed the mark away with her thumb, its claw-like nail not even grazing the spot.

"There we be time later in our chambers for further affections. Now we must return you to your throne. There is still court to be held."

Vez nodded and put his mask back on. Smazeph turned to the Gavis and raised her hand. Both of them obeyed the unspoken command and turned around. As they began walking toward the entrance, the soldiers rotated position to watch and let their rulers pass. They themselves would follow behind the other Ginearals. Fite and Crosta kept pace behind, not glancing at even one in the lines. In turn, none of the soldiers took notice of Fite's expression. She was still glaring hard at the queen.

5

The Last Cloch was a castle of opposite aesthetic. While its exterior suggested that it was a ruin with impeccable endurance, the interior rang something of extravagance and the idea that Vez had everything. Walking up the porch into the main entrance, the king and his Ginearals entered the spacious anteroom. The stone floor was accentuated with four massive burgundy carpets, each embossed with a giant pale blue hornet in the center; the same design that was Vez's ornament. A rustic lamp chandelier and wall lanterns served as the means of nighttime lighting. Neither Vez nor Fite had to worry about wiping their feet on the mat placed in the entrance's overhang, as that they had not picked up any dirt from the battlefield. Even if they had tracked anything, the servants around the castle would take care of it.

Before they had entered, about half of the Eaglaceal ventured to the perimeter nests on Fite's command. The others followed both of their masters inside. Awaiting them all were three of the castle staff. They were all Danucs, Smazeph's people. Like her, they had round ears, brown fur, and striped tails. These servants wore plain dark uniforms that had a degree of elegance but nowhere as glamorous as the queen's dress. The uniform consisted of a blackish-blue robe and a matching coif hat that had holes for the ears. There were Gavi servants around the castle as well, but they did most of the outside work. No doubt there would be a few already tending to Crosta's horse and returning Vez's platform to its rightful place in the South Hall.

The Danucs were accompanied by a young Shade soldier who seemed less built than those in the escort. This was Aamjunta's orderly. The only weapon he was carrying at present was his commander's own sword, a large curved blade

53

known in his homeland as a *tegha*. Since the sword was meant to be carried by someone of Aamjunta's size, it was quite large and heavy. The orderly had the loaded scabbard slung on his back. It was about his height and clearly too heavy for him to carry. Regardless, he kept to attention and followed the others in kneeling once the king was in sight. When the four of them returned to standing, the orderly noticed Aamjunta's disapproving leer. He didn't flinch, as his commander always gave him that look.

"Orderly, to me!" barked Aamjunta. His sandpaper voice was harsh and jagged on the ear. The orderly shuffled over to the group. He went around two of his fellow soldiers and the gleaming bulk of Kavanchi to reach Aamjunta in seconds. He bowed his head to him in a too quick motion, and was then met by a slight but abrupt shove to the side by the Ginearal. Aamjunta unsheathed the tegha and inspected it for imperfections that were no way present.

"You better not be mistreating him, Aamjunta," said Vez, looking sideways. "Soldiers do need discipline, but I will not stand for abuse of any of my people." Aamjunta looked to him quickly.

"Not at all, my king," he replied in a much calmer tone. "Just making sure he is doing his job as my sword-carrier." Vez frowned. Aamjunta was a proud warrior, perhaps too proud. Under the Gavis' caste system, he and the orderly were technically equals regardless of rank, but Aamjunta treated his subordinate like a common worker.

"It looks to me like he is doing just that," Vez answered, his tone a little warning now. Aamjunta flinched a little, but his crocodilian face made it hard to see such expression. He returned the tegha to its sheath. Vez turned his attention back to the other servants. "Is the throne room ready?"

"Yes, my king," said one. "Dusted and polished as always."

"Good. Let us go then. The prisoners may be here sooner than expected."

***

Turnie Mave's litter touched down outside the castle about fifteen minutes later. The rest of the caravan was making its way through the village in the meanwhile; at least that's what Turnie saw when she last looked out the window. Liam was not given the chance to see it for himself. Still sitting on the litter's floor, he just stared at his feet. He was feeling a bit fortunate that the Wheel had not decided to bind his legs together as well. When they landed, he kept the concentration on his feet, although he did glance for a moment to watch her stand up. It was hard to look away at how tall she was. If she saw his glance she didn't appear to notice. She opened the door across from him and stepped outside. The hornet that carried her spear came into view. Turnie took it gently and sent her mount on its way. She then turned her attention back to Liam and jabbed the litter's step with the spear's butt. The metal knob hitting the wood made a ringing noise.

"Stand!" the Wheel commanded. Liam, not seeing any other alternative, urged himself forward. He tried to move his arms to his back, but then remembered the manacles. He thrust forward instead and got on his knees, with his palms on the floor. He pushed himself slowly with hands then feet, and in moments he was standing. Turnie jabbed the step again.

"Out!" Liam did so, but as he was stepping out he saw his hat on Turnie's seat. He stopped to retrieve it only to be met with another ringing jab signal.

"I said out! You won't need that for now." Liam frowned and resumed exiting the litter. When he stepped out and down, he got a good look at the castle before him. To him it looked rather old; *how does a king with this much power not live in something a little more grand?* Turnie coming up next to him pulled him from such query as she leaned in to whisper.

"Stick close to me and follow what I do. If you are asked anything you are to answer. Do not make me start having second thoughts about you." Liam roved his focus to her for a moment, then only replied with a nod. Without any further prodding, he followed by her side to the entrance.

The two of them walked straight inside and through the anteroom. There were mainly just Danuc staff going about their business, but Shade guards and soldiers were present at every entrance. Liam was already accustomed to the appearance of Shades, but this was his first time seeing Danucs. Turnie figured this as much when she noticed him looking around and not bothering to hide it.

"At Cliar, they educate you about not just the native enemy but our foreign allies, yes?" she asked. Liam's attention was brought right back to her. He nodded fast in response.

"They say such things like that the Danucs are warmongering and covetous, while the Gavis are savage, bloodthirsty beasts?" Liam nodded again. "Well, this may not surprise you, but there is a grain of half-truth to all that."

"Half-truth?" Liam asked. His voice was but a whisper, but Turnie still heard him.

"Yes. The details are complicated, but it was the Danucs who created the arms that his Majesty's people now use. They invested many resources that are exclusive to their homeland to perfect these weapons. They're also the ones who discovered the Tíorafhoi and made them the backbone of our military force." Tíorafhoi, roughly translated as "tyrant hornets," was the general name for the hornet force. They came in a total of seven different varieties, each with names and powers of their own. Seven Swarms under Seven Ginearals.

"I… I have learned that," said Liam, still timid.

"As a warrior, I am not one to focus on such things as finances or coffers, but even I can tell that there are number of costs and debts amounting to all this conquest. Some of these extend to more than just weapons and troops. However, not one Danuc in this castle has thought to bring it up. In short, they're quite lenient on collection periods. For now."

Liam's wandering gaze shifted back to the servants moving about. He was hoping they were not listening to this open talk.

"As for the Gavis," Turnie continued. "While they may look beastly on the outside, they are quite spiritual and organized. They have many deities, much like the Shades do. And neither of them argue over whose is superior because they've managed to find commonalities between some gods. That's not to say that there aren't any Gavis who are savage in battle. Ginearal Kavanchi, as you'll soon see, is especially feared."

By this point, the two of them were out of the anteroom and in the Nexus Tower. This was the central most structure of the castle. On each side was a pair of enormous oak doors that led to the other larger places. The door to the South Hall was closed, but the North Hall's doors were wide open. More servants were moving about. The corners of this ground floor were marked by overhang notches, each filled with a spiral staircase. The Wheel was about to address their purpose when one of the guards by the eastern doors came forward.

"Ginearal Mave, His Majesty is waiting for you." The guard's tone suggested that this was no time for a tour. He dared not say such aloud to a superior, but Turnie still took his meaning and without offense. She just nodded and prompted Liam forward.

The throne room was a long open space. While the anteroom and the Nexus' ground were decorated with appealing base essentials, this room was filled to every end with quality ornamentation. The reinforcing columns were olive-colored marble, combined with other sturdy unseen materials to support the castle's original stone. More covered lanterns hung from the ceiling. The windows were small and deep, embossed with pale yellow stained glass; they were set in to prevent any likely ranged attack from coming in. Burgundy banners that were the same as the anteroom's rug were along the walls, the biggest one in the far back, above the platform where the throne stood. At the far end of the room, just below the platform was the Ginearals' council table. Five of those other six were seated in large, cushioned chairs. Kavanchi was standing beside the throne, on guard for the king. Standing to Vez's right was his queen. Liam had heard of her and that she was a Danuc, but what Cliar's instructors had known of her was minimal. Any information the Earths had on Smazeph was mostly rumor and speculation. The one thing closest to a fact that Liam was warned about was her presence, how as the chosen queen she looked intimidating. There was a time where they assumed she was some kind of sorceress, but that was disproven because no one had yet encountered a Danuc that possessed a Wart. Although, if anyone set out to investigate, they never came back to tell the tale.

King Vez's throne was the one thing in the room that was not of an intricate craft, at least not at first glance. While the wooden framework and the layback cushion were of a rustic form (one that originated from the Shades), the seat cushion was stuffed with cotton instead of hay. Vez was sitting back in a comfortable position, the kind that suggested attentive peace as opposed to lethargy. He sat up just a little as

58

Turnie and Liam came closer. Even with the mask, he could still be seen expressing calm approval.

"Turnie, right on time. How about you and this young man step forward?"

"Yes, my king," she said aloud. Nudging Liam just a bit, they both went around the council table from the left, passing Turnie's empty seat. Liam wanted to get a better look at the other Ginearals but decided not to risk a harsher prompt from his captor. He kept his eyes focused on Vez, coming closer to the most feared Shade alive. Vez looked straight at him the second he reached the long carpet. Liam was startled in an instant, fumbling behind. Turnie did not ignore that and prodded Liam's foot with the butt of her spear. Liam snapped back to the present and regained his pace. Turnie bent her knee to the king and Liam followed with the barest delay. He was looking right at Vez again. Opening one eye, Turnie noticed this.

"Head down, eyes closed," she whispered through clenched teeth. Liam did as he was told. Vez sat up for a better look. Smazeph followed her husband's movement and saw that his face was neutral now. He uttered neither word nor sound as he looked at this nervous Earth prisoner. Vez eyed the cloth on Liam's pinky very carefully.

"Show me his Wart," he said at last. Turnie raised her head in response and then tapped Liam on the shoulder. With just her eyes, she instructed him to present his shackled hands. Liam did so without resistance. Turnie put down her spear and rose just a little so she could remove the cloth. Vez then rose from his seat; that made the queen and the other Ginearals react. He stepped down from the dais and came closer to the presented hands. Standing tall and hands behind his back, his pose of choice, Vez eyed the wart upon the left pinky base. Now Liam was keeping his head down on his own accord.

"Laoch tier, indeed," he said with confidence. "Raise your head and tell me your name, young man." Liam raised his head and looked Vez in the eye. He waited a second for Turnie to prod him, then blurted out an answer.

"Private Liam Pairc, Cliar Base," he uttered. No stammer, but the strain in his voice showed how afraid he was.

"How long have you had this Wart?" Vez asked. Liam didn't answer. Turnie gave a muffled "ahem."

"Never noticed it up until now," he said quickly. Turnie ahemmed again. "Your Majesty." Vez leaned in for a better look. He saw no black spots in the Wart. It was common knowledge that long-standing Warts, like regular warts, had these spots to indicate clotted blood vessels. No spots meant a newly grown one, regardless of rise or hardness.

"Look here," Vez commanded. His order was casual. Liam looked at the king's now raised left hand. With his right Vez prompted Liam to look closer. Liam lowered his shackled hands a bit but still kept them in presentation. Vez was presenting his hand with the palm facing himself, and with that Liam noticed a tiny tab on the pinky armor of the gauntlet. Vez then slid the tab with his free hand. It made an almost mute click. He removed the metal sleeve from his pinky and then turned his palm to Liam. The private saw on the purple finger a wart that was in the same place as his own. This Wart distorted the skin it was made of, coming off as both pink and white. In the center were a healthy cluster of black spots.

"We may not look it, but you and I are the same," said the king. Liam bit his lip in offense at that statement but said nothing. Vez saw that but pretended not to notice.

"I amend my statement from earlier, Turnie. You have picked a reasonable prize. He just needs a little work. Build on his established training, yes. Maybe even teach him a new weapon. But training his newfound power, that is priority."

60

"Yes, your Majesty," said Turnie.

"And I will be joining you personally in instructing him."

The room was filled with a collective gasp from Turnie and almost everyone else. Liam made no noise himself but his eyes widened. Kavanchi only turned their head to the king, the only sound made coming from a shift of their armor.

"My king!" Smazeph exclaimed. Liam turned to the sound of her mature, feminine voice. Other than Turnie's, he had never heard anything like it. "Thi-that is unprecedented."

"And unwise," said Aamjunta from his chair.

"I see your concern, yes, but this must be done." Vez returned the armor to his pinky as he spoke. "A power of that level is to be trained by like minds. Like minds that are tempered with wisdom. So in a way, it is wise."

"But other than Ginearal Mave, you've never taken another Earth in," Aamjunta added. "Our campaigns have assured that."

"Mind you, Turnie came to us, and that was because of how she was trained. Despite her power, her kind wanted it to fit their specifications, their goals. Namely the goal of wiping my people from existence. And it is not just our campaigns that have kept other defectors from coming forward. It is because the whole of the Earths' military is trained to believed they are the masters of this whole land. Turnie was wise to see things differently. Furthermore, it is better to have this fledgling power in our hands rather than theirs."

A Shade trooper entered the throne room in a rush.

"My king! The baggage train is returning, along with the other prisoners."

"Thank you," replied the king. "We will further discuss Private Pairc's future affairs later. For now, we must deal with the other prisoners." He then looked to Turnie. "I will need you for that. Your prize is adjourned from this meeting for now." He turned back to the trooper. "Take this young man to Ginearal Mave's quarters, and make sure he stays put there."

"Yes, my king." The trooper walked closer to the throne, stopping about three feet from Liam. Turnie rose from her kneel and signaled Liam with her eyes to go with him. Liam's eyes widened in protest. Turnie tapped the butt of her spear, much more gentle than before but still enough to prompt the strict message. Liam relaxed his eyes and conceded to follow the soldier out of the room. As he walked past the council table, he glanced at Aamjunta. The Gavi made no growl but still bared his teeth in such a subtle way.

6

The throne room doors were closed gently behind Liam and his escort as soon as they stepped out. The two who did so were long practiced in opening and closing that entrance. Liam followed the trooper without further question or resistance. The two of them quickly returned to the Nexus Tower's base floor. Guards by the staircases and the hall doors were the only ones present when they entered, but one of the Danuc attendants from earlier emerged from the back left stairway. She saw Liam and the trooper and came forward.

"Lieutenant, is that prisoner of some importance?" she asked.

"Yes, ma'am," he answered. "This is Ginearal Mave's new apprentice. I am taking him to her quarters."

"Then allow me to assist in escorting him. We shall go through the North Hall around the back. The other prisoners will be brought through the anteroom. We can't risk the possibility that seeing their separated comrade will inspire them to fight back, even if they are weakened. Just a precaution."

"Very good, ma'am. Lead the way." The trooper's answer was quite stock. The attendant walked up to Liam and took a look at his manacles.

"I'll get a key from the guard to unlock these once we get you settled, not before. Another precaution." Liam looked away from her but said nothing. "Both of you follow me."

The three of them entered the North Hall. Now Liam got a better look of this space. Three large oak tables and several chairs were stored off in the back of the room, their obvious use for gatherings and events. It would seem that Vez kept these at the ready should diplomatic or celebratory events become necessary. No one could say for certain when that would ever happen. On the right were three more stairway entrances, all guarded. The furthest one was a spiral climb, indicating a tower. It also had five guards stationed whereas the others had three. Liam dared not to ask, but he could guess that tower led to the king and queen's apartment. Neither the trooper nor the attendant caught his glance at these places.

The attendant led them to the hall's far left corner. She turned to Liam and placed a finger to her lips, staring at him in an unblinking do-you-understand. Liam nodded quick. The attendant did not have to tell the same to the trooper. The corner was decorated with a long, varnished credenza. Atop it was a burgundy cover and a tall, gilded oil lamp. The attendant walked to the credenza and removed a bell-like snuffer from a sconce on the lamp. She put out the flame and then looked to the lieutenant. He nodded and then turned to the guards behind him. The second they saw him look towards them, all eleven guards turned their backs to him and gave their attention to the walls behind them. The movement was seamless and disciplined. The lieutenant turned back and watched the attendant twist the snuffer's wooden handle. The teeth of a key emerged from the tip. The attendant inserted the secret key into a lock on the credenza's inner left door. She opened it and held out the entrance in invitation for Liam. He took the cue and walked toward her.

"Enter but wait to move further after I join you," she whispered. "Watch your head." Liam, in silent obedience, crouched down and went inside the cabinet. It was a snug fit, but the lack of shelves or racks inside made it easy for him to settle in. It was stuffy but not unbearable inside. Liam looked at the interior. He noticed that the other doors had no hinges. They were fake. The rest of the inside looked just like it should on such furniture, except for the small, unusual hole on the back part off to the far right. The attendant entered, no longer carrying the snuffer; she obviously put it back in place. She looked at Liam to make sure he was there, then produced a pewter knob from her uniform's pocket. Inching further inside, she made for the hole. She placed the knob in the hole and turned. A rustling sounded from the back. She quickly removed the knob from the hole, just as that piece of the credenza's back paneled and then slid away. A secret passage.

She crawled into the hole first but beckoned Liam to follow her. He did so just as the only thing sticking out of the passage was her feet. Something prodded Liam from behind. If he had to guess it was the lieutenant prodding him with his gun. Liam crawled into the passage. A bit tricky to do with shackled hands. The passageway was straight and looked meant for a crawler of any size except the Gavis, and it was made of smooth, polished stone that seemed brand new in comparison to the weathered blocks that made up the whole of the castle. Lighting was dim inside this tunnel. Liam caught sight of the attendant feet away from him, her striped, bushy tail sticking out of the gown and twisting about like a ferret. She was moving so he followed her without any pressure; he had a feeling that the lieutenant was close behind and decided not to make him shove himself further.

Seconds into moving through, Liam paused when he heard the rustling again. This time it was behind him and it echoed into a rumble. Something clicked back into place as the passage suddenly became pitch black. Now another rustle, more of a swishing, sounded in front of Liam. He took it to be the attendant's tail brushing the wall. A wordless instruction to keep moving, which he did so. He crawled through the dark until he came to a slant in the passage; it was now moving upward. Nothing else he could do but follow the pathway.

Liam only had to inch up the darkened slope for a short distance, but with the manacles progress was slower. The pathway then went straight again, and inches later it took a turn to the left. Follow the attendant, that's all he could do. He wasn't thinking about anything else. Not how he joined the Earths' army, not how he kept to himself there, almost blending in with the other privates. He was not even panicking. Any panic was taken away by the exhaustion of using that power. *That power.* Now that was the last thing he wanted to think about.

The tunnel took another turn. Another left. It was straight but much longer now. The passageway was still smooth, but even in the dark it seemed wider than before. Liam kept on crawling in silence, although as he moved he could hear muffled steps from above him. Muffled heavy steps. Likely more Shade soldiers. Any heavier would suggest Gavis. After what seemed like hours, more turns abounded. Left, then straight, then right, then another long straight. It was unclear if time was slowed or just stopped altogether. Then for a moment, Liam was starting to see the outline of his guide's backside once more. Faint light was pouring into his vision. He saw the Danuc suddenly drop out of sight through the square opening at the end of the tunnel. Alarmed that she just fell like that, he inched up faster, stopping just to the opening to avoid falling out himself. He looked to see that the drop was only about five feet down, and that the attendant was standing up with her arms out. Her knees were bent, implying that she somehow landed on her feet. It also seemed like she had just backflipped out of the tunnel. She lowered her arms and turned around to notice Liam sticking his head out of the opening, staring at her.

"Alright, since you're still bound, you'll need to come down slowly." There was actual concern in her voice despite her mouth was bent into a humored smirk. Liam backed a little and checked to see if the lieutenant was right behind him. The soldier must have had really good hearing to hear the attendant from his position, as he was a good distance away from Liam. He could make out the lieutenant's facial features, and they were telling him much more politely now to go forward. Liam turned back to the exit and looked below. The attendant was now standing at the bottom of the small drop, arms out and looking up at him.

"Don't worry, I'll catch you." She was only a couple feet taller than him, and he assumed she must be physically stronger than him. Not vibrant strength and muscle like his chief captor but strong enough. He had much less choice now. He brought his head back into the passageway and inched his feet forward. Hesitant as he was, Liam still managed to launch himself out of the shaft. He plummeted for seconds before colliding torso to torso with the attendant, the force almost tackling her to the floor. She regained her balance as she held him in a near-bear hug and brought him to his feet.

"Good thing your cuffs didn't get me in the face," she said humorlessly. It was then that Liam noticed his shackled wrists were resting on something that was a tad soft. His eyes widened and his face began to color. She looked him right in the eye and smiled.

"I won't tell the Ginearal if you don't." Liam turned his head away in embarrassment.

"Could you… remove your arms from me, please?" he uttered.

"Ah, so you can talk." She let go of Liam and looked to the shaft again. "Lieutenant, you can follow now." The lieutenant slipped out the shaft in a much slower fashion, his gun slung on his shoulder. He rearmed himself once he was on his feet. The attendant was now stepping across the wide room. It was made out of the same smooth stone as the passage from floor to ceiling. There was a rack of keys embedded on the far-left wall. At the other end of the room was a single large wooden door, guarded by another Danuc, this one sporting light armor and carrying a spear. The attendant nodded to this guard, and he returned it, granting her permission to select a key from the rack. She walked over and selected four; two big ones from the center peg, a medium one from the inner left peg, and a small one from the rightmost peg. She turned to the private and lieutenant and jangled the keys toward them. The guard stepped aside and she unlocked the door with the heavier-looking big key.

"This way," she said to the other two. They followed.

The hallway they entered was much wider than the passage but nowhere as wide as the previous room. And it was also made of that ubiquitous smooth stone. If there were wooden braces holding it up, they were very well hidden. This passage was also lit with metal and glass lanterns. Instead of flame, these were lit with an unknown source, which Liam could easily see because the lights did not flicker. The hallway was a short straight, about twenty feet, then took a right turn into another straight that was double the length. It ended in a smooth stone porch of steps. In the wall above the top step was another hole like in the credenza wall. To the left of the hole was a welded ladder that ended at the ceiling. The attendant signaled the other two to halt the second they approached the steps. She walked up and took out the knob once more, placing it in the connection point. A new, more earthen rustle sounded from above. She removed the knob and the square of ceiling over the ladder opened up, letting in outside light.

The attendant signaled again for the other two to stay as she climbed up to look around. She was looking outside for less than a minute before she brought her face back into the tunnel.

"Coast is clear. Come on up," she told them. They followed her up the steps and out the hole. Liam squinted as his eyes tried to readjust to the daylight. Once he was able to see again, he looked at these new surroundings. To his surprise, he could see the castle just yards away. Even more surprising was that he was looking at the front of the castle. The angle from where he was standing showed that off to the left in his view was the cobblestone pathway to the main entrance. If there were any soldiers about, they were likely further up the path. They had gone in something of an underground circle. Liam looked behind him now and saw a tall stone obelisk marking this secret exit. Its base was just inches from the hole.

"The Ginearal's quarters are this way," said the attendant. She was pointing to a diagonal section attached to the right of the bulk piece. Another heavy door was present in the center of the smaller section. The three of them walked away from the obelisk and headed for the door. No one saw the hole's panel close, its attached turf completing the concealment. The attendant came up to the door and unlocked it with the lighter big key. She ushered Liam inside, with the lieutenant close behind, then went in herself.

Turnie's quarters were an organized split interior. The left half of the room was a training and exercise space with racks of weights and a small sparring ring that was cut into the floor and filled with sand. The right half was a furnished but basic sleeping space. A large bed and a sofa were the only furniture present, and above the bed on the wall was the place where the Ginearal kept her spear. There was a small washroom further off right. Two windows of yellow stained glass were on the back wall, letting only a small amount of light in. The lieutenant walked ahead of Liam and directed his attention to the sofa. Wordless instruction to sit down. Liam did so, and the attendant came over and unlocked his cuffs with the small key.

"The Ginearal will be with you once His Majesty has finished the council meeting. You are to remain here until she returns. Lieutenant Ulices here will be standing guard outside. If you need anything, please give a soft knock on the door and ask him to fetch me. My name is Sumiko, by the way. Remember that. You understand all this?"

Liam gave a solemn nod. He cooperated this far. Sumiko nodded approval and walked back to the doorway with Ulices following her. When they reached the door, Ulices took one more look at Liam to make sure he stayed put before following Sumiko outside. The door closed shut. The lock sounded. Liam did not lean back on the sofa, frozen with exhaustion and uncertainty. He did lay his now-free arms on the cushions. Aside from wondering the obvious of what Turnie planned to do with him when she returned, he was curious about what that medium key was for.

7

While Liam was being led through that hidden passage, the other prisoners were brought into the castle. The expediency in which Vez's subjects kept the private out of sight from his fellow Earths was successful. Reeth, Xanthe, Irelan, and Gert were clapped in irons of their own, along with Privates Ochtó and Grocer. Private Reoite was cooling down in one of the fever tubs. Of course, the medic made sure to clean up his bloody nose first. They were all placed in the prisoner wagon and had taken the long, slow travel to NightPeace. No one said a word, not with all of the troops and hornets making up the procession.

Irelan was especially worried after Liam was taken away to the Wheel's litter. She tried to ask both of her superiors on what to do about him, but they gave her a firm shush about it. Gert sneered at that response; to him it was nice to not be the one getting harped on this time.

They had passed all of the village farms just as the king's entourage had. None of them had any idea what the farmers' reactions were when he passed. All they noticed was that the attention that these Shades were giving them was quite negative. The huts' pennants were raised, but that was for the king's forces, not them. Those farmers that were nearest to the road gave cold stares, aimed in particular at the general and the sergeant. A flash of pity was given to the privates. Venturing into the city itself was uneventful, although Irelan was surprised how civilized it looked. She was the only one looking around without preemptive judgment. Reeth and Xanthe looked around as well, but they held looks of contempt and loathing at what they saw. Returning looks were much briefer here. Those among the barracks seemed accustomed to the sight of prisoners of war.

The caravan stopped at the start of the cobblestones. Two Shades from another part of the train escorted the sitting prisoners up the path. Three more were removing Private Reoite from the tub. The upper half of his uniform was put aside when he was immersed, but he was still wearing his pants and they were now drenched. The medic inspected his temperature before he was led off the wagon. He was frigid and exhausted, only emitting a low groan to indicate he was conscious but hazy. No cuffs were needed for him.

Reeth and Xanthe were fixing their gazes on the Last Cloch as they were all led closer to it. Irelan was looking at it as well. Liam had to be somewhere in there by now. Gert and the other two were more focused on the perimeter nests. In silence they agreed it would be a miracle to get past all of the occupants in those during an escape situation.

"Real nonsense, playing king in a wreck like that," muttered Reeth. The soldier escorting him shot a look close to his face. Reeth made a snort in her eyes. She flinched from the air but chose not to discipline him for that. Xanthe watched them both, looking for an opening to defend him. No chance came.

Up the path, through the anteroom and into the Nexus Tower they were brought. They all waited outside the throne doors until Reoite was brought in. A Danuc servant was following behind the troops who carried him. She seemed to have been rushing back from a task in another part of the castle. The sentries opened the doors as the procession readied itself to enter. The servant tapped her foot to get the sentries' attention. She signaled to them by clapping the heels of her palms together fast. A sign of something urgent, something that could not be mentioned in the presence of these others. The sentries nodded and looked to the troops, who understood the message and backed themselves and their prisoners from the door and back to the center of the room. They then let the servant pass into the throne room.

"Hey, what's going on here?" said Gert with indignance. "I thought we're going in…"

"Shut it!" Reeth and Xanthe both said through clenched teeth. Their command did not stop the soldier next to Gert from hitting him in the side with the butt of his gun. No one else, not even the two next to him, came to his defense. They all knew how undisciplined speaking out of turn was.

***

"Pardon the sudden intrusion, my king," said Sumiko in a low voice. "I only wished to inform you, and by extension Ginearal Mave, that the young private is well secured in her quarters."

"Very good," answered Vez, in moderate volume. "I would have accepted waiting until the prisoners were dealt with, but you were in the right to bring this to my immediate attention."

"Agreed," said Smazeph. "Who knows how long it will take to judge them?"

"I heard some disturbance outside," said Crosta. "They sound restless."

"One of them certainly was," Sumiko replied.

"You may return to your duties, Sumiko," said the queen. "I suggest you use the side door back there."

"Yes, my queen. Oh, and you'll be needing this." Sumiko produced a key from her sleeve. Smazeph beckoned her forward and held out her hand. The key was transferred without disturbance. The court then waited until Sumiko left through that sole door behind the pillars. Vez looked over to Kavanchi in that interval. The guard Ginearal was presently

73

clenching something tight in their armored fist. Vez then faced forward once more.

"Bring in the prisoners!" he called aloud. The doors came open again and the procession slowly entered. The escort looked around the room to make sure Sumiko was long gone. None of them gave the side door too long a look. Could not risk the prisoners catching on. The seven Earths were brought past the council table and before the dais. Reoite, still in a haze, was placed on his knees. Irelan and the other privates began to bend theirs as well.

"Do NOT kneel!" Xanthe ordered under her breath.

"Is there a problem?" asked Vez.

"No problem." The general spoke this time, his voice even. "Only that we don't acknowledge your rule, you filthy cor-KAAHH!" That soldier next to him gave him no chance to utter the full slur as she stomped hard on his leg, making him buckle. She could have snapped it with that much force. The other guards got the rest of the prisoners to their knees with a swift boot to the back. Hard but not as hard as the stomp. Xanthe, Irelan, and the boys winced nonetheless.

"I will not have that word slung around by anyone in this room," said the king, his tone dangerous. "Do so again and I will order immediate execution!" Kavanchi gripped their weapon, waiting for the order.

"Geh... I don't fear dying... CORCRA!" A bronze-coated thunder came from the dais. Reeth felt an immediate wind that followed coming toward his face.

"HALT!" Kavanchi's blade was stopped midway into the general's cheek. He bit his lip hard in terror. A trickle of blood was already sliding down his chin.

"Return," ordered Vez. The Longcroc did so, their blade slowly leaving Reeth's face. The gash was deep. His right eye had almost been taken. Kavanchi returned to their place. The others looked wide at the blood upon the blade.

"You will state your name last," said Vez to Reeth. "The rest of you do so first, and one of you give me the name of that one there. I will not bother to wake him." He pointed to Reoite. Xanthe looked at her commander. She looked away, hesitating, then stood up.

"Sergeant Xanthe Toll, Cliar Base. That one over there is Private Skylark Reoite, also Cliar."

"We're all Cliar," said Gert. His guard kicked him in the backside.

"Acknowledged. You next."

"Ngh… Private Gert Norl."

"Private Mason Ochtó"

"P-Private Abram Grocer."

"Private Buí Irelan," she stated last, with a newfound boldness and no stalwart emotion in her face. "And that over there is General Orthur Reeth."

"Insolent underling!" shouted Aamjunta. "His Majesty asked for his name from him, not you!"

"Hold, Ginearal," said Vez. Longcroc impulse was beginning to grate on him today. He looked at Irelan. "Thank you for that input, young lady."

"Where's Liam?!" Now she was overstepping. Aamjunta rose to speak again, but this time the queen stopped him. She then looked to Irelan and gave her an answer.

"He is dead." She cut to the point. Irelan stumbled back on her knees.

"W-what?"

75

"He was most unresponsive, even when he stated his name," Smazeph continued. "An affront to His Majesty that is just as unacceptable as speaking out. He was removed from here and executed outside."

"You're lying!"

"Kavanchi, show her." Kavanchi looked at Irelan and tossed what was in their clenched fist to the floor. A rumpled Cliar kepi. Irelan looked in horror at it. Her lip trembled and a goggle formed in her throat. The others were looking at her, not the hat, in surprise. The council watched with feigned neutrality. Turnie included. Vez held his own feign, mixed with a little tiredness.

"We did not wish to stain this room with blood," Smazeph added. Her face was of a more arrogant indifference.

"Didn't mind staining it over there," blurted Gert. The order of "shut up" was very much not in his vocabulary.

"This is becoming unproductive, my king," said Smazeph.

"Agreed. Guards, take them to the dungeon. Fite, Hurch, please assist them. Have General Reeth's wound cleaned but do not patch it up. Let him live with a reminder of his defiance." The two Shades stood up and moved at once.

"You are an abomination!" screamed Xanthe. She said no further than that, as now Fite had one of her sabers just below her chin. Xanthe looked up at those black and blue eyes. They dared her to say more, but she would not. The prisoners were brought to their feet and led away back to the doors. Hurch gave Reeth's guard a rag from his pocket and she applied it to his cut. One of the guards who carried Reoite stood frozen Irelan up. He was assisted by the one in charge of the sergeant, since Fite was taking over in moving her. The exit was much slower and more ponderous, but soon they were gone.

76

"Let us pick this up around dinner," said Vez. "And have someone clean up that blood."

8

Ginearal Runkc took the initiative in walking down and examining through the open entrance to see for certain that the prisoners were out of sight. She returned to the council table and gave the wordless all-clear. Kavanchi was wiping Reeth's blood off their weapon, not even having to take a knee to do so. Once they finished, they returned to attention. Smazeph stepped forward and spread her arms out, signaling the official dismiss.

Sumiko returned from the side door as the Ginearals were getting up from their seats. She had been on standby the whole time.

"I will get that cleaned up right away, your Majesty," she said as she approached the dais.

"Get Jun'ichi on it," Smazeph commanded. "We need you to return to the South Hall and check in with Aya on the progress."

"Yes, my queen." Sumiko bowed and followed the Ginearals out of the main entrance. The doors closed slow and shut once they were all out. Only Vez, Smazeph, and Kavanchi remained. The queen turned to her husband and smiled.

"Do you wish to stay here and watch Jun'ichi clean?"

"Of course. You know as well as I do that having both of us in his presence motivates him to get it spotless. Though he his dedicated all the same."

"Indeed." Smazeph then looked firm. "That was reckless of Sumiko to barge in that way, though. It would have been risky if the prisoners heard where that young man is being held."

"Yes, but urgency took precedence. Next time something like this happens we shall have her wait."

"A wise decision. If I see her, I will make that clear to her."

"Give it time before you do. Is my leadership to your satisfaction, my queen?"

"It is, my king. So satisfactory that it shall be well rewarded later." Vez shifted in his throne. A sudden tingle had run up his spine.

***

"That was unbelievably reckless of you!" Turnie followed Sumiko through the passage to the South Hall and stopped her halfway through. "Do you have any idea how close we were to having a riot in the throne room? You should count yourself fortunate that the queen made that statement to halt escalation!"

"I got your new toy to a safe place though. Doesn't that count for something?"

"They could have figured out he was not too far away if they heard you. You heard how his friend reacted."

"I practically whispered it. Those doors are too thick to listen through, anyway."

"You have too much confidence in your people's so-called improvements."

"As a servant, I am beneath you, Ginearal. But as a kinsman of the queen, I still take offense to having the Danuc principle of quality being doubted, no matter how high a rank of whom delivers the insult."

"Offense noted. Now perhaps it would be best for us to return to our own duties before council resumes."

"That much we can agree." Turnie said nothing more in response and walked away from Sumiko, taking the left-side passage to the armory. Sabers and rifles adorned racks and shelves throughout this room. One corner held some of the older rifles. Their crystals had been long removed and their storage space had begun to gather dust. A notice that read the Danuc characters for "emergency" was nailed to the shelf. What was the real chance anyone would have to use an obsolete gun during an invasion? Turnie had joined both her king and his people in learning their allies' language during this kingdom's beginnings. It was a struggle for even Vez to know that certain characters meant more than one word, not to mention the intricacy of some characters' form. It had been common for those in lower ranks to express frustration and some close-mindedness on that education. But Turnie dared not to do so. The mind was just as important as any outside muscle, and she made sure all muscles, hers and her troops, were fit and flexible.

Turnie took a left into a passageway with its own sign on the wall. It read (in Danuc) "Ginearal Mave Only." No guard present or necessary. Turnie made her way through the passage and came to a dead end. Stationed at the wall were two Earths wearing nothing but faded pink rags. Unique prisoners of war they were, Earth soldiers who were sting victims of Turnie's own hornets. The Slaver's presence never fazed them, but when she came down this hall they moved with precision, each turning to the walls and pulling down the slide switches on them in unison. Another secret mechanism of the queen's people's design. The stone walls parted to unveil her quarters. Liam was lying on the sofa. At first she thought he was napping, but he sat straight up at the sound of the shifting wall.

"Follow," she whispered to the slaves. They obeyed without a word. Liam swung around in surprise.

"Wh-where'd you come from?!" he stammered.

"A route that only I am allowed to pass," she answered. "Did you think I would return through the front?"

"W-well…"

"Of course, you did, so you let your guard down and anticipated the obvious. If you're going to serve under me, you'd be wise to note that not all is as it seems around here, even with the partial truths you were trained under. Now stand!"

Liam was about to hesitate again, but then he saw she still had that spear in hand. He hated that ringing from the butt when it was thumped on something, and now he wished to not hear it again. He stood up right away and looked Turnie in the eye, face neutral as he had to the drill instructor at Cliar. Turnie scanned him up and down with her own eyes, then nodded.

"Undress him," she ordered to the servants.

"Wait, wha?" Liam stiffened up as they walked toward him. Their movement was stiff as well but they moved with uncanny speed. The one on his left, a girl with dark brown hair, removed his glasses. The other servant, a young man who was about a couple years older than him, went to unbuttoning his uniform jacket. The girl then unbuckled his belt. Their movement was steady and methodical.

"Wh-what are you doing?"

"I need to get a better look at you," Turnie said as she walked past Liam and made her way to the locked front door. "See how healthy, how fit you are to be trained by me." She rapped on the door with her free hand. "Lieutenant, fetch a medic and report back here at once."

"Yes, Ginearal." Turnie waited until she could not hear the lieutenant's footsteps behind the door. She turned back to see that her servants had now just about removed everything. The young man was putting his boots off to the far end of the sofa while the girl was taking Liam's leg out of his pants. Turnie looked over Liam's body. He was lean but had substantial muscle. There was no visible bruising. His beige undershorts looked thin and starchy. The girl was making her way to remove them.

"Wait!" Turnie commanded suddenly. "Take him to the washroom and remove those there. Then draw him a quick bath. He'll need to be clean for a proper examination." The girl nodded to her and then took Liam's hand. She and her partner led him away to the washroom. "Keep the door open, in case he tries to fight," Turnie added. Liam looked at her for a moment. With his near-sighted vision, he couldn't easily see the focused but bewildered expression on her face. She kept watching him as his boxers were removed, and only turned away seconds after his backside was exposed, then retired to the sofa. For no real reason, she decided not to sit in the same spot he did.

Liam made no attempt to fight off the slaves as they scrubbed the minimal dirt and sweat off of him. Turnie soon felt she would not have to intervene and laid her spear in front of the couch, instead of its hold above her bed. Minutes passed, and then a knock on the front door.

"Ginearal, I've returned with the medic," said Lieutenant Ulices.

"Enter." The locked sounded and the lieutenant entered, followed by the medic. Turnie leaned back toward the direction of the washroom. "Is he ready?" The male servant leaned out of the doorway. He made a motion as if he was scrubbing something, then moved his hands back and forth through his hair. "Alright, get him dried off and bring him out here." The slaves brought Liam back into the room, drying off the rest of his back as they went. The door unlocked and Lieutenant Ulices entered, followed by the medic. Liam had not seen the field medic when he was unconscious, but he imagined that this was not that one because the one present here was another female Danuc. She was wearing a thin white buttoned coat over a form-fitting bodysuit made of black leather. The suit's collar covered almost all of her thin-furred neck. Both articles, like all Danuc clothing, had an opening for the tail. Her hair was formed into a pair of buns fitted with white silk covers, and her glasses were horn-rimmed. She was carrying a wooden board with an unusual metal device holding the parchments. Liam had seen boards like that used by instructors at Cliar, but the parchments were held with a long nail through holes in the contents. This device was clamping them without damaging them. He was postured straight as she scanned his naked body up and down with her orange eyes.

"Looks healthy from here. Let me get a better look." She walked up to him as Turnie ordered her servants to back away. Liam stiffened in place as she came closer. She gave him a look with a raised eyebrow, as if detecting his nervousness. She did not ask. Immediately, she looked at his left hand and took hold of it to see his Wart. She also took note of the marks on his wrists from the manacles. The skin was not broken.

"And he has no hornet or gun wounds?" she asked as she began looking at his shoulders.

"No," said Turnie. That question was obvious but still procedure.

"That's good," the medic replied under her breath. She put her hand on Liam's chest and gave it a gentle press to feel the density of his pectorals. Liam shook a little as she produced a stethoscope from her pocket. She slipped the board under her arm so both hands were free.

"I suggest you remain calm," she told him. "Can't read your heartbeat as normal if you make it go fast with worry."

"Uh, right."

"Do they not subject you to examinations at your base?"

"Y-yes, but in a medical wing, not a sleeping quarters."

"Do you never get a woman medic?"

"No, we get a fair rotation of men and women."

"Just never a woman of my sort before?" A hint of a smile was forming on the right corner of her mouth. Liam frowned as if to say of-course-not. He tensed up a bit more, and now he felt a delayed shiver up his back from being unclothed for this long.

"You'll have to get accustomed to being naked when you train with me," said Turnie. Liam shot her a look of surprise.

"What?!"

"Hold still." The medic turned his head back to her as she moved the stethoscope over his chest.

"I train and exercise in the tradition of certain ancients from the Old Continent. They lifted weights, sparred, boxed, and wrestled with little to no clothing. All of that is what the sandpit back there is for. I had reserved it for his Majesty's kinsmen under my command, but they have trained well under the prescribed, clothed regiment. So, you better be prepared for that, as you'll be the first trainee of mine to do so."

"And you look to be in prime condition to do so," the medic added. She had removed the stethoscope and crouched down to inspect his abdomen. "How old are you?"

"N-nineteen. I joined the army two years ago."

"Family obligation?"

"Not really."

"I think you should leave me to ask the personal questions, Doctor," said Turnie.

"Yes, you're right, Ginearal. You chose him as your responsibility after all, so getting to know him better is your obligation. I am only here to measure his health." She moved her hand from Liam's stomach to his inner thigh, then looked up at him. "Please don't flinch, it's procedure."

"Uh, sure." Liam was no fool. Medical examinations required inspecting everything. He never had issue when they did so at Cliar, why should there be issue here? He took a deep breath as the medic gently clasped his organ with the tips of her fingers. They felt cooler on his skin here than anywhere else she touched him. Her thumb ran over, tracing for unseen lumps or other afflictions. Liam looked down at her for a moment. The lower buttons of her coat were opened, so he could see the outline of her stomach tightly framed by her suit. A prominent sheen was on her leather-clad thighs as she crouched. He then felt another shiver on his back. To brace it, he curled his toes. This resulted in an invisible weight suddenly dropping in his stomach and making a splash inside. He felt his heart beginning to beat faster, and then he swallowed; his mouth just now felt dry. His large throat fruit wobbled up and down. Turnie took notice, as did the medic.

"Thirsty?" she asked. She smirked again, this time not bothering to hide it.

"A little," he croaked. Turnie looked to the girl servant and directed her attention towards a cabinet by the washroom door by nodding at an angle. The servant walked over there and took out a tall clay cup, then went to the washroom and filled it with water from the sink. She returned and walked over to Liam without a prompt from her master. The medic watched the servant pass the cup to him. He took it slowly with one trembling hand and brought it to his lips. He tilted his head back with care to sip it and almost doused himself. The water was swallowed in five large gulps without so much as a dribble. Liam handed the cup back and resumed his stance. The medic gave a quick touch-exam of his scrotum with one hand while grasping a handful of his buttocks with the other. She gave a surprised look at what little cushion was felt. Liam began to feel a stiffness between his legs and curled his toes even more.

"Alright, he's good to go." She stood up and went to the back to wash her hands, then came back over to Turnie. "I will give my report to his Majesty. You'll have no trouble talking to him about this later."

"Thank you, Doctor." The medic retrieved her board, having put it down when she needed both hands, and left the way she came. Lieutenant Ulices followed her after giving a fast salute to the Ginearal. When the door closed shut, Liam finally relaxed himself. He noticed the stiffness had remained present. Turnie looked at him with indifference.

"Did I do something wrong?" he asked nervously. Turnie's face softened but she kept a professional air on it.

"No, you did quite well. Expected for someone under your training status. Although, I have to admit the doctor was exercising a bit too much liberty. Arrogant liberty at that. If this was her way of seeing you need an outlet for certain matters, she'd have done better to tell me off to the side." Now

Liam was looking puzzled, and a little uneasy. Not of what the medic would have said but of what Turnie was thinking now.

"There will be time to address and discuss all things with you later. I will be a hard teacher but not a heartless one. For now, you will rest, and the intensity of your training will depend on what his Majesty says next. Now let's get you into some fresh garments."

9

Evening would soon be upon the Last Cloch, but there was daylight to spare. The seven prisoners were escorted to the dungeon, which was not part of the castle at all. It was in an enclosed area below and behind the hill, away from the eyes of Vez's people but known to all of his forces. The dungeon itself was a sturdy stone and wood building, not unlike a warehouse. Its perimeter was a fence composed of thick, high trunk poles wrapped in metal wire with sharp-looking barbs. More of a stockade than a dungeon. There was a nest to the left of the entrance and a small guardhouse to the right.

Hurch led the way, keeping Reeth close. Fite still had her saber trained on Xanthe, who had no choice but to calm down but seemed to want to lash out again. Irelan had to be led by two soldiers. The shock of Liam's fate had not worn off. The rest of the seven were coming quietly here and now.

When they were just feet away from the prison entrance, two guards (one armored spearman and one trooper) stepped out from the guardhouse. At the same time, three pink hornets emerged from the nest. The spearman, whose chest armor had a large pink hornet sigil on it, signaled the hornets to hold position by raising his spear up and looking straight at them. The trooper's kepi bore a patch with three stars behind a horizontal line. He was a colonel.

"Colonel Blare," called Hurch. "New residents have arrived." Colonel Blare was a few years older and a couple feet taller than either of the Ginearal siblings. His face showed that he did not seem thrilled that two youngsters outranked him. He stepped forward anyway to look at the prisoners.

"Intern or press?" he asked. The hornets behind him buzzed a little louder upon hearing this question.

"Internment until further notice from his Majesty," Hurch replied. Blare looked away from Hurch for a moment for a better look at the Earths. The two high-ups looked defiant, one private was dead to the world, another seemed paralyzed, and the remaining were just staying put. He turned back to Hurch.

"We should keep the command ones far away from each other, and their troops. One in the upper cells, the other in the lower. Those other two in the lower, together. The rest for the center cells."

"Wise idea, Colonel." Hurch's tone and compliment were genuine, but Blare read it as arrogance. Reeth frowned at this arrangement but dared not to protest. Blare turned to the spearman and raised his chin. The spearman nodded and then signaled the hornets to back away. Once they returned to the nest, the spearman stepped aside to let the others pass. It was all very quiet out here, save for the buzzing inside the nest and beyond. There was also the faint sound of machinery coming far away from no clear direction. Vez was up to something, and the prisoners who were able to listen to the noise now wanted to know what it was. But this was no time or place to ask questions. Colonel Blare led the line straight to the building. Two soldiers and two FearStings were posted at the massive double doors. The spearman approached them and tapped his weapon on the ground once. The varnished wooden butt made no ring. The FearStings inched back and the troopers holstered their weapons to reach the large iron rings on the doors.

***

The North Hall was being prepped for dinner as sundown came. The kitchen was somewhat quiet that afternoon, but had been bustling for the last two hours. The staff were always coordinated, from those in charge of the dishes to the runners who'd bring extra portions to the barracks. The tableware was all set and the dishes were almost ready to go out. Vez's rule and his alliances had insured over time that food was relatively plentiful in NightPeace. The Shades' traditional staples were corn, potatoes, beans, and fish, but they had come to accept the meat and poultry choices of the Danucs and Gavis. Danucs were partial to pork, chicken, and duck. Gavis would eat any meat but their specific choices were lamb, beef, and the barkdeer of their homeland. Commoner Gavis ate their meat raw, while higher-caste like Aamjunta consumed them with mixes of spices and through long established cooking techniques.

Tonight's fare was varied but substantial for the king's entourage. Roasted ears of corn seasoned with dwarven cilantro and crumbled horse cheese, braised duck in a sweet plum glaze, leavened bread (naan) paired with skewers of mint-and-ginger seasoned barkdeer and fermented yogurt, and salad composed of varied greens and cucumber. There were also regular servings of rice imported from both the Danuc and Gavi nations. Vez and his people had come to enjoy the foreign grain.

Vez was seated at the head of the table as usual, with his queen sitting right beside him on his left. Fite and Hurch always sat next to each other, still in uniform but with hats and gloves off and laying on the benches. Aamjunta, sitting across from them, did not have to do the same for his turban. He had his orderly standing beside him to pour him more water. Kavanchi ate outside in the anteroom, as their job of guarding the king extended to mealtimes. The kitchen staff always managed to put together a combination of everything being served for them, always on a sturdy tray that they rested on their knees as they sat on the guard bench. Runke and Turnie sat on the same side as the siblings, while Crosta sat a few feet

91

away from Aamjunta. The rest of the bench space was for chosen guests, usually servants whose duties required a semi-regular report. And Jun'ichi, Sumiko, and Aya were those usual servants in attendance.

They all had started their meal with a thin-broth soup with green onion and dumpling, a personal favorite of the queen's, before partaking in any of the bigger dishes and rice. Vez had a mask-bearer standing to his right, a Shade girl who wore the same uniform as the attending servants minus the hat. The king ate his soup with a spoon while Smazeph preferred her people's chopsticks. Midway through the soup course she prompted her husband to take a dumpling she held out to him from between the sticks. He leaned over and took the dumpling in his mouth, sliding it off the lacquered clamp. He chewed it and smiled at her while doing so. She then reversed the sticks in her hand and passed them to Vez. He took them and watched her slowly open her mouth, beckoning him to do the same. Vez swallowed the one she fed him and picked up one for her from his bowl. He fed it to her in the same fashion, then a second after returned the sticks to her. She chewed for a few seconds and then swallowed, just as he did. Her tongue peeked out and slid across her blue lips as she gazed with longing at him. He deepened his smile and raised his small cup of hot tea. Cheers to her. Hurch grinned with interest at the display. Aamjunta averted his eyes and made a silent groan. Fite's glare was trying to burst out, and only Turnie saw that. The dwarves and servants kept to their own soup.

Once the bowls were cleared away, they all began to dig in to everything else. Vez and Smazeph each had an attendant serve a slice of duck to them. The Ginearals and the other Danucs passed around the other dishes to each other. Aamjunta immediately grabbed two of the skewers and a big piece of the naan when it came around to him. He slid the deer meat off the skewers and onto the bread. The orderly put the water jug down on the table without a command and spooned some yogurt onto the wrapup. Aamjunta made a growl of approval and stuck the whole thing in his long jaws. When he looked at his hand, he saw a fleck of yogurt near his thumb and pinched the orderly hard on the shoulder. The orderly took the napkin from the table and wiped it off.

As soon as everyone had something on their plate, Vez rose from his seat and tapped his teacup with his fork.

"Everyone, now that we're all well and eating, shall we proceed to further business?"

"Yes, your Majesty," they all answered in low unison. Vez resumed his seat and looked over to Fite and Hurch.

"Are the prisoners all settled in?"

"Settled as best as possible, my king," Hurch replied. "Leave it to Colonel Blare to figure out how to space them out. They're lucky we don't overcrowd that dungeon."

"Their sergeant seemed more than willing to die in defiance right then and there," added Fite. She took a slow bite of the naan on her plate before continuing. "But the rest went quietly into their cells. Not even that loudmouth fought back."

"And what of that one young lady?" Smazeph asked. "The one who could say no more after the news of her comrade?"

You know damn well what, you're the one who broke her, Fite thought. "She had to be moved by us, my queen. Her spirit looked shattered." Smazeph nodded and looked to Turnie.

"Ginearal Mave, do you think we should have them all pressed in?" Turnie was the only Ginearal who had changed clothes. Instead of her regular warrior garb, she had dressed in a custom rose gown, well-suited for her tall stature and greater musculature. She still wore a headband, though one that was matching and embroidered with elegant pattern. Vez had great respect for her heritage, but even he could not turn a deaf ear to his queen's insistence and Aamjunta's seconding for her to dress more conservative at dinner. Turnie was not fond of the queen for that. She did not, however, share Fite's specific hostility.

"I will discuss it with the colonel, my queen. Some of them will serve us better in the slave quarters, especially that so-called loudmouth. However, I would not recommend pressing the general or the sergeant. As for the young lady, we must wait until she can grasp her surroundings again, and we must keep her far away from Liam."

"You're absolutely right, Ginearal. We can't risk her knowing the truth. You will be responsible for keeping him from knowing her fate."

"As you wish, my queen." Turnie already knew that would be hard. "Training him and his power will keep him busy."

"Excellent, though perhaps you would be wise to take an accelerated approach. Isn't that right, my king?"

Vez was savoring his corn but paused when she asked. He lowered the ear to his plate and finished chewing.

"What do you mean?"

"Sumiko, Aya, would you care to deliver your report from the war engineers?"

"As you wish, my queen," they said together. Neither one of them was a novice at their job. If Queen Smazeph asked one or both of them to give a specific report, they were more than prepared. Aya had the written elements of the report on her own clipboard, which she had kept on the bench to the left of her until the time was right. She finished chewing her bit of salad, picked up the board and stood up, facing the king and queen. Sumiko was up seconds before and stood to Aya's right so they could both be seen.

"Ten new assault machines, ordered last week, have been assembled and ready for both yours and his Majesty's approval. They just need to be fueled and armed and they will be ready for deployment."

"That was the second order that I put in, correct? We have exactly twenty in place?"

"Yes, my queen."

"And none have been tested yet?"

"No, my queen. The assembly team thought it would be better for his Majesty to see the demonstration once he was finished inspecting the recent encroachment, as is what he was doing today."

"Chief Engineer Aka was the one who decided this wait?"

"Yes, my queen. To give time to assemble the crews from our forces, with yours and his Majesty's approval. Although…"

"Although, what?" interrupted Smazeph. Her tone was low now. Aya stiffened a little. She knew any drawback no matter how small could be a problem.

"Deputy Chief Engineer San wishes for the machines' designer to be present for any demonstration. He asks for the Crown to charter a ship for him."

"The designer you are speaking of is my cousin, Lord Zharve, head of the Deshomino Yokei Arms Company. I saw his plans for these machines long before the parts were shipped here. Aka and San have been in his lordship's employ for years. Is this request from Lord Zharve himself, or is San asking for this on his own initiative?"

"San presented no written word from his lordship for this request," said Sumiko. "So yes, San alone was asking this."

Smazeph frowned. It was improper for a Deputy Chief Engineer to exceed his authority out of loyalty to his employer. She clasped her fingers together and pondered for a moment, then turned to the king.

"What do you make of this, my king?" Vez had been at complete attention to this report. He had met Lord Zharve in person during his rise and considered him family, but he also knew that Zharve ever rarely traveled unless he had to, and that travel was for the sole purpose of seeing if a weapon of his was ready for action.

"As fast as your homeland's ships are, it would take more than a week for his lordship to reach Uaine, and our navy is not strong enough yet to spare a ship for him. We also cannot ready a blockade to patrol the waters to guarantee safe passage for him if he is to come by personal ship. And with the Cliar soldiers having come upon the encroachment, that base is bound to send more troops out if they get none or even some word of what became of Reeth's battalion. They may even request to send forces from one of the Forts, maybe even a Laoch. We have to consider striking back while the enemy is in the dark. Having these machines assembled is a sign that we must do so."

"How much time should be taken to mobilize, my king?" Smazeph asked. Vez turned away for a moment and thought hard. Everyone else was silent and at attention for a minute and a half.

"Four days," said the king.

"Mobilize in four days, you mean?" his queen asked.

"Yes and no. We need at least three days to assemble an invasion force, including the machines. In that time, we scope the barracks for further troops, the crews, and those who will stay behind to guard NightPeace. We must also give complete consideration on the mix of hornets that will make up this force. True we have plenty overall to spare, but as to which Stings will be in the field is more important than ever. I have confidence that we can spare many of the ones we use most of the time, but as you all know, two of our swarms have some issues." Most of the Ginearals nodded in agreement.

"Does this mean that we can use the Faigceal for this campaign, my king?" Aamjunta asked. "My swarm's caretakers last reported that they are less impulsive with their stinging. Even just a small number should suffice."

"Just because they're less impulsive as you claim doesn't mean they're less inclined to friendly sting," said Crosta, high objection in his voice. "Last time we used them in the field they harmed more than a dozen of my troops. Half of them are still recovering. They still can't fully eat!"

"At least my swarm actually does something, horse-dwarf. Your Mioscaceal don't do much except turn enemy soldiers into frozen gimps that stare off into space. So and so that they just sit around in the cells of the dungeon. We put too many of them in the field and Colonel Blare will have his hands full!"

"We are equals, Aamjunta! I am not a mere horse-dwarf, you pompous lizard!" Aamjunta growled.

"ENOUGH!" shouted Vez with a single pound on the table. "I will not have infighting among this council, not while we are approaching such a crucial juncture!" Aamjunta stood up and lowered his head toward Vez.

"A thousand apologies, my king." Crosta stood and bowed as well. "I apologize for the outburst, my king," he said, much less flowery than his peer. Both Ginearals raised their heads to see the king nod, a signal of his forgiveness. All three returned to their seats in unison.

"You are most right that we need a strategic concentration of Stings in this force, my king," said Smazeph. "But remember, the Tíorafaoi have the collective title of the Seven Swarms. If we are to use that title to the effect of striking fear in the enemy hearts, we should have strategic but noticeable concentrations of all seven."

"Hm, my queen, as always, makes a valid point. And so, we will use the next three days to rally such a concentration. On the fourth, we march on Cliar. Once we capture it, we shall see which of the Five to target first. This will take much timing and cooperation. Let us all keep that in mind. In the meantime, let us resume our feast."

10

The council's feast went on for another hour without so much as a quarrel. Crosta and Aamjunta did not exchange further hostile glances to each other, and Fite even steered her gaze off the queen for more than a minute and enjoyed her meal. The official ending came when Kavanchi returned to the king's side. The king and queen dismissed all except Turnie and the servants. The other Ginearals took their leave at their own pace. Fite, Hurch, and Runke gathered leftovers from the table to bring to the subordinates who guarded their quarters. When Vez looked upon Turnie she immediately rose from her seat and faced him. She had brought her spear with her to dinner, and it was still between her feet under the bench. Normally this was to pacify violent arguments in a meeting or the slim chance of invaders or assassins coming upon the king. Turnie had added the new reason of keeping her charge from taking it and using it to escape, even though she doubted he was strong enough to carry it for a long period of time.

"Ginearal, do you think you'll be able to get that young man ready to join us in three days?"

"Of course, my king. I will let him rest this evening but will give him no such extensive relief that could be considered pampering. Just the basics. First thing tomorrow, we begin training. Just me and him."

"Very well. Although, I wouldn't go so far as to wake him at dawn. He may still need some recovery from using his power. Getting him to use it for battle will need to be expedient but reasonable. He only just first used it in the heat of battle."

"Understood, your Majesty. Is that all?"

"Yes, you may go." Turnie bowed to Vez and retrieved her spear, then stepped out of the room without delay. Vez and Smazeph then turned their attention to the servants.

"As to the matter of getting my cousin to Uaine, tell the engineers that I will send a letter to him personally, detailing of when and how he shall get to travel here. That should warn them that decisions concerning kin are always by my word. I would suggest that you tell them immediately. Tomorrow you will also check in with both Ginearal Crosta and Ginearal Aamjunta on the progress of their swarms and report back to both of us. Do this while covering your new duty of assessing which of our soldiers can be assembled into the machine crews."

"As you wish, my queen," said Sumiko, speaking for all three.

"You and Jun'ichi may go. Aya, I would prefer if you would remain in the company of myself and his Majesty tonight and tend to our quarters. Consider it a mild penalty for your oversight in the report."

"Y-yes, my queen."

"Do you need me to give her instructions, my queen?" asked Sumiko.

"No, she has done stewardship around this castle just as long you have. I am certain she can figure it out. Now leave." Sumiko nodded in response to the icy command and left the room with Jun'ichi following behind, but not before handing over the special key to Aya.

"Do not worry, Aya," said Vez in a more assuring tone. "Tidying up a ruler's bedchamber is not difficult. There is at least one outside task that we will ask of you, but you should be able to handle it. I assume Sumiko has told you of it at some time before?"

100

"At least once, my king," Aya answered. "She was often always the one to do so. Guess that's why she asked about instructing me."

"I assure you it is anything but difficult, and most painless even to me."

***

The king and queen opted to digest their meal by taking a walk around the inside of the castle while Aya was sent to their apartment tower. They allowed her to finish the last bits of her meal before doing so, as the stumble in her report had put a small strain on her appetite. She had to wait for the guards to clear the table and benches as well as wait for the maids who brought the linens up to the tower.

When Sumiko had handed her the key, she had also whispered to meet her outside the door once the king and queen were asleep. Nervous as Aya was, she knew where they had to go later. There were no secrets among these servants, although ironic compartmentalization assured that they alone worked the areas of the castle grounds that few others were permitted. The linen maids came down the tower stairs. The guards let them leave before allowing Aya to go up. The base interior was wider on the inside, with the stone spiral steps making an immaculate display in the center. The sconces held closed lanterns on strong wooden rods instead of torches. Their placement gave anyone walking up these steps a greater sense that this is where the rulers of this kingdom settled in for the night.

Aya reached the top of the staircase and faced the small platform of hallway that led to the chamber. To her surprise, Jun'ichi was waiting for her. The chamber's entrance was to his left. He had been resting his eyes while standing up, not even leaning on the simple bench that was against the wall. He raised his head and opened his eyes just as Aya came into the passage.

"I take it you didn't see me come up before the maids earlier," he said, alleviating her of the obvious question. "Then again, you were a bit fixated on trying to eat something." That was most true, as Aya had her eyes glued to her plate when she was finishing up. It was amazing that she kept her food down after the queen's words had bored into her.

"You didn't think to bring this up with you." Jun'ichi brought Aya's attention to a large and unusual container that was by his side. It was a cylinder on top of a large box, both made of pure steel. The cylinder's lid and the box's front both had keyhole locks on them, but Sumiko's key was only for the lid. The whole container was frosted from a perfect-fitted slab of ice in the box beforehand. It would stay cold for a long while.

"Sumiko gave you the key, surely you would have known to get this." Now Jun'ichi was beginning to sound more unfriendly.

"Y-you're right," Aya stuttered. "Is there any word on when they will return to…?"

"He's going to tell you right now," Jun'ichi interrupted, pointing at who was behind Aya. On of the tower's guards had appeared.

"His Majesty and the queen are approaching," he said. Panic was now flooding Aya's face, and Jun'ichi could see it. He strode up to her in wide paces and gripped her shoulders hard, looking her straight in the eye.

"Pull yourself together! This is our most important duty! It is most likely the only time they will get to do this before the invasion. Now get over there and stand at attention!" Jun'ichi swung her over to the chamber door. She almost collided into it, only stopping so by getting her hands up against it. Her colleague looked at her with warning and suspicion, hoping there was no scratch from her claws on that door. Aya righted herself and stood in front of the door with her hands behind her back. The guard stood against the wall as Vez came up to the top, guiding his queen lovingly by the hand. Following them was a Danuc from the kitchen staff, whose uniform was much plainer than Aya's, carrying a pitcher of water.

"Right this way, my queen," said Vez to his confidant.

"Steady, my king. You know that my favorite part is the slow anticipation that comes from the ascension. Please do not rush this." Her gentle smile faded when she saw Aya stiffened against the door. Aya turned her head just a little and was met with a demanding stare from the queen. Smazeph said nothing but her look read "Well, are you just going to stand there or are you going to open it?!" Aya got the message and stepped away from the door, flailing her arms out to open it. She grabbed the door with her right hand and tried to pull it open. She then remembered it was a push and did so. Her left hand swung forward for no reason and hit the door's edge hard. She winced. The pain was keeping her from seeing that the queen was doing all she could to avoid reprimanding her.

"A-after you, your Majesty. My queen." Aya stepped back after the address. Vez and Smazeph walked forward, keeping their eyes only on the entrance and nothing else. Their bedchamber was a wide half-circle lined with fine fabric and only the best comfort. An enormous vanity was on the far-right side, with enough room for both of them to look in its mirror. The washroom was off to the left, doorless entrance right next to the chamber's own doorway. The bed was large and plush, and its canopy was winding drapes of burgundy and blue. Vez and his queen stepped in to the center of the room and looked to the vanity. Aya, Jun'ichi, and the kitchen servant promptly fell in.

"Aya, get two cups for us from the vanity. We will take our water in them," Smazeph ordered. "Jun'ichi, you brought the container, so you will assist me in the washroom. When you are done with the water, Aya, you alone shall assist his Majesty." Aya's hands were shaking. Smazeph parted from Vez's hold and went into the washroom, with Jun'ichi following behind. The pitcher holder, whose name Aya did not know, came up beside her when they were out of sight.

"Cups are in the bottom left drawer," she whispered. The king and queen had no wine in their room, as there were all kinds of risks associated with having such. Aya went to the drawer and produced two ivory cups from it. The pitcher holder walked over and waited for Aya to place the cups on the vanity. She walked over to it but did not fill the cups. Instead, she turned around and faced the king, pitcher still in hand. Aya noticed this and did the same.

"Come now, Aya," said Vez. "Disrobe me." His voice was kind. Aya slowly walked over to him, a little calmer now because of how he spoke. He was only a few feet taller than her, but she could still reach what had to be removed. She reached for his horned crown.

"Ah." It was only a faint click from his mouth, but it was still a warning that that was not the first thing to take off. Aya pulled her hands back and thought for a moment, then she looked to the king's mask and its ornament. She then looked in Vez's eyes and he gave her the faintest nod. She unfastened the mask very carefully, exposing his bearded face, then spotted the nightstand by the bed and the open wooden box with a molded cushion inside that was resting on it. Immediate deduction led her to place the mask in the box and close the lid. Next, she went to work on removing his chest armor. No problem. She was just about to walk around to behind him and remove the under-suit when another "ah" sounded from him. Aya thought for a moment and then looked to his right arm, where his blades were carried. She spied the fasteners at the end of the gauntlet and went around the other way to his arm.

Aya unclipped the fasteners around the area. The under-suit had no full sleeve there because Vez's right arm was a prosthetic. She took off the arm in both hands, revealing a long-healed stump with light purple, almost pink discoloration. Aya held the arm carefully, keeping her fingers away from the blades. Beside the mask box were two long black velvet sleeves. Aya placed the arm on top of the box and then took the sleeves and slid them over the blades, matching their curve.

Now she went around behind him and unzipped the back of the under-suit. Such a convenient device, that zipper. Metal fasteners were not an option, as they would have dug into his skin if he was hit from behind in battle. Vez's left arm was less prosthetic than his right; he still had all his fingers and all his tendons. As such, the left sleeve had more length that slid out from under his forearm plating. Aya pulled the suit down off from his right shoulder, freeing his stump. Vez lifted a leg out of the suit, then the other. Aya removed the extra plating from the king's left arm, just so he could get it out of the sleeve. She returned it once his was fully unclothed.

"Always a wonderful sight to look upon," said Smazeph. Vez slowly turned around to see his queen standing in the washroom entrance as naked as he was. The fur around her breasts and abdomen were as light as that on her face. Her dark brown nipples were erect and peeking out of the fur. She stood firm and prominent, hands on her hips and legs well-spaced. Her eyelids were hazy low and she was breathing with an open mouth. Vez looked her up and down with great interest, his excitement rising fast. Aya was looking at the queen herself, but she began to turn away as if she was unworthy of this sight.

"Do not look away from me or him!" Smazeph ordered. "This is an honor for any servant who tends to their rulers' nightly needs to look upon their bodies as they consummate." She closed her eyes and raised her head to the ceiling just a slight. "You may remove our crowns now." Jun'ichi removed hers first, then Aya removed Vez's. It was heavier so she had some difficulty. She placed it on the vanity, and then Jun'ichi placed the queen's next to it and then stood next to Aya.

The three servants watched in silence as their rulers walked towards each other in slow, rhythmic steps to the center of the room. There was enough light to see them coming from the lanterns on the walls. Smazeph kept her stride as she walked. It looked stiff at first glance but then appeared manageable as she kept moving. Aya was so busy watching her and the king that she did not notice Jun'ichi's smile, satisfied with his preparation task. Smazeph stopped in the middle of the room first, followed by her husband. Face to face once more, with him looking up at her. His eyes moved lower again, looking to maintain his desire by looking upon every detail of her form. There was no chance of it weakening now.

Smazeph brought her hand to his chin and gently raised his head up to make him see her eyes. Her mouth was forming unspoken words. A command to not dawdle. Vez stepped closer to her as she bent her knees just a little. Their mouths came together, followed by their bodies. Only their lips and torsos were connected at this point. Vez then pulled back away and cupped his queen's breast with his one hand, running his plated thumb around the nipple. Her exhale was shuttering. She then put her hand on his right shoulder and gripped, looking at his stump at that time. Look but don't touch. Her claws dug into his shoulder.

Vez continued rubbing her nipple while kissing the other. There were no words from either, just heavy, long under-breaths from him and short, rising pants from her. With every clockwise rotation of his thumb, she widened her stance. When she was just about bowlegged, he looked down again.

106

The lips of her sex were glistening and open. He began to crouch down. She noticed this and dug her nails in his shoulder. He stopped and looked to see her shaking her head just a little.

"You may taste that later," she whispered. "When all is done." She leaned in and licked the top of his head in one long streak. That motion seemed to send word to his mind, for now Vez moved his hand to her hip and directed her towards the bed. As Smazeph laid down, she could see his member was at its full length. She put her head back and spread her legs wide. "Begin... now," she stuttered.

11

The union was long and satisfying. Vez and Smazeph's screams from their pleasure-making had sounded through the whole chamber. No words, just sound. If the guards below heard it, they kept to their posts. Whether anyone else around the castle or its grounds heard them was impossible to determine. The servants in the chamber were the only ones who saw as well as heard them for those twenty long minutes. The pitcher holder was keeping the vessel firm in her hands the whole time, although she could feel a tremble in her hands when she watched the king thrust deeper inside his wife. The tremble came even more so as she stared at Vez's firm, purple backside and the marks in his shoulder where the queen had gripped him. Aya's eyes were wide open as she watched the process. Her mouth had become dry and her lip was shaking. She wanted to ask for water herself but could not look away, and even if she did her peers would have hushed her. Her ears picked up on a faint drip near her feet and that made her bring her knees together. Jun'ichi appeared the most composed in this audience, wearing a calm smile on his face the whole time. He did look down at his feet for a moment here and there, but the others didn't notice. Under his smile he was gritting his teeth because he wished his robe had deep, flexible pockets.

When Vez finally released, both he and his queen let out the loudest cry they could muster. The room slowly filled with both of them catching their breath. Vez took the most miniscule of steps as he backed away out of her.

"Water," he said. The kitchen maid turned back to the vanity and poured a cup, then put the pitcher down and brought the cup over to him. Vez's body was drenched in sweat, giving his nocturnal skin the shine of amethyst. He turned around and took the cup in his one hand, nodding his thanks. "For her, too," he whispered. The maid went back to pour the queen's cup.

"Jun…'ichi," said the queen. He took that as his que and walked around and off the right to the bed. The maid had the filled cup ready but did not follow him. This was priority. Smazeph raised her hand and leaned it in Jun'ichi's direction. He took but did not pull her up. He let her sit up on her own. She stared off into space at first, then centered her focus on Vez and the other servants.

"Legs are still tingling," she said. Silence followed. Vez took that time to drink in the sight of his wife. Her face made it seem she was tired, but he knew from past experience that it meant that he performed well. Smazeph caught him staring and smiled.

"I'm glad that you sound less stinted than you used to," she said. "Even through my cries, I could hear the change."

"Well, I doubt I could ever reach your pitch, my dear."

"Give us the time to sort this out and you shall have your after-treat, my king." Vez nodded with a smile of both understanding and confidence. She had not steered him wrong yet. He turned away to take a long sip of his water as Smazeph and Jun'ichi left for the washroom. When he parted his mouth from the cup, he turned back and sniffed the air a little.

"Her scent will become more prominent once the sample is taken out of here." Another louder sniff (not from him) came out.

"You give off a pleasant scent yourself, your Majesty," said the pitcher holder. Her voice was quiet but casual. That made Vez swing around.

"A bold statement for you to make, Nin," he said with warning in his voice. Nin lowered her head in guilt. Her nostrils were still flared as she did so.

"I did not mean to offend you, my king."

"It is fine. You are a young kinsman of my queen. It is impossible to not have some envy of her being the one who joins with this realm's lord and master." Jun'ichi returned from the washroom, carefully holding a long pouch full of unmistakable contents. He was now wearing a long pair of gloves that appeared to be made of the same material as the pouch but thicker.

"Aya, the key," he called.

"You may go and assist him, Aya," said the king. "Penance fulfilled." Aya gave a bow and left the chamber following Jun'ichi. "Nin, the door please." Nin put the pitcher down on the vanity and closed and locked it. Smazeph emerged from the washroom, looking more livened up again. She leaned an elbow on the doorway.

"Easy as always, no?" Vez smiled and nodded. He took another drink as Smazeph walked back over to her spot on the bed. Her motion was not as stiff now. Nin saw her taking her seat and brought over her cup, then retreated back to the vanity. Smazeph took a long gulp and then looked at Vez.

"I never get tired of seeing you stand like that after we fuck."

"Standing like what, exactly?"

"Oh, just that calm stand that would look pathetic on somebody else. Head up but not too high, face at ease, legs not straight together. And best of all you look like you're ready to go again." True, Vez was not at full mast like earlier but he was not flaccid either.

"We should make another round more regular."

111

"I do not think so. Then they'd never leave. No, we have our ways to purge the excess, my king, and it is better to do that in near privacy." She finished her water and place the cup on the floor. "Now come here and partake." She then looked to Nin. "Turn around, cover your ears and shut your eyes. I heard you. You do not deserve to see this tonight."

12

Aya and Jun'ichi returned to the bench where the container was left. The guard watching it closed the bedchamber door. He then stood in front of it, paying no attention to the servants' task. Aya took out the key and unlocked the lid. She was met with a slow burst of cold vapor and a faint hiss when she opened it. The cylinder's inside contained a thin tube that was fixed in place by three ribs of sturdy, sterile material that was neither metal nor wood. Aya stepped aside without prompting to let Jun'ichi come forward and slide the pouch into the tube. Even at a distance, she caught a quick whiff of it before it entered the cold placement, and the faint scent she caught told her that the pouch had been inside the queen for almost half an hour. Jun'ichi closed the lid once the pouch was secure. He nodded to Aya and she locked it.

The two of them proceeded to descend the stairs. The guards below let them pass as soon as they heard them come down. Jun'ichi was carrying the container, still wearing his gloves. He and Aya walked side by side. It would seem that he silently awarded her that courtesy for how steady she handled the duty earlier. The table and benches had long been put back in their place, so the North Hall was open space once more. Jun'ichi began to lead the way when he and Aya were about halfway across the hall. Aya sensed this and made sure not to lag behind. She heard low rumbling from the ground floor apartment as she crossed. That had to be Kavanchi, off duty and resting but still in reach of protecting their rulers.

They exited the North Hall and moved straight into the Nexus Tower. Standing in the center of the floor was Hurch, posing like a spearman. He noticed them approach and smiled.

"Ah, there you are. Assisting in the delivery tonight, Aya?"

"Yes, Ginearal."

"Well then, let's be quick about it. My sister's watch on the dungeon will be over within the hour." Hurch clasped his axe in both hands and took the lead. Jun'ichi and Aya followed him as he made his way back to the throne room. The guards opened the doors for him at once. The throne room was quite dark, the lanterns extinguished hours ago. Hurch could manage to navigate through here because of his nightly rounds, and Jun'ichi had gone this way plenty of times. There was also some moonlight peeking through the tinted windows, and it faintly reflected off the edge of Hurch's axe. Aya used that to guide herself through the room. She took it slow but managed to keep up with the other two as they walked around the dais and off to the far-left corner behind it.

The nestled door there led to outside, and down that slope was their next route, between the gardens and the training grounds. Faint lantern light showed the moving shapes of the gardens' night attendants, who were busy watering the more nocturnal blooms deep within. The training grounds were empty and unlit. A small barracks was on the close end; that was for any cadets who were in charge of setting up equipment. On the far end, locked up tight was a large shed for the training gear. Hurch and the servants made their way down the slope and took the gravel path that began at the base. Illuminated by a small covered lantern was a sign at the start of the path, message in Danuc.

AUTHORIZED OFFICERS AND STEWARDS MAY USE
THIS PATH

There was no guard by the sign, but a lone senior cadet with a long rifle in hand was sleeping on the barracks' porch. Hurch saw him resting and frowned, beginning to think this should be reported. He had stopped just before the sign when he noticed this. Jun'ichi came behind him and politely "ahemmed" him to move on. Hurch glanced at the container and nodded. The two of them set off on the path without further delay, with Aya coming close behind them.

The path was straight for all of its length that was open and visible. Once it reached the tree line it led to a small dip and a left turn. Another sign, without an accompanying lantern and reading the same notice as the first, was staked at this point. After the turn, the gravel went a few more feet until ending at a dirt path that was bordered by thick shrubbery. Two Shade spearman were posted here. They saw the Ginearal's unmistakable outline approach and kept still, allowing all three to pass. Down the dirt trail they went, taking care not to drag their feet or go too fast, lest they kick up anything. They moved through this patch of woods until at last they came to what lay below in the clearing.

Beyond these woods was a settlement along the coastline. More nests and barracks were present, but there were also civilian huts much like the ones among the farms. A medium sized harbor lay among the edge of the settlement; it was quiet but its active status was evidenced by the good number of vessels in port. Fishing boats and a few prototype warships. This place was known as Cuan, and it was NightPeace's sister village.

Hurch, Jun'ichi, and Aya set off into the village. It appeared that just about everyone here was fast asleep by now. The only others who were awake were the guards on the barracks porches. Hurch was too busy making his way through now to approve. Their final destination was a facility at the top of a hill that was embedded into the cliff face and well enough away from the sea. Like the warships, it was constructed and plated almost entirely of steel. There were three sets of a dozen concrete stairs leading up to it. Another Danuc import. The guard tower at the base of the stairs was a restored ancient watch-post made of hard bluish stone. Its sentry, wearing a uniform but also a spearman's helmet instead of a kepi, held out his lantern on a wooden pole. He looked down at the trio as they came closer and waved them on. They each looked up to the light and nodded their obligement.

***

The three of them made the climb up the stairs without delay. Aya still lagged a little behind but managed to follow without spurring. The stairs were not steep, so she had no trouble moving one leg in front of the other up them. By the time all three got to the top, the sliding metal door of the facility was already opening in a slow rumble. Emerging from the entrance was Sumiko, Lieutenant Ulices and the Danuc medic who examined Liam earlier.

"Good evening, Lieutenant," said Hurch, tipping the brim of his hat.

"Sir," replied Ulices, saluting.

"I take it you've remained as Dr. Ren's guard for the last few hours?"

"Yes sir. Ginearal Mave did not require me to further watch her quarters upon her return to them. She would have said otherwise."

Dr. Chika Ren stepped forward. "Let us not further burden ourselves with your military formalities. I take it that what you have there is another sample from the king?"

"Yes, Doctor."

"Then let's bring it inside."

All of them entered the building. The heavy door slid back closed behind them as they walked straight through the antechamber, which looked just as sterile as the outside. On either side of them were five doors that led to private rooms. The doctor had Cuan residents, civilian and soldier alike, visit this place during the day to use those rooms. Only men used them, but there were some who brought their wives along for support.

They all walked down the central hall. No doors of any sort on either side. They reached a block of metal with low cage doors. It was guarded by Shade soldiers that only carried revolvers. No doubt they once belonged to Earths who were now enslaved. Functional trophies. The guards nodded to the doctor as she came closer, then they turned their attention to the keyholes on either side of the block. Both of them presented a key that they wore on a band wrapped around their non-shooting wrists. They inserted the keys in the holes and turned them at the same time. The cage doors opened in a slow, precise swing. Dr. Ren led the others into the lift. The guards turned the keys back and the doors closed. The internal mechanisms clinked and rumbled and the lift began to descend. Aya had only ventured to this facility on occasion, but as it was something her people built for the king, even she had passing knowledge of its purpose.

The lift made its smooth descent down the shaft, lined with more smooth metal. It was getting colder as it went further down. Fortunately, the metal was chill resistant, so no frost formed on the walls or the doors. Aya shivered a little. She looked at the others and was surprised to see not one of them make a single twitch. Dr. Ren did button up her lab coat a little. The lift reached the bottom and stopped with a lurch. Cold mist greeted the group through the opening. Aya shivered more. No one took notice. The doors made another careful swing open, and they all exited.

The belly of the facility had been carved out long ago, bringing a number of small caverns in the cliffs together to make a single massive chamber, reinforced and plated with that ever-present steel. Other Danuc medics and Shade soldiers moved about the aisles formed by the enormous refrigerated shelves. The power source for this refrigeration and all the mechanization was known only to the Danucs, and it was well hidden and well-guarded somewhere in all this.

Dr. Ren led the group around the lift's bottom block and past the aisles to an isolated storage room on the far right. Her fellow medics who were nearby saw her approach and they nodded to her. She returned the nods in such a casual manner. Another sliding door to this room was opened by an unseen guard on the other side. The group entered. It was even colder in her, as Aya could feel. This time Hurch noticed her shiver and just gave a friendly tilt of his head, gesturing her to keep moving.

They all reached the exact final spot. An empty shelf space in the far back. The occupied ones were lined with sample cylinders, minus the ice boxes. There were still spaces for more, but only a few shelves left.

"Jun'ichi, if you please."

"Yes, Doctor." Jun'ichi placed the container on the floor. He crouched down and carefully grasped the cylinder, then turned it to the left. It unscrewed with a click. He stood up again and brought the cylinder to an empty notch in the shelf, placing it down in there and turning to the right. Another click, followed by a hiss that was visualized by a burst of chilly mist.

"Splendid. The sample is accepted. A lengthy hiss, too. His Majesty must have been very proficient tonight."

"He was. Saw it myself," said Jun'ichi.

"Any indication when His Majesty and the queen wish to produce their heir?"

"Not yet, Doctor," answered Hurch. "If they did, my compatriots and I would have been told so at tonight's meeting."

"Uh-huh." Dr. Ren was checking the notes on her board for a moment.

"Something wrong, ma'am?" asked the lieutenant.

"No, nothing wrong." She gave a slight chuckle. "Just wishing I had a chance to extract a sample from that young Earth I examined today."

"I'm not sure Ginearal Mave would've allowed that," said Hurch, humor in his voice.

"And you had no container on hand at the time," added Ulices with sternness. "Very much against procedure."

"Yes, you're both right. But you should have gotten a look at him. In his prime but so nervous. You can bet I would correct that if I handled him then and there. And if the power of his Wart is just as strong as Ginearal Mave reported, just think of the strength we would gain if we had the means to replicate it."

"Perhaps," said Jun'ichi. "But still, extracting his sample on a whim would still be against procedure, and our queen is particular about that."

"Well then, I'll just have to ask Ginearal Mave's permission next time I see her. For the sake of our queen."

Aya shivered again, but not from the cold.

119

13

The dungeon building was quiet that night. As Colonel Blare had instructed, Reeth was taken to the upper cells, while Xanthe, Irelan, and Reoite were placed in the lower ones. The rest on the middle floors. Furthermore, Xanthe was given a corner cell in the front left. There were two dozen cells on each of the four floors, accessed by sturdy metal stairs and catwalks. To the prisoners' surprise, this jail looked somewhat empty when they were first brought in. It was only when Xanthe was placed in her cell that she saw a single imprisoned Earth next door, sleeping. No doubt there were two or three more spaced around the floors. The ones who had yet to be pressed.

Fite and Hurch had confiscated all of the prisoners' hats before locking them up. Xanthe's lone neighbor was missing his kepi, too. It was likely they'd deliver them back to Fort Lightwing to send a message, but who could really guess what that abomination Vez was planning at this moment? Xanthe was silent but her mind was racing with the fact that that private was just executed for little reason. She leaned forward and tried to look out of the bars of her cell. The only light coming in now was the moonlight from the high window in the back. The guards had doused the lanterns hours ago; what was odd is that there were no flames in them, and the guards turned off the light just by laying a hand gently on the lanterns' tops. The enemy's simplest technology was just as strange as its weaponry.

The sounds of the castle's activity were distant. There was no way anyone could hear the specifics of what was going on in that place. There wasn't even the sound of any hornets, as they had likely all settled into their nests for the night. Those guards who were there to greet them before remained outside, and they would react to any noise made by the prisoners. A few hours ago, Gert, who was on the second floor, continued to not keep his mouth shut. That was corrected by a few hard jabs with both spear and rifle butts. Gert's protest utterances were turned to faint groans, then silent breathing.

Xanthe leaned back into her cell, then took a closer look at the other prisoner. He was sitting in the center of his cell, legs crisscrossed and head low, appearing to be asleep.

His neck's going to be strained in the morning, she thought.

"Psst." Xanthe stiffened and looked around for who uttered that. It couldn't have been Irelan or Reoite because they were on the other end of the ground floor, and this noise was close.

"Psst. Here." Xanthe looked at her neighbor again. His head was raised now, and he was looking at her. From the details she could see from the moonlight, his face was fairly round, and his general frame appeared stocky. His hair was brown and he was squinting his eyes.

"Are you speaking to me?" she asked, her voice all whisper.

"Please speak up," he said aloud.

"They'll hear us."

"They're likely resting. Even they get tired on duty. Don't worry." Xanthe looked back to the front door before she answered.

"Alright," she said a bit louder. "Sergeant Xanthe Toll, Cliar Base."

"First Lieutenant Liam Birrsova, Fort TwoShips, 2nd Coastline Battalion."

"TwoShips? You're a long way from home."

"Yes, they sent us inland to the front lines instead of assisting the navy. Not a smart idea, in my opinion."

"Wait… Birrsova? As in relation to…"

"… Andrew Birrsova, the current FortChief of TwoShips? Yes. I'm his younger son."

"Where's the rest of your unit?"

"All but gone, ma'am. Two soldiers up in the center cells and me are all that's left. One boy, one girl."

"What happened?!"

"Two months ago, we were sent to the border of the dwarves' herding grounds in the Green West. We were to seek out any further dwarven sympathizers to the enemy, besides those two who became Ginearals. The Tiarnabhac's official statement, as you may know, was that his people were neutral in this conflict. The FortChiefs weren't buying it, particularly my father. So, they ordered our battalion out there to assist patrol with the small outpost near the West. It should have taken a third, no an eighth of our force to patrol. Not the whole thing. Didn't send even one of our Laochs to assist. Then again, they're better suited to assist the navy. We got there, and both of those Longcrocs and their forces were waiting for us!"

"*Both* of them?"

"Yes. I guess that big silent one isn't always joined at its king's hip. Anyway, it was the both of them, the bigger one with its grey hornets, the fancy one and his tan hornets. Even one of those two dwarves. The male one. His hornets were green."

"I've heard in reports that they were green."

123

"Yeah, well we were seeing them in person, firsthand. Short version is, the enemy got to the borderline just before we did. Outpost's forces were light. They came out to meet us, then we charged the enemy. Never stood a chance."

"They slaughtered you all?!"

"Not quite. Anyone who didn't get gunned down or sliced up by the Ginearals was stung, and that's what happened to most of them. Although, good bunch of those poked by the SlugStings somehow got close enough to the big one. Then it split them in half." Xanthe flinched. "Everybody else who got stung was taken prisoner."

"Intel's mentioned that the SlugStings are the grey ones. What about the tans?"

"Didn't really know what they did at first either. We didn't learn until we were all locked up. And you can bet we were all pretty horrified when we heard. There were a lot of them who got poked by the tans. Danuc medics were visiting non-stop to treat them. I listened in when they did. Those tan ones, they call them the StarveStings. Their venom blocks the victims' digestion process. Makes it near-impossible to take in nutrients from what they eat. Medics checked them and had them taken away. Haven't seen any of them since."

"So, they took them for further treatment elsewhere, away from other prisoners' eyes?"

"That's what the medics said. Me, I'm thinking they just took them somewhere near the nests by the castle and let them starve to death. Then they let the hornets eat them. Can't prove it from here, but that's my best guess." Xanthe found herself biting her hand. This just became all the more disturbing. What was just as disturbing was the lieutenant's tone. There was no sign of fear or distress in his voice. He sounded so casual it almost seemed like he enjoyed this hypothesis. Xanthe removed her hand from her teeth, taking a glance at the bite marks. Not hard enough to bleed. She looked back at Birrsova.

"At least you seemed to have survived all this time in captivity."

"Survived, yes. But…" He unbuttoned his jacket, lifted up his undershirt and angled himself so that the sergeant could see better in that minimal light. A faint mark was on his side.

"… I got poked, too."

Xanthe jumped back at that. "Wh-which…"

"Don't worry, it wasn't a StarveSting. It was a green one."

"What does their sting do?"

"To be honest, I don't know," Birrsova answered as he put his shirt back down. "Nobody said anything about it. Doesn't seem like it did anything, other than kind of relax me. No terror, no fever, no other kind of adverse effect. Just relaxed me. Not to the point of knocking me out, thankfully. And my two friends up there, they got the greens' sting, too. We're all okay but imprisoned."

This did not add up at all for Xanthe. Fear, fever, sluggishness, enslavement, and now starvation. How were the hornets' venom effects so specific? Just more evidence to her on how terrible Vez and his retinue were.

"And by the way, there were more in here that weren't starving. You just couldn't see them. I imagine some of them might still be in here. Heard the other dwarf's hornets did that."

So those clear hornets don't just make themselves invisible. Their venom makes whoever they sting invisible.

"Cliar base, you said you were from, Sergeant?"

"Y-yes."

"And I take it that's your commander upstairs?"

"Yes. General Reeth."

"And the others?"

"All privates."

"Just you seven?"

"We… had another private with us. The Wheel took him. And that so-called queen had him executed before we arrived. I believe his name was Liam, too."

"Oh, really?" Xanthe turned away and shook her head. This was way too casual a response. "What was he like?"

"Don't know a lot. A hesitant but model soldier, I guess. No disciplinary problems. Never really stood out… at least not until he got his power."

"He got a Wart? Right then and there?"

"Yes, during our fall back." *Not retreat.* "It was all so sudden. Surprised the enemy, too. Electric force field."

"Hmmm… well, that's a shame that he's dead. That could've have helped our side immensely." A rapping sounded from the front door. Birrsova swung his head toward it.

"Best you pretend to be asleep now, Sergeant," he whispered. Looks like they're starting to hear us. I've been here for some time now. You and the others stick close to me and my friends, and you'll survive." Another rap. "Good night."

Xanthe laid down on the hard wood floor and turned onto her side. When the doors unlocked and opened, she shut her eyes hard. She pushed herself to relax her face so the guards wouldn't catch on to her act. Easier thought than done.

Despite her training, she was becoming more afraid. Afraid of the enemy. Afraid of the stings. Afraid of the guards.

Afraid of Birrsova.

And now she was afraid of the coming morning.

14

It was about an hour and a half before the crack of dawn. Vez stirred gently from sleep. His face felt so much lighter without the mask, and that feeling was most prominent when he was lying down. He licked his lips, still tasting the sweet-salt of his queen on them. She was most eager in feeding him last night. At first it was just him leaning between her bent legs, one hand on her knee and her other hand clutching the back of his head as gorged himself. She had squeezed his tongue a little every time she throbbed. After a few minutes of this, she pulled his head up and wordlessly instructed him to lay down. He did so and then she stood up on the bed and turned around so her backside was facing him. She backed up so her feet were parallel to either side of his head, then raised her tail. The next thing he saw was her sex slowly descending to his face. He then resumed his meal for perhaps another hour before they both collapsed into sleep. Sometime during the night, he woke up and got his head to the right end and onto his pillow.

Smazeph was now lying next to him on her side. Her fur was slick with sweat, and she had the sheet all to herself. Vez lifted up his right stump, attempting to brush her back with it. A quick squirm with his own back helped him make contact. Whatever nerves were still alive in his stump could never replicate a finger's touch, but he felt the texture of her fur somehow. It was a pleasant feel. Looking at her and feeling her made him twitch again. He turned forward and saw that his member was still erect. No signs of her lipstick on it, and this made him sigh. All the time they had been married, she had never once put her mouth on him as he did with her, and for some reason he had always wanted to see her azure-coated lips wrap around head, shaft and all and suck on it. He had suggested this at least twice (the first time was on their wedding night), but she refused. She told him, in her polite intelligent way, that it was unbecoming for a queen to service her king that way, since they ruled as equals.

"It's better for a queen to offer herself in a way where she is on top," she further told him. "Besides, if you wanted such service, I could ask Sumiko or Aya to do it for you." He never requested such.

I suppose I can only dream, he thought. *But she could still do so while she's sitting on me.*

Thoughts on what was coming soon and what needed to be done were starting to return to the forefront of Vez's mind. He sat up to assess these thoughts, still rubbing his queen's back with his stump. The machines had to be tested. Their crews had to be gathered. And above all, he had to monitor Turnie training that young Earth. What were the chances he'd get another night like before within these three days? If he wanted more of these nights, these tasks and this coming battle came first.

Vez rotated his stump against her back one last time, then he sat up and swung his legs over to the edge of the bed. With further motion his member settled down. He stood up, walked over to the door and gave it two sharp raps.

"My king?" said the guard's voice. A different voice. They rotated overnight.

"Yes. Have any maids who are up come to prepare my bath. Find Sumiko if you can."

"Yes, my king." Vez heard the guard exit. Smazeph made a faint groan from behind him; she was stirring now. He turned around just in time to see her sit up and rub the slumber fog from her eyes.

"Good morning, my queen."

130

"Eh… my king, the sun has not even risen yet. Why are you up?"

"I am preparing to set out to observe Turnie's training. You do recall yesterday that I said I would personally see that, yes?" Smazeph sighed as she became more awake. She looked to her nightstand and retrieved her emeralds from their cushioned box, much smaller than the one for her king's mask. She put the gems in her ears while showing a look of mild disapproval.

"Is something wrong?"

"I don't mind that Ginearal Mave is training this boy, but I'm still concerned about you being out in the open near him. How do you know he won't just use his power against you when he gets the chance?"

"Turnie will make sure that doesn't happen. And so will I."

"How?"

"Learn more about him, just as we did with Turnie. As meek and unsure as he appears, there's no way he's completely bought into his superiors' hatred of my people. We appeal to him, and he'll be much more willing to use his power for our side."

"But whatever unfolded in his life is bound to be wildly different from Turnie's history. And remember, Turnie came to us, when she could no longer stomach all she was put through. Her choice was conscious and on her own initiative. This boy may have nothing to motivate him to serve you."

"Cannot be sure of that unless we try. Again, my queen, you worry too much."

"Wake up." Turnie voiced the command with calm force. Liam slowly opened his eyes. He had been sleeping on the sofa the whole night, wearing the fresh linens he was given after the examination. A loose, plain beige shirt with yellow trim and matching pants. They seemed comfortable, as he fell asleep right away. He actually napped after he dressed. There was very little he could do then, and Turnie had sensed he was not up for deep conversation. The servants had brought him soup and bread for dinner while she was eating with the council. He managed to eat, and was surprised at how good the soup was. The dumplings were new to him, but he enjoyed it nonetheless. All he could think about doing afterwards was resting. When Turnie returned, he half-awakened to see her enter, then turned his back on the sofa to sleep on his side. The rest of the night was as blur to him.

Turnie was about to say "Wake up" again when Liam sat up. He squinted and shook his head to adjust to the faint morning light before looking in her direction.

"Your glasses are here," she said, holding them out. Liam remembered that he left them on the small table in front of the sofa.

"Thank you," he muttered hazily. He took them and put them on, and was then startled when he looked at her with clearer vision. Turnie was standing naked right in front of him. She was not even wearing her headband, and her hair looked smoother now. It was also tied in an enormous knot. He could only surmise that she combed something into it during the day to make it spiky. She didn't have her spear on hand, and he took a quick look to find it hanging on its rack. He then stared at her once more.

"Well… stand up and strip," she ordered.

"Wha…"

132

"I did tell you that we would be training in the old ways yesterday, didn't I?"

"Y-yes, ma'am," he sputtered.

"Then stand up and remove those garments. Now." Her tone was rising. Liam stood up immediately and removed the nightshirt. Its collar was wide, so he didn't have to remove his glasses in the process. He put the shirt on the other end of the couch and then removed the pants. He had been given fresh underwear to go with the night clothes; plain grey shorts with no trim. He started to remove those but paused to notice her looking close at him, face indifferent. Sensing another command, he finished taking off the shorts.

"Stand straight." He did so. "Alright, what size weight do you wish to start with?" Liam looked over at the rack of weights. Numerals representing the pounds were etched into them.

"Uh… ten, I guess. Ma'am," he finished, straightening up once more.

"Very well. Follow." She walked over to the rack, with him following close. She took the pair of weights marked "XXXV" and moved to the sandpit. Liam took the "X" weights and joined her. She looked at how he held the weights. He seemed to manage.

"Those weights are too easy for you. Put those back and take the two-X."

"Y-yes, ma'am," he said. No sense arguing. He walked out of the pit, taking care to wipe his feet on the soft mat ring on the edge, and returned the X's. He then reached for the XX's. The bigger weight pulled him off balance a little, but he recovered. Liam returned to the pit and resumed attention, arms and weights at his sides.

"We will begin with the biceps and shoulders," said Turnie. "Watch closely." Liam turned his head to look. Turnie curled her arms up, then raised them high above her head after a second, then in a bending midpoint, then back to her sides. All in steady motion with a single half-second in between.

"Now let me see you do it."

"Yes, ma'am." Liam faced forward. He was familiar with these exercises; cadets and privates alike did these as routine. He took a deep inhale and did the curl, exhaling as his forearms came up. He inhaled again and exhaled as he raised high. Inhale, then exhale at midpoint. Inhale, then exhale as the arms came down. The movement was slightly delayed, but he did the exercise just as precise as hers.

"Very good," said Turnie. "Now let's do five of those. No stopping."

"Yes, ma'am." They both assumed starting position and began the set, breathing at all the proper intervals. One. They lifted again. Two. Again. Three. Again. Four. Inhale, exhale, curl. Inhale, exhale, up. Inhale, exhale, mid. Inhale, exhale, back down. Again. Five. They stood in place for a couple minutes, breathing recovery. Liam was beginning to feel heat on his back.

"Now we squat," said Turnie. "Five, no stops."

"Yes, ma'am." Liam and Turnie stiffened their arms and widened their stances. Inhale. And…squat. Exhale. Up. One. Repeat. During the third squat, Turnie roved her eyes toward Liam, checking his movement. It was near flawless, with only the faintest struggle in the bend. He took no notice of her watching him. She looked forward again as they both took on the last squat.

"Weights on ring," she said. Liam turned to his left and placed the XXs on the mat ring. She put her XXXVs on the opposite edge.

"Now we stretch."

"Yes, ma'am." His response was automatic.

"…" She looked closer at him just as she began raising her right arm up and bending her torso to the left. He was doing the same, in synch with her own motion. It looked like copying on the surface but was not. Turnie looked forward again as she raised her left arm and bent the opposite way, holding it for a few seconds like the left stretch. She then got out of that stretch and put her arms forward, palms out. She counter-rotated her forearms to stretch them. A fast glance had her seeing Liam do the same. She did not even command him this time. *He knows routine and has basic discipline*, she thought. *And no urge of defiance whatsoever.* She returned her arms to first position and brought them down. Liam made the same motion. Turnie stayed put and looked at him for a long moment, waiting for him to speak up. He just stood in place, not looking back.

"Alright," she said with some unease. "Now we stretch our quads, then we repeat the weight sets…"

A knock on the door interrupted her instruction.

"Ginearal." Lieutenant Ulices was behind the door. "His Majesty is here to observe your protégé."

"A moment, please," Turnie replied. She got out of her stance and turned to Liam.

"Stay in place for the moment." Her order was softer this time.

"Yes, ma'am," he answered once more.

Turnie sighed faintly and walked out of the sandpit, wiping her feet on the mat ring without having to think to do so. She walked over to the passageway wall and reached for a small gold button on a plaque. A faint whine sounded from the walls when she pressed it. Liam kept his position but now he decided to get a better look at Turnie from behind. His eyes widened a little. It was not her rippling back muscles and firm gluteus that fully surprised him (though those were the first things he gazed on), but the unnatural, bronze-gold device embedded into and across her upper back. The device consisted of a flat, horizontal oval with its own installation. A bulbous, plain sphere of the same metal was in turn embedded in the center of that. This whole component seemed to be latched to her very spine.

15

The passageway opened once again, and Turnie was met by two different slaves on the other side, both women. They entered the room and the passage closed up as soon as they were in. Turnie motioned them to stay and then walked up to the front door and opened it. The king was standing a few feet behind Lieutenant Ulices. He was dressed in a long, draping robe that hid his right arm. It was a light, amethyst violet that stood apart from his darker purple skin, trimmed in both yellow gold and jade green. Turnie saw Jun'ichi and Sumiko standing off even further, carrying the king's crown, suit, and armor.

"My king," she answered with a bow. "An honor that you can join us this morning."

"I did tell you yesterday I would be joining you," said Vez. "There's no need for complete niceties for mere exercise. Seeing as you're unclothed, I can imagine that I've caught you between sets."

"Yes, my king."

"Any other king would have asked his general if they were decent before entering. But then again, no other king has generals who values root custom equal to physical fitness as you do, Ginearal Mave."

"Thank you, my king."

"Now, may I please enter? I wish to see you both in action."

"This way, my king." Turnie led Vez and the attendants inside with a wave of her hand. Lieutenant Ulices resumed guard position outside the door as soon as it was closed. Vez saw Liam, as unclothed as his master, standing firm with his back to him.

"Pairc, turn and face his Majesty," ordered Turnie.

"Yes, ma'am," Liam answered, a little louder this time and not as mechanical. He turned around and looked in Vez's direction, resuming his stance and neutral expression.

"Good morning, young man," said the king. "You look rested and better than before."

"Thank you, your Majesty," said Liam, bowing his head. Turnie frowned at this. The attendants looked interested. As in whom no one could clearly say, but Vez saw his Ginearal's hostile expression and became concerned.

"Is something wrong, Mave?"

"Indeed, there is something wrong," Turnie answered. And with that she strode up to Liam, her bare feet making slapping thumps on the floor. Liam still had his head bowed. When she came up to him, she grabbed him hard by the chin and forced his head up.

"Why are you acting so willing? As an enemy prisoner of war, you should be resisting and defiant to my authority! Is this your way of biding time before you can strike at my king?!"

"No, ma'am." Stutter-free response this time. Conviction.

"Then why are you just following everything I order to you?"

"I guess I'm accepting that I'm under your command from now on. Ma'am." More conviction and no sarcasm. But this did not satisfy Turnie. She gripped Liam's chin hard and instantly wound back her free arm, hand already a fist.

"GINEARAL!" For Liam, this was the first time he ever heard the king raise his voice. Turnie did not fire the punch. She swung her head back to Vez instead.

"What is the meaning of this? Are you willing to hit him in front of me?"

"No, sir. I only mean to enact discipline as is appropriate to one in his position."

"For what? He has done nothing disrespectful or insubordinate. In fact, he has completely followed your instruction to this point. Last I checked you have shown disapproval of how Aamjunta treats his orderly. Now you dare to attempt to act like him?! Unacceptable!"

Turnie lowered her arm and looked away. Vez was correct; there was a fine line between instructive discipline and downright abuse. And she, like her king and the others on the council, had always felt disgusted by Aamjunta's behavior towards his sole assistant (Kavanchi might have approved because of kinship, but they never made comment). Turnie removed her grip from Liam's jaw. She turned back to him and bowed, her long, toned arms at her side.

"I am sorry. I do not expect you to forgive me. I have failed you." Liam was speechless but not alarmed. He just stared at her as she kept her bow.

"You must understand, young man," said Vez. "Ginearal Mave has been through much. Just about as much as I have. For both of us it was too much. Those that she once served did the most awful things to her to further their own goals. Surely, you've seen the evidence of their work? They put her through torment to make her a Laoch, and now the consequences of that are that she rightfully broke herself free from their hold. She came to me, and my queen, and we have helped her since. The one challenge we now still face with her is how to show kindness and empathy to the unfortunate, or those who have been numbed by what the enemy has done through their greed and arrogance. I sense that you have become one or the other, and I do wish to hear your story." He fixed his gaze back on Turnie. "What about you, Mave? Do you wish to hear his story?" Turnie rose from her bow and looked to him, then bowed again.

"Yes, my king. And I wish for him to know mine. The real story if those in Cliar have told him different."

"Then it will be so. But not now. We have much to do in these few days and must use every second of time to do it. Now, as I understand it, you both were about to do another set, yes?"

"Of course, my king."

"Then please make room and allow me to join you in this next set. Sumiko! Jun'ichi! My arm!"

And with that the servants helped disrobe the king and reattach his right arm. Turnie and Liam returned to their positions with their weights. Vez took the XXXs from the rack.

16

Smazeph had her own important duties to see to. Her husband was all the more eager to supervise this prisoner's training. She could no longer attempt to change his mind. As soon as his bath had been drawn and he immersed himself, she finally got herself out of bed. She would have been more well rested had she not reacted to him waking up so early.

She was feeling an ache. A mild, tolerable ache but she still wanted to be done with it as fast as possible nonetheless. Mere stiffness in her thighs from the night before. She appreciated her husband's vigor; he was in no way weak either on the battlefield or in the bed. While Vez bathed, she instructed the one who drew it (Nin again), to leave the room and leave the washroom door open. Vez made no objection. As soon as Nin was gone, Smazeph stood outside the door, leaning her back against the wall and stretching out her legs. It wasn't that the door was open so she could watch him bathe. No, she could visualize him in her mind well enough. It was the sound of the water and the lathering of his body that she wanted to hear. She felt herself throb again as she listened, along with a dry lump in her throat. She ever so wanted to rub herself to the noise. Put wetness in sync. Nin returned with a towel and his robe when he was finished, accompanied by Sumiko and Jun'ichi. They collected his crown, suit, and armor. Smazeph stayed in place against the wall when they entered. They glanced at her as they gave her nods in lieu of a bow, which she acknowledged. Neither of them stared.

"Are you going to join them in the exercise, dear?" she asked, calling to Vez from the doorway corner.

"A little," he answered.

"Then wouldn't it make sense to bathe until after lifting weights?"

"Not really. I do not sweat much anyway. I will be fine." He emerged from the washroom in just the robe. Smazeph wiped off the remnants of her lipstick and came toward him.

"Do not be too light on him. He still hails from the enemy."

"I'll be as firm as I can." He leaned in and kissed her on the cheek. She did the same for his forehead once more. He gave his own nod, turned on his heel, and left the room with the attendants following.

***

The sun had long risen by the time the queen had bathed and came down to the North Hall for breakfast. All of her dresses were blue but they all had different styles. The particular one she wore this morning was lighter than the one she wore yesterday. It had less yellow-green trims and exposed her shoulders. Ideal for a warmer morning.

Smazeph was having a simple meal of rice porridge and fruit, both locally sourced from a farm that was not amongst the ones on the capital's main path. It was north of Cuan, up on the cliffs but well far away from the shore, as the sea would damage the crops if it were close by. A combination of orchard and paddy, secured and well hidden from enemy eyes. It had taken careful examination of the soil there to produce something that was near close to what was grown back in her homeland.

Ginearal Aamjunta and his orderly were the only ones present and dining with her. The orderly had been allowed to sit on the bench. His commander's *tegha* was lying beside him in its sheath. No one spoke, but the queen kept one eye on Aamjunta the whole time. If he did anything to his charge now, she'd let Vez know right away. The orderly took no notice of her gaze. He just kept his head down and tenuously ate his fried eggs. The queen finished before either of them. She stood up and nodded to take her leave. They both answered with their own nods.

Nin was waiting for Smazeph in the Nexus. The queen had appointed her as her aide for the day. No doubt an extension of punishing her for her thoughtless comment last night. However, Smazeph had to admit her husband was right; this pitcher-bearer was bold, to admire her king in such a way. She wouldn't hear such things spoken by Ginearal Fite, even with her clear, hostile jealousy. The queen knew of it but said nothing because Fite kept to duty first.

"Where to first, my queen?" Nin asked.

"To the South Hall, and then the training grounds. We are to witness the preparations for the machines."

***

The South Hall was in the same state as it was days before, littered with charts and schematics of the new weapons. Chief Engineer Aka and Deputy Chief Engineer San had been summoned in advance to get things organized in preparation for their audience with the king. Ginearal Kavanchi, having awoken and broken their fast much earlier, was in guard position, watching the two Danucs sort these scattered parchments into sensible fashion. Their helmet's visor was up. The double doors opened and Kavanchi turned to attention. Smazeph noticed them standing firm, visor still up.

143

"Very good, Ginearal. You may now resume normal duty state." Kavanchi nodded, propped their weapon against the wall, and lowered the visor. Their scales and scars were concealed once more. The engineers heard the queen's voice and dropped their papers in hand. They both bent the knee and lowered their heads.

"My queen," they said together.

"Rise," she said, wearing a look of disdain. They complied and stood up. "Are you ready to present the machines?" The Deputy Chief Engineer stepped forward to answer, twitching his slight, elongated nose.

"Yes, your Highness. They were assembled in the hangar yesterday and we are ready to deploy any number for testing."

"Then shall we proceed to the testing grounds?"

"Of course." This answer came from Aka. The bloodshot in his sclera linked with his crimson irises, making it look like his eyes contained miniature octopi. They shifted from looking at the queen to seeing a stray parchment off to the left that seemed to contain something important. Aka leaned forward and snatched it up.

"Is his Majesty joining us for this demonstration?"

"He is busy at the moment. Something else pertaining to the coming campaign. If all goes well, I hope you will be willing to repeat the demonstration for him when he has the time to see, yes?"

"Absolutely, your Highness."

***

The hangar was at the farthest end of the training grounds. It was a wide, flat building with a high roof, made entirely of the same stainless metal as the roofs of the barracks. A hundred Shade soldiers were standing in formation nearby. Fite and Hurch were keeping an eye on them. These hundred were the greener troops under their command. On a normal day, they were practicing their marksmanship and their melee thrusts with the bayonets. Not yet ready for the new automatic lasers. Today the time on those exercises was shortened to accommodate the machine test. Behind the siblings were forty more experienced troops. Unlike the cadets, they were grouped in a looser fashion. Fite and Hurch allowed them to be at ease so long as they came to attention when need be. A large square of the thin grass in front of the hangar was being flattened by Gavi workers. They wore drapes and turbans of plain white, and were using long, rectangular paddles to accomplish their job. Two more of those workers were standing guard by the hangar doors. Between them were five Danucs dressed in shabby, oily garments. They were engineers who would act as the test crew for the demonstration.

Hurch looked up the hillside, in the direction of the grounds' guard-post. He saw Smazeph, Kavanchi, and the Chief Engineers on the horizon. He nudged his sister to look. Her eyes widened but she kept any expression of detesting the queen in her mind, not on her face. Duty called.

"Her Highness approaches! All to attention!" The veteran troops behind her and her brother snapped into straight lines of ten (some had already done so once they looked up the hill themselves). The hundred cadets kept still, though at least one or two looked above for a split second to make sure. The Gavis by the hangar stepped to the doors' handles, while the ones prepping the test field sped up their flattening. Smazeph and Kavanchi were leading the way as they walked down the slope. They walked at such a slow pace. It was an indirect way of testing those below, to make sure no one broke rank in their presence. Aka and San were close behind, moving faster but checking their pace so as not to bump into either superior. Doing so to these two in particular would certainly mean death. The papers they carried were much more organized, but they still fumbled with them as they jogged.

All of the cadets kept still as the queen passed them, her hands clasped in front and together in a queenlike way. Those who were closest dared to rove an eye to look at her. They were surprised to see no blue on her lips. Smazeph had elected to keep all things simple this morning and chose not to reapply her lipstick. She looked beautiful both with and without it anyway. And while she could not read the soldiers' minds, she had no doubt some of them were thinking impure things about her. She walked on, not even glancing back.

The four stopped a few feet away from the siblings. Fite and Hurch bent the knee in quick succession.

"Your Highness," said Aka. "How many of them do you wish to see?"

"Bring out one for now," she answered. Aka and San nodded and then made a rounding arc for the hangar. They nodded to the door-Gavis once they were close enough. The workers gave a simultaneous heave as they pulled back their respective sliding doors. The engineers stepped back from the door a regrouped to the left, out of the one worker's way. Their bosses then guided Smazeph and Kavanchi over to the doorway as it widened more and more. From here, Smazeph got a better look at the finished product.

The nearest war machine was in just the right spot, facing the door. It was a tank that stood on four elevated sets of treads, braced with fortified springs and shocks for the purpose of all-terrain movement. The main chassis was a whale-like bulwark of strong armor. Four sets of ladders were attached to either side, leading to the trapezoidal dome on top where the crew would enter. The main gun on top was a long-barreled shell loader, while the two support guns underneath were double barreled lasers on sliding tracks. The whole vehicle was painted in the Shades' burgundy.

At the moment the doors came to a stop, more Danuc workmen came running over to the machine, carrying enormous boards with small sturdy wheels. They worked as a team to slide the boards between spaces in the tread units. The boards had interlocking teeth and spaces. When they had been fitted into place, the boards were secured with small attached chains.

"Chief Engineer, having seen his lordship's designs, I was under the impression that this machine's treads would be able to withstand any ground, including this hangar's floor." The hangar floor was smooth concrete.

"You are correct, your Highness."

"Then why are these strange boards beings slipped under them? I fail to see a purpose."

"Those are my towing boards, your Highness," said San. He directed her attention to the long thick ropes attached to the front boards. Ropes that only the Gavis could pull. "It's only to preserve the treads until the first test. We will remove them before the test crew takes their positions."

"Remove them now."

"But, your Highness…"

"They serve no real purpose… unless that purpose is to waste time. Remove them now and have the crew take position and start it from the hangar."

"Y-yes, your Highness." San ran up to the tank and stopped the Gavis before they could take the ropes. He then signaled the workmen to disassemble the boards. They all looked annoyed as they went to do so.

"The Deputy Chief Engineer's prudence is questionable and his initiative is becoming a hinderance, Aka. Why are you allowing him to do this?"

"He is merely committing himself to his job anyway he can, your Highness. Overzealous but admirable."

"You are his superior, Chief Engineer. You are to keep his commitment in line. In line with the wishes of his Majesty, and by extension, mine. You are both fortunate that I do not instruct the Ginearal here to discipline either of you for your impulsiveness." She directed Aka's attention to Kavanchi. Their cold, red eyes bore into his now-frightened face. San came back over and showed the queen that the boards were clear of the tank.

"Instruct the test crew to take their position." Both of them nodded to her command and did so.

17

One of the workmen informed Aka and San that the tank had been fueled and its ammunition stocked in advance, while the rest of them took San's boards back to the hangar's storage space. They exited the hangar as the test crew was presenting themselves to the queen, giving her their names and positions. One driver, three gunners, and a commander. Smazeph asked them if any of them had secondary duties. The driver and commander replied that they shared the duty of lookout. The queen nodded approval of this.

All of the observers backed away from the hangar, regrouping with Fite, Hurch, and their soldiers. The crew climbed up the tank, led by the driver. They stopped as soon as the driver came to the top. He produced a chain from around his neck that held two keys, then took the bigger brass one and unlocked the deadbolt on the hatch. Once that was opened, the driver carefully swung aside and kept a stance with one hand on the ladder. The gunners were to enter before him. The first one climbed up and went down through the hatch. The second and third followed soon after. As they climbed in, the commander made periodic looks forward and all other directions, to simulate the duty of keeping a lookout. He then climbed in seconds after the driver did so.

The closest of the audience heard muffled commands from inside the tank's hull. Words unintelligible from here. That meant the crew would be able to communicate with each other without the enemy getting an idea. The faint sounds of latching metal came next, and seconds following that was an ominous rumble and some spit-length hisses. The tank began to move. It slowly rolled to the edge of the hangar's concrete, then dipped just slightly onto the grass. The Gavi workers moved aside and grouped with the siblings and their troops. In

149

less than a minute, the tank had exited the hanger and moved onto the testing square. On the far end of the square were the targets. A small platoon of dummy soldiers, dressed in the enemy green and led by a cavalryman on a wooden horse, were positioned on the far edge line of the square. On the small, two-level elevation behind them were two high walls. The one on the first level was a number of tall pointed logs lashed together and staked into the ground. The one above that was made of large, mortared stones. Both were to simulate fort walls.

The tank stopped just as it was halfway across the square's width. It had been running alongside the close edge line. Two more spittle hisses came from it as soon as the treads ceased moving. More muffled commands sounded inside as it started to move again, followed by the squeaks of something being turned. The audience watched as the tread houses shifted to the left, making the tank itself turn left. The houses were straightened again as soon as the chassis' front was pointing at the distant targets. The audience could now see the dual trails of grey smoke that came from the exhausts on the tank's back. Smazeph looked away a moment to see the head engineers rustling through their papers again as they watched. They appeared to be checking all details of the tank as depicted in the plans. She said nothing and resumed looking toward the test field. The demonstration would speak for itself.

The tank approached the near-center of the square, still keeping a good distance from the targets. Noise from inside was fainter at this distance. The tank's main gun was raised into position. Hints of clanking from the inside followed, then a brief silence. A muffled shout then came from inside that sounded like "Fire!"

PA-HOW! The main gun fired its shell. The payload soared into a faint arc toward the target zone. In a split second the wooden fort wall was pulverized in a fiery blast. Some of the shrapnel knocked down some of the dummies below. The ones in the back. More commands were shouted inside the tank. It started moving again and as it did, the laser guns underneath moved on their tracks until they pointed out in front. Another shout followed, this time sounding like "Open fire!" The left pair of guns fired first, then the right. The laser rounds came out in rapid succession. PEW-PEW-PEW-PEW! It was a steady sequence of four beats from four rounds, left to right. Each one of those rounds hit a dummy, blowing it apart at the legs. The guns were also on a rotation disc that worked independent from the track. It turned ever so slightly as the rounds brought down more dummies on the line. Half a set of shots destroyed the cavalryman and the two soldiers behind it. The queen lifted her gaze just a little to the untouched stone wall on the top.

Her concern was answered as the lasers retreated back into position while the tank itself reversed. The clanks from before were heard once again. Another muffled "Fire" came a soon as the tank stopped, having moved only a few inches.

PA-HOW! The shell came up in a higher arc. It smashed the center left of the wall. Whatever incendiaries were in the round made the surrounding stone and mortar crack deep. It fell apart in seconds from its own weight. The tank started moving again, its tread houses adjusting so it could shift to target the half-intact right side of the wall. Small, finite turns of left and right that allowed it to change position. Smazeph turned to Aka.

"The position adjustment looks cumbersome." Aka bit his lip hard. Her tone wasn't just concern. It meant unsatisfied.

"Yes, you are right, your Highness. It is not ideal. A 360-degree rotation of the houses would be better suited, but Lord Zharve's design has not accounted for that. Instead, we opted for drilling the test crew on how to sense making a change in position to aim at unmarked targets."

"And Lord Zharve had found no way of correcting this flaw before sending the components our way?"

"N-no, your Highness."

"…" To Smazeph, this lapse in contingency did not sound like her cousin at all.

Another shell was fired at the rest of the wall. Smazeph was not looking at that. Her eyes were on San's disorganized parchments. The tank straightened itself out and stopped in place. The workers went off to get some water to put out the flames on the destroyed targets. The test crew emerged from the tank and were met with mild applause from Fite and Hurch, as well as their troops. Some of the cadets joined in, but most of them were staring at the wreckage, stiffened beyond mere attention. The crew noticed the queen was not looking towards them. The commander stepped forward.

"Your Highness." Smazeph looked up at him, then glanced at the test field.

"The weaponry is effective," she replied. "However, as I was just discussing with your superiors here, I have concern on the drive and movement of this machine." She then turned her gaze to San for what seemed like the umpteenth time.

"San, that one sheet you're holding…" The Assistant Chief Engineer looked at the pile in his hands.

"W-which one, your Highne…?"

"Fifth highest from the bottom." San, eyes still on her, moved his hand to what he hoped was the requested sheet.

"No… look! Fifth! With the bent corner." San looked at the papers now. He located the sheet, and it was visibly dog-eared. He pulled it out and held it up in front of his face. Smazeph came forward and snatched it from his hand before he could even look. She turned away and fixed her eyes on the image on the plan. Aka, standing a couple feet away,

152

attempted to peek. He bit his lip again when he saw part of a thick disc depicted on the parchment.

"What is this?" Smazeph asked the question in a low voice, one word at a time. San's hands began to shake. He gripped his other papers to try and stop them.

"I... I haven't looked right at that one. Your Highness, if you could please..."

"Aka, you said that the houses would work best with 360-degree rotation, yes?"

"Work better, yes, your Highness. But as I just said, Lord Zharve's design did not..."

"What is depicted on this plan?" She swung around and thrusted it in Aka's direction. San goggled to regain his voice.

"It's a..."

"I'm asking him, not you!" San retreated. Smazeph looked back at Aka. The papers in his hands were beginning to slip.

"It... it's the plans for the rotation mechanism. F-for the tread houses."

"And was this mechanism installed on the tread houses."

"No, your Highness." He answered without hesitation. Smazeph lowered the parchment from Aka's view and held it at her side. She raised her head a little. Her gold eyes bared down on the Chief Engineer.

"Ginearal." Fite, Hurch, and Kavanchi all straightened up at the word.

"Hurch." He heard his name and stepped forward, only walking a pace and a half.

"Have two of your soldiers escort the Assistant Chief Engineer to Cuan. Now." The command was soft and low.

"Yes, your Highness," he replied, bowing. Hurch did not ask where in Cuan to take him. He already knew. The Ginearal turned around and beckoned two troops with a snap of his fingers. They nodded and walked around the queen and came behind San. They seized him by the arms.

"Take his papers and give them to me," Smazeph ordered. She saw that they were about to drop. The soldier at San's right grabbed them fast. San's hands were open, both clenched and trembling.

"Wha… no! NO! Your Highness, please! I-I didn't mean to…!"

"Take him away."

"NO! YOUR HIGHNESS! MERCY! PLEAAAASE!" The soldiers began leading him away as he screamed. Smazeph suddenly halted them after a few steps. She came to them and took the papers, then placed the one sheet on top where she could see it. Her free right hand struck out like a viper and latched onto San's jaw. She leaned in close, her face emanating veiled lividness.

"Your foolishness will not delay his Majesty's victory." She shoved him back hard and stepped away. The soldiers resumed escorting him. He said nothing more.

"And as for you," she said to Aka. "You will rectify this at once." She passed the top sheet to Hurch. "And you and your sister will supervise him."

"Of course, your Highness." Hurch answered with conviction but even he was bewildered.

"Your Highness, please. In hindsight, we should have had these in an order from the start…"

154

Her left arm swung in a backhand motion. The smack she landed on Aka's face was hard and loud. All the others saw it. All but Kavanchi winced.

"My hands will suffer no further insult." Low but not a whisper.

18

The second set was accomplished without trouble. Turnie led Liam into putting the weights back in their proper place before they stretched once more. Vez, on the other hand, did his own second set by himself. He concentrated hard on doing it, not even watching as Turnie instructed one slave to bathe Liam while the other left to bring him new clothes. Jun'ichi was about to take the sets from the king when he finished, but Vez shook his head as soon as he approached.

"You don't want to get sand on your robes now, do you?"

"No, my king." Vez put the XXXs back, wiping sand off his feet onto the mat along the way. His sweating was minimal, and he bent forward and held his knees to catch his breathe before doing his own stretching.

"Ginearal, do you have any water?"

"Over there." She pointed to a large waterskin by her bedside. "Allow me to get it for you, your Majesty."

"Thank you." Turnie retrieved the skin in a round trip of four long-reaching steps. She opened it before passing it to him.

"You should drink first."

"You are more important, my king, and I know how to regulate my hydration," she countered. Vez nodded and took the skin from her. He held it over his head and poured a fast stream of water into his mouth. A few droplets sprayed his chest, but he did not dribble any of it. Turnie went about putting her battle garments on. The same ones from yesterday. Vez never questioned when she bathed. For her that was after all duties, training and practice highest among them, were complete. The king handed the skin back to her as soon as she slipped her loincloth up her thighs. Only the belt and headband

needed to be put on. She nodded her thanks before she drank. A smaller draw and she put her lips on the opening.

"I take it he has shown no objection to being bathed twice in almost half a day?"

"Not at all. You are most right that I am to treat him with respect, as he is no mere prisoner. I only seemed to act harsh because of my loyalty and duty to you, my king."

"At least you are honest about your behavior towards those you outrank, rather than deny as Aamjunta tends to do." Vez signaled Sumiko and Jun'ichi to come over and dress him. Jun'ichi removed his prosthetic arm, then Sumiko handed him the suit. He proceeded to slip it on.

"So, any idea on how we are to train him in using his powers within this short time?" Turnie froze as she was putting on her belt. This was the most important, if not the only important question of this day.

"Well, since it is a defensive power, we need to see if he can use it at will to counter oncoming attack. And since that first field he gave off was so wide, we will need a large amount of space for him to use it."

"Very good, Ginearal. And what is the most ideal area here with such space?"

"The training grounds, of course, your Majesty."

"Ginearal," interrupted Ulices. "I apologize if I am speaking out of turn, but the training grounds will be occupied this morning. Her Highness the queen and a few of the other Ginearals are to watch the test for the finished machines."

158

"No, you are right, Lieutenant. I was informed earlier last night of that." Turnie sighed in embarrassment of forgetting that detail.

"Can you think of an alternative place to train, Ginearal?" asked Vez. Turnie looked at him again for a second, then turned the other way to think.

"Hmmm… oh, the beach northeast of Cuan…"

"Yes, continue…"

"It is secluded from both the castle and the village. I and the other Ginearals use it to train when the regular grounds are unavailable." In truth, the only other Ginearals who used this area other than Turnie were the siblings. Most of Kavanchi's duties were in or near the castle, and Aamjunta disliked the saltier air. The dwarves could never get their horses past Cuan's entrance border. However, the king was not asking for specifics.

"Absolutely correct, Turnie." Just then, the one slave returned through the passageway with Liam's new uniform, exactly like his own but burgundy instead of green. A pair of new, grey under-shorts and matching socks were stacked on top of the uniform, while new boots were carried underneath. The uniform's kepi sported a dark grey patch that was in the shape of Turnie's spear. Liam himself had finished bathing and was being guided out of the washroom by the other slave. He had a towel wrapped around to cover his privates.

"Perfect timing, young man," said Vez as his servants equipped him with his arm and crown. "Now you can get dressed with the rest of us."

***

After Liam got himself dressed, Turnie summoned five SlaveStings to accompany them to the beach. Vez placed his mask back on his face when they arrived, and the others watched for almost half a minute as he leaned in and cast his eyes on the pink hornets. He seemed to be giving them silent instruction of sorts. Liam thought to ask but knew Turnie might hush him, so he said nothing. Vez then turned back to the others and broke down who was riding with who. Turnie would lead the way with him riding with her. Liam would go with Ulices. The servants would take a hornet of their own. The two without riders would be rearguard.

The flight path was up and over the castle, making a straight, diagonal line towards Cuan without leaning too close to either the training grounds or the dungeon. Minimal risk of distracted eyes in those locations looking up. The only eyes that would see them were those in the port. The day watchman heard the group's buzzing from the ornate wooden tower by the docks. He looked in the small mounted lens tube that faced the sound (there were a dozen all around his post) and saw that the king was in the air. Immediately, he removed the large conch shell horn that was hitched to his belt while turning around to face the village. He sounded a long, deep blast from the horn, then pursed his lips and followed with a short, high pip. A signal to the villagers that their king was flying overhead.

Pennants shot up on every single roof of Cuan. Citizens, workers, and policing soldiers all went to their knees and lowered the heads just before the king's group arrived. Liam watched the spectacle below. He had not seen the farmers' display from Turnie's litter yesterday, so this was all a new sight to him. Vez, Turnie, and Ulices were all looking ahead. Sumiko and Jun'ichi peeked at the kneelers below just for a little. Liam kept staring as the air procession passed over the village. Ulices noticed this but decided not to order him to about face. The hornets began to descend as they flew into a turn past the village. The beach was behind that particular cliffside. Vez looked down at the nests at the furthest corner for about two seconds. He looked forward again as the horn sounded once more. The same two notes but inverse.

The beach was a wide enough area, filled with plenty of sand. The curved cliffside and the jutting rocks at the water's edge gave it the appearance of an ancient arena. The procession landed in the one space where the rocks lessened. The arena's entrance. The Ginearals who trained here obviously knew where to enter without struggle or injury. Turnie dismounted first, then Vez. Ulices dismounted next, with Liam following him. The servants dismounted last. All five of them stepped away from the SlaveStings and entered the main area, minding the smaller rocks; natural booby traps. The hornets themselves kept their position. Vez stopped and looked back towards the landing space. Liam saw him pause but Turnie beckoned him to keep moving, much more polite than before and not having to ring her spear on anything. Just a slight wave of it.

A trio of FearStings came flying from the village. They were carrying a rifle box. Liam looked around the beach; there were no targets set up. If Turnie wanted to see his marksmanship, why would she not set up any firing targets? The Eaglaceal landed just feet away from him, unlatching their legs from the box and backing away from it.

"Open and assemble, Private," Turnie commanded. "It's unlocked." Liam stared at the box for a few seconds. It was a long rifle, like Gert's. The FearStings chorused a low buzz, prompting him to do as he was told. He dared not to look in their eyes. There was a trembling in his hands but he hid it by bending his fingers into eagle talons. He opened the latch and threw open the lid. His fingers became relaxed as he reached in and pulled out the rifle. The bayonet, sheathed and placed below the rifle, was taken out right away. Liam unsheathed it and snapped it onto the barrel. He leaned in to retrieve the ammo only to find the place in the box's molding where it would be was empty.

"Ma'am, where are the…"

"HUAAAAAAH!" Liam looked up to see Turnie charging toward him with her spear. She thrust it right at him once he was close enough. He jumped and rolled away as the skull-sized spearhead jabbed into the wood of the box, splintering it. Liam got to his feet again and saw the FearStings backing away to the edge of the circle, joining the king and the servants. The box was flung away from the spear's force, clattering on the rocks and damaging its wood even more from the impact. Liam heard the sand shuffle in front of him and saw Turnie charge him again, this time winding her arms back in a swing motion. The spearhead's edge, not its flat, was at the ready. A swing like that would cut his face deep. Liam sprung to his feet and ran sideways to his right. The spear came whizzing forward, the force of the swing making the metal give off a high whine. It made no contact with Liam as he moved away, but he still winced as if it did hit.

Liam's feet changed from moving sideways to backward. The shift almost made him stumble. It took a second to regain footing.

"Ha!" Turnie shouted as she then raised her foot and try to bring it down on Liam. Tall as she was, she could reach him from a fair distance. Liam backed away again, nearly tripping as he did. Turnie's foot slammed the sand, peppering the air between them. Any closer and her foot would have shattered his kneecap. Little more to the right and something else would have been squashed.

"What are you doing?!" Liam found his voice all of a sudden.

"No questions," shouted Turnie. "This is training!" She lunged her spear at him again. He brought up the rifle.

162

The spear's point tilted up at the end of the lunge and left a deep gash in the butt. Liam was surprised that it didn't get stuck in there. His feet were shuffling in the sand to keep his balance.

"There were no bullets in that gun because I am testing your close combat skills. She followed up with an under-swing. Her spear's butt just grazed the rifle a slight. An impact was still felt. "And despite whatever discipline you have, I don't trust you enough to demonstrate your marksmanship with his Majesty present." Liam frowned. He had no desire to shoot Vez right then and there. It would be both stupid and suicide to do so. He said nothing in response because she might not believe it. Instead, he lowered the rifle and assumed an offensive position.

Turnie hardly paused to notice this shift. She just readied her own position and ran forward. Liam started moving again. He would have to move in an instant with her easy strides. She was keeping the spear in quarterstaff position, the flat of its head displayed. Any second now and she'd either swing or thrust once again. Liam started moving back, but only a little. In the back of his mind, he was wondering why he wasn't just dropping the rifle and running off. *That's easy, she'd catch me no matter how fast I run. A fighter with her strength won't stand for cowardice.*

She wound back the spear for another thrust. He got ready to dodge it. *Move to the right.* He shifted his leg to do so, but in that split second Turnie flipped the spear back so that the butt was pointing. She angled it fast and jabbed his shoulder.

"Geh!" That butt felt almost as bad as the ringing it could make. Liam winced and almost lost his footing. He looked down and saw his legs begin to entangle. Fighting through the blunt pain he corrected his left leg's course. He glanced up at his assailant and saw her flipping the spearhead forward again. He aimed the rifle's butt at her midsection and jabbed as hard as he could. He did not get a good look at her expression from the contact; she looked away from him and inflated her cheek, giving the impression that she was in the middle of chewing something. What he did see was her grip on the spear faltering. He took the chance and spun away from her. He didn't roll, at the risk of hitting his likely bruising shoulder or stabbing himself with the bayonet. His feet churned up the grains.

Liam kept spinning around for about five and a half turns until he was certain that Turnie's shadow was not above him. He braked his feet and spread them apart once more, as well as bending his knees. He was breathing audibly, and he was feeling the sweat develop on his back. It would soon make the material of the uniform stick to him. As this uniform was made of the same half-starch material as his old green one, he knew that sticking would be uncomfortable. He looked up and saw that Turnie was a good distance from him, catching her breath but not as hard as he had to.

"Huh… you have decent reflexes," she uttered between breaths. He looked her in the eye and flicked his head once to message a thanks. Turnie gave a faint smile. In her mind, manners could still be noticed even in a fight.

"Let's see how you handle these." She flipped the spear to point down and jabbed it into the sand, then proceeded to spread her legs out into a formidable stance. She backed away from her weapon a little before setting in. As she began raising her right arm, she looked in Vez's direction.

"My king, perhaps it is best that you step back for this next part."

"I will be fine, Ginearal. Fire away."

Liam gripped the rifle once more and stood on the balls of his feet. He would have to get moving again; the Wheel was

164

about to charge. The blue energy circulated around Turnie's raised forearm. The crackles and hums reached Liam's ears, and he responded by getting his feet flat again. He was ready to move at any second. Turnie looked straight at him, attempting to read which way he would make the dodge. The energy wheel was formed and spinning. Its hums became a screeching whine. With instant reflex, Turnie wound her arm back and hurled the wheel forward. It left her arm and sliced across the sand, making a slight turn to the left and heading for Liam. He got moving once more, stepping away from its path. But no sooner did he start running that he saw another, smaller wheel angling toward him. In seconds it be shortly parallel to him, then collide! He picked up his pace; the second wheel zipped past him, about half an inch from his raised ankle. The movement was so fast he did not notice it. He did, however, glance and see that Turnie had fired that second wheel from her left arm.

The first wheel sped through a gap in the arena rocks and crashed into some shrubbery by the cliff face in the back, while the second angled off in its turn once more and hit the perimeter. The practical stalagmite that it hit broke its movement, and in turn the wheel blew it to pieces. Liam dodged the shrapnel as best he could, but some of it bounced off his shoulder and another stray piece clacked on his glasses. It was this close to cracking a lens. Liam shook his head a bit to loosen any other errant debris. Just a piece or two that landed on the brim of his kepi.

Turnie yanked her spear out of the sand. "Your agility is most above average," she said aloud.

"Thhh-aaaanks," Liam replied. He was uncertain if this was a time for politeness but felt a sudden need to show it.

"Manners and chivalry have their place in the chaos of battle… but not in the middle of the fight itself." Here tone lowered to dangerous on the end of that sentence. Vez's eyes widened as Liam looked and waited for Turnie resume her firing position. But she kept the spear in hand, not moving her arms at all. Liam returned to his own sparring position, not bothering further to check for debris on him. Distinctive rattling sounded in the arena. Liam looked around a moment to find its source. Only when he looked back in Turnie's eyes did he determine where the noise was, and it both puzzled and frightened him just then.

It was coming from her back.

19

Remembering the embedment in her back, Liam gripped the rifle harder than ever. He winced just a slight because the sole thought in his head was to run and he was not obeying it, and to him the command sounded like a million different voices shouting almost all at once. His mind was full on screaming for him to run away. Vez looked at him while the other spectators were keeping their eyes on Turnie. The king could see that Liam's feet were slowly beginning to shuffle again. He leaned in to witness the inevitable retreat, and as he did so the FearStings that were off to his left looked as well. They started beating their wings in time with the rattling from the Wheel's back. If Liam ran, that was their cue to attack him.

And then Liam ran towards Turnie. The king's gasp of surprise was somehow unmuffled by his mask. The hornets mellowed off in turn. Liam did not usher a battle cry as he charged. He did not shut his eyes either. He just ran head on, eyes forward at her. Turnie began moving forward herself, but she took slow, easy steps as he came closer. She gripped the spear and raised it up a little more, as if she was going to spar with him right then and there. Just as Liam was on top of her, the rattling changed to smooth whirring. All but Vez and the hornets had eyes on the source. The ball in Turnie's device was making its plating vanish in a tilted fashion, like an orange peeling itself. Inside were shifting, metallic, blue-black grains. The rattling resumed, and it was louder with the shell exposing it.

A grainy tendril shot out from the orb. It lashed Liam across his face. He reeled back and landed on his rear five feet away from Turnie. Sand's softness had done nothing for his tailbone. Now he was wincing from the sudden pain both in front of and beneath him. Turnie wasted no time and ran up to him, bringing her spear into a downward thrust. The spear head caught on a piece of Liam's sleeve, snapping him out of the nerve distraction. He felt the edge grazing his arm and flinched away from it as one would pull their finger back from a paper's edge. Liam moved to his left on his knees, eyes now closed. The biting lip exhales he took as he moved indicated that he was still fighting the sting of the previous hits. A fresh new lash nearly made contact with his temple. He heard a click near his eye; the motion put a chip in his right lens. Now holding the rifle one-handed, he used it to push himself back. He opened one eye as he moved, looking to see if Turnie would try to stomp him again.

To his surprise, she was still again. She was looking at him, and her words mouthed "On your feet!" The whirlwind of pain and alarm deafened him to her voice. He got to his feet regardless. The two tendrils that she had out now were poised to attack. Liam opened his other eye, ready for them. Instead, the tendrils whipped back and merged together. Within seconds they began forming a solid, jointed arm. That end of that arm then began forming two branches, and those branches arched and telescoped. Altogether it formed what appeared to be a large grapple. A bright blue spark formed in the center of the clamp's open space. In seconds the spark began to whirl, changing into another wheel. The clamp widened as the wheel grew bigger and spun faster. Now it was Turnie who charged forward. The arm leaned back as she moved, but its wheel kept forming. Liam was ready for her this time. He took his own steps forward, rifle still in one hand, not running at the exact speed as before. Much more cautious now. Turnie caught his movement and aimed her spear's butt at his exposed chest. Liam put the rifle in both hands once again, but with its own butt being aimed. The second they were close enough, Turnie made the thrust.

CLACK! RONG! Liam swung the rifle up. The butt met the area of shaft above the spear's and knocked it away. Liam then proceeded to bring the rifle up and knock down the spear.

ZZZZZZZZOWW! A sharp blue flash came in Liam's line of vision, followed by a splintering explosion between his hands. The arm came down on him and destroyed the rifle. Liam violently stumbled back and lost focus on what was in front of him. He felt his feet starting to leave the ground. In seconds he'd land on his back. He made himself roll left and regain his footing before bringing his hands to rest on the sand. It was then he noticed something; his face felt lighter and his vision was slightly blurry. That attack had destroyed his glasses! He then saw five large drops of blood hit the sand below him. Liam brought his hand to his face. His palm was smeared with blood. A sudden blunt force from behind him almost made him smash his hand into his face. Turnie kicked him. He rolled away just in time to see her try to land another kick. Her foot blasted the sand. Liam was now crabbing about as Turnie pressed her attack. Her wheel arm was pulled back as she thrusted and stomped at him.

"DEFEND!" she shouted. "DEFEND! DEFEND! DEFEND!" Her tone was louder and harsher than any ordinary Earth drill officer. Even in the rapid chaos around him, Liam could hear it at full volume. Turnie pressed her attack. A jab, "DEFEND," a flip, a point thrust, "DEFEND", another flip, a jab, "DEFEND." This went for a short, uncountable cycle. With every step of this violent dance, Liam was being backed more and more to the arena border. The FearStings were only just around the border's curve.

The meaning of Turnie's pressing command became clearer as Liam was backed to this edge. He briefly looked at his left hand, at the pinky base. This fight was to encourage him to bring out his Wart ability. He then started remembering the discomfort that signaled using his newfound power, and

169

what came after it. He'd protest right now but this was not the time, as he found himself being pressed closer to the rocks.

"DEFEND!"

Liam's eyes darted everywhere but front and center of him. He then saw feet away was the rifle's bayonet. It was much out of reach. The spear point flashed out at him again and he dodged accordingly. His space for further dodges was very thin now. His heels would soon touch the rocks.

"DEFEND!"

With the rush of all that had been happening at this moment, Liam missed the sudden change; this time the spear's butt did not come at him. Instead, it was that third arm. Its energy wheel had been extinguished the moment Turnie shifted into this routine. Just took a slight closing of the branches. She was now attacking him with an open clamp. The clamp flew over her shoulder and stretched out to him. He ducked down, and the clamp's tips made hard contact with the wide-faced outcrop behind him. The force and impact made the rock crack in its center. White stone dust peppered the clamp.

"Ngh… hrr…!" Turnie struggled to pull the clamp out. The tips were well stuck in the rock. Her focus was off Liam, and her spear was put to standby position. Liam saw his chance.

"HAAAAAH!" Liam crouched and made a run for Turnie's midsection. He flung out his arms to attempt a tackle, and found himself slamming right into her torso. Tall as she was, he managed to get his arms around her. He chose not to headbutt her, but he got his face close enough to make her stagger. Liam smelled a large hint of dried sweat. The Wheel's exercise odor was stale but prevalent. Somehow, Liam wasn't repulsed by it. It even seemed a little sweet to him, and it didn't stir his stomach like the grass air. He gave another whiff but did not press his face on her torso. She would notice that.

Turnie did not take immediate notice when Liam got his arms around her. She was giving her support arm another tug. Only after that did she see her opponent wrapped around her, pushing with all his disadvantaged strength to knock her down. In hindsight, this would have looked pathetic to her. She couldn't see his face well at this angle, but she heard the strain in his breathing. He was really trying to push her back. The stuck arm was between her center and her spear arm; she was unable to counter with the weapon. Her left arm was free, though. She answered his tackling with a hard punch to his side. Liam gritted his teeth from the hit, keeping whatever wind she was trying to knock out of him. She went to punch his side again, but he upset her movement by wiggling as he hugged her.

"Hrr…ghhh…GET OFF!" She thrust forward, trying to shove him off her, and the push pressed the clamp tips into the rock. It cracked once more, and she heard it. She thrust again, this time from the hips. The motion shook him but he held on. She put her arms out and thrusted from the chest, winding her arms back. The force dug the tips in more. Another crack sounded. She did it again. And again. Liam gripped tighter as she thrust. At this point he looked down and saw that her bare foot was right near his boot. He angled his foot left, just so his heel was touching her foot's side, then he raised his leg and stomped on it as hard as he could.

She was about to fire another thrust when he did so, and the resulting pain made her let out a shout to go along with the extra force she put into it. Liam lost his grip and his balance, landing on his back. Turnie saw him on the ground and readied to attack again. The clamp was still in the rock. She looked at it for a moment and then dropped her spear. Taking a deep breath, she got into a firm, bending stance and used every ounce of leg strength she could muster.

"NRRRRRRRGGHHH!!!"

She ripped the rock out of its place. As she lifted it, thinner tendrils came from her back sphere and wrapped around the arm, fortifying its build. Liam looked up and saw the arm gain strength and lift the rock higher. In seconds Turnie had lifted it right over Liam's head. He began scrambling to his feet. The sand hampered his sit-up, but he managed and ran almost on all fours for the bayonet. Turnie slammed the rock down where he was just as his feet left it. The rock was pulverized and the clamp was free. Pieces flew everywhere. A moderate piece struck Liam on the ear. It threw him off a little, but he still reached the bayonet and grabbed it. He stood up and faced Turnie. There was rock dust all over her right side. She let out harsh exhale and clenched her fists. Two more energy wheels began forming around them. A third then started to form from the clamp, now pointed at the fighting target.

"Enough!" called Vez. Turnie saw him walk into the arena, two FearStings following behind. Her new wheels were almost at full capacity.

"That's an order, Ginearal." Turnie looked at him, then at Liam, and back to Vez. She let out a hard sigh.

"Yes, my king." She lowered her arms. The clamp's ends flattened out and snuffed out the energy. The wheels around her fists dissipated.

"I'd say this was sufficient progress."

"But we did not figure out how to activate his field, my king. We progressed with nothing."

"And during all the training bouts with your regular subordinates, did you ever ask them to display power, even though they had none?"

172

"No, your Majesty. Just to hold their own and put up a good fight."

"And it was that request that made your fighting reasonable. That's also what kept you from killing them in a fight, yes?"

"As well as telling them to fight knowing the possibility that they may die at any moment in battle."

"Correct. Inform them of that inevitability but never make it a reality." Turnie knew that was easier said than done. Almost half of the soldiers that fought her in the ring did not come of out of it without a broken limb or a concussion.

"This young man has proven his close-quarter skills. That is sufficient… oh, you can put that down now." Liam looked at the bayonet and slowly placed it back on the sand. One of the hornet guards scuttled up to him and retrieved it with its jaws. Liam stiffened. Being up close to it all of a sudden was to him more frightening than whatever its sting could do.

"You just have to be patient with him, Mave," Vez continued.

"But that field power of his could swing things in our favor for this coming battle."

"And it will, but only when he figures out how to activate it. When we all figure out how to activate it. Remember, he just got the Wart. It will do no good to have him force it."

"That… is a reasonable point, my king."

"Good. Now, let us return to the Cloch. And let us go on foot this time. A procession. My people in Cuan will want to see what we have been up to." The servants and the lieutenant heard him say this. They all looked at each other, wondering if one of them should ask the king if that was a wise choice. Vez looked at them and sensed their concern.

"Do not worry, friends. It is always important for the people to see their king. Now let's go." Vez and his guards took the lead. The other hornets followed, grouping with the servants. Ulices beckoned Turnie and Liam to come along with a shift of his head. Liam waited for Turnie to retrieve her spear. She stopped and brought her gaze on him, then shoved the heavy spear into his hands.

"Do not drop that at any point of the walk. You may polish it when we return to my quarters. I will show you. Is that clear?"

"Yes, ma'am," Liam replied. He fumbled with the spear in his arms for a moment before managing a salute. Turnie exhaled from her nose and walked away.

20

The Shades of Cuan were carrying on with their day. Farmers from the hillside above were selling their apples and rice, fisherman were making their catches on and around the docks, and the soldiers on police duty were keeping an eye out for trouble. They were accompanied on patrol by either a FearSting or a FeverSting, and they wore armbands with the same patch as the Ginearals who commanded these swarms. The marketplace was the main street of Cuan. Along with the farmers' stands, the huts, the hives, and the barracks, three larger buildings were interspersed along this route. Like the watchtower, they were constructed in the style of buildings from the Danuc nation; all made of high-quality wood, built with complex interlocking pieces instead of being held with nails and sealing material. One building was a school for the Shade children living here. Another one was a fusion temple for both Shade and Danuc. The biggest building, which was close to the cliffside facility, was the town hall.

The farmers in the market were assisted by Danuc workers, who dressed much less fashionable than the castle servants. The worn, weathered clothes they sported made them brethren of the fields. They were all engaged in friendly barter with the other citizens, as a permanent currency for this village and the sister capital had yet to be established.

A SlaveSting flew over the marketplace and made its way to the watchtower. Those who stopped to look at it noticed that it was coming from the hidden beach. Some of them immediately began prompting those around them to watch it go. Important duty was about to be communicated. The pink hornet flew into the open space of the watchtower. No one in the market could see the watchman's reaction from here, but they all assumed that he welcomed it without hesitation. In less than a minute, the watchman came into view. The fishermen had the best view of him. He took out his horn and signaled the populace. Six high pips, followed by a deep rumbling drone. This was the signal for a royal procession.

In that instant, the calm and casual tempo of the whole village changed. The officers on duty made the first move. Firm but non-threatening, they issued a simple order to the civilians.

"All prepare! His Majesty approaches!" The farmers and patrons assisted each other in decluttering the street and closing the stands. Bartering items were sheltered inside for later. The wares were quickly but carefully stored for protection. At least two fishermen let go of their recent catch, while another just tossed his empty line in the water. Those on boats rowed to the pier as fast as they could. Most of them opted for a small beach space that was reserved for emergency mooring. The assistance from the Danuc dockhands expedited things. The school building and the temple opened up, and the occupants rushed out to join everyone else on the main street. The students, all of various ages, stayed together in an uneven cluster.

"Clear the street! His Majesty is coming! Stand on either side!" the officers shouted. The procession signal sounded again. The officers commanded more. No one objected, but those who were slower to get in place were told to directly. The patrolling hornets stationed themselves at different points of the crowd. A Danuc dressed in temple robes and carrying the sticks for a large drum took a place near the students. Two Shades wearing the same robes brought out the drum, a varnished wood cylinder placed on a stand formed with two X-crosses. Another Danuc stood next to him, ready with a much smaller drum around her neck. They both looked out to the end of the main street and the path downhill to the beach. Another SlaveSting and a FearSting were flying their way. That was the drummers' cue to start beating.

BUM BUM BUM BUM BU-BU-BUBUM BUM BUM. The one with the bigger drum started off. Those around where he stood gave him a wide berth so he could beat effectively. *BU BU-BU-BO, BU BU-BU BO.* The Danuc with the smaller drum followed his lead right away, rapping with open, gentle palms. Her nails did not touch the skin.

TH-TH-TH-TH-TH-TH-THUM, TH-TH-TH-TH-TH-TH-THUM! An older youth from the school broke off from his classmates and joined the temple drummers. He was playing the native drum of the Shades, a large, one-handed drum that was beat with a carved beater stick. The beater had two bulbous ends and a twisting grip. The Danucs looked at him for a moment, then nodded invitation. Other temple workers and those who had been praying with them began to sing a low, wordless hymn in time with the drums.

The hornets that escorted the procession descended to the crowd's eye level as soon as they arrived on the route. The hornets running security flicked their wings to them as they passed. Vez followed the two hornets in front of him, walking in the center of the road. The crowd cheered as he came into their view. He looked at them and waved, smiling even though they could not see his mouth. The rest of the hornets that were accompanying him flew above. The servants followed behind Vez, one to either side of him. Turnie and Liam followed them, with Ulices bringing up the rear with rifle out.

Liam was concentrating on carrying Turnie's spear. He held it at a diagonal, the point far from its master but close to the crowd from his right. Holding it horizontal as if he were walking a tightrope was out of the question because the citizens being so close on either side made the street too narrow. His face was clean of his blood, as Turnie had him rinse it off in the ocean before they left. He still was not comfortable tasting saltwater afterwards. The front of his wine-coat was still wet. Sumiko had recovered his broken glasses, then quickly mentioned to him that she knew a lens-maker in NightPeace; he'd have a new pair just before the march. Turnie gave his shoulder a tap with the back of her hand.

"Point it up," she whispered. Liam tilted the spear up as best he could. The head made it somewhat top heavy, but he made an effort to get his hands to grip the shaft in a sufficient position.

"Flat facing the street, your own head up and forward," Turnie added. Liam twirled it into place fast, then looked ahead. Even with his near-sightedness, he could make out the expressions of the crowd. All were cheering loudly but dialed back a little when they caught a glimpse of him. Some of the Shades present stopped cheering altogether. Others then looked at Turnie, widened their eyes, then continued cheering for the king as if nothing was happening. The drummers kept on, not missing a beat. Liam got a sense of how loud they played as the procession came closer, beats hammering on his hearing space. The cluster where the band stood was on the corner of the street's turn. Liam wanted to ask Turnie if they would stop there or would they keep going.

His answer came when he saw Vez stop and raise his hand; everyone else stopped the second his arm came up. Vez's fingers were already crossed and the green lightning was sparking around his palm. He closed the pincer grip for a second, then opened it as his arm shot up. A modest ball of the energy flew up. It cracked an exploded into a single firework before it could touch the lowest cloud. Although it was now just about the middle of the day, the crowd could see it most clearly. They gave a momentary cheer as the drums died down. Vez uncrossed his fingers and stepped forward. He took a position in front of the big drum where all on either side of the corner could see him.

"Kin and allies of Cuan! I am walking among you today for a simple but important reason. This late morning, I was just observing a training bout between Ginearal Mave and her new apprentice soldier, a prisoner of war who was selected by her on the battlefield just yesterday!" The crowd started muttering in surprise. Vez turned to Liam. "Come forward and join me, young man."

Liam needed no further prompting. He carefully passed Turnie's spear to her, then walked toward Vez. Jun'ichi and Sumiko moved away to let him pass. He kept his head up, eyes forward, arms to the side. He dared not to look at any specific faces in the crowd, as all their eyes were on him. Vez put out his arm as he came close and brought him to his side.

"It's okay, just loosen up a little," he whispered. Liam unclenched his hands and lowered his shoulders. He gave a most audible exhale and hoped no one took offense to it. Vez's arm came around behind him, and his hand, the one where he generated his power, clasped his shoulder.

"This youth is a prime example that not every single one of the Earths are our enemy. There are always bound to be those who are pressed into service regardless on where they stand on both us and their own so-called society. What stands before you is a blank, unrecorded slate. Both I and Ginearal Mave, and eventually our peers in my council… eventually all of you and those of our sister village… will see his history carved out by his deeds in aiding us for the battles to come. But first we are learning his past history, not as an enemy soldier, but as a simple person." Liam looked away at that moment, and he felt like tensing up again. He had not yet been asked about his life before at all. If this was the king's way of getting his people to sympathize with him, he doubted it would work.

Vez paused and looked out to the crowd. He kept his eyes wide and alert, looking for someone to step in and object.

He gave no such expression to warn the audience of doing so. Seconds passed, the silence growing. He looked at Liam, still averting but glancing once. Another second and Vez cleared his throat to continue. He thought of reaching for his mask. His free hand did not rise.

"Now, I can see in your eyes that some if not many of you may seem doubtful that this Earth waif could serve any purpose to our kingdom." That made Liam swing his head back to the king. Vez was taking no notice. "Some of you may even have ventured a wild guess as to why we have him serving us, and I will neither confirm nor deny that you are right. Whatever use we have for him, whatever he can contribute, all of such will be to ensure that the war against our long, true oppressors will reach a fast end, and never reach our doorstep! Remember, it is not just your king, not just the army, not just the hornets that protect this land. It is everyone who has lived or come to live on this continent and loves it so… that makes the road to absolute peace a reality!" The crowd roared cheer and approval. Liam was even more surprised by this, as Vez had spoken all that with no bravado or exaggeration. He said it so plain.

The high squawk of a seagull was heard from the king's left, followed by a single hornet's wings. It dampened the cheering. Vez looked up and saw the SlaveSting descend toward him. Those standing above it backed away to let it land. It was the one that flew to the watchtower. Sitting on its back was a Danuc in a wine-coat but no kepi. A brass badge in the shape of a scroll was pinned on his left side. The gull was alive and clutched in his hand. It made further, periodic cries that were well spaced apart.

"What is this, watch messenger?!" Vez was firm but not annoyed. The watch messenger dismounted immediately and knelt. He still held the gull up high as he did.

"Your Majesty, an urgent message from Lord Zharve is to be deciphered." Vez took a closer look at the gull. It kept silent but turned its head right and left. Just looking around and not attempting to bite the Danuc's hand. There was a small line of medical stitches on the back of its head.

"I see," said Vez under his breath. "This is no doubt part of that new system he was promising." Only Liam and the messenger heard him say this. The crowd was silent and curious. Vez let go of the private's shoulder and turned to the rest of the procession.

"We must go to the watchtower at once!" he called.

***

It took only a few minutes for the crowd to disperse. The drummers played more as the procession departed, but not at the same intensity. The messenger mounted up again, his hornet now flying close to the ground. They led the way. Liam walked by Vez's side with Turnie and Ulices walking behind them. The servants brought up the rear a few paces away. They all left the main street and started moving toward an embankment that led to the dunes around the watchtower. A wooden walkway with railings stretched across to the flat area where the watchtower's base stood. The walkway began with a latched gate.

The procession slowly made for the part of the embankment that was worn down over time to allow a safe descent. The SlaveSting touched down by the gate and allowed the messenger to dismount. He nodded to it and it flew off. It was then that Liam took a closer inspection at the messenger's sleeves. They sported patches much like the ones that the Ginearals had. Three on one sleeve, four on another. It was easy to see that this insured he could ride any hornet in

181

the Seven Swarms. The messenger, gull still in hand, undid the latch and beckoned everyone else to follow. They all began stepping down the embankment trail. Nobody noticed who was coming down their way from the other direction; Ginearal Hurch and two other Shade soldiers, escorting a silent, nervous Danuc dressed in both practical and official garments.

It was a hundred-foot walk to the tower's base. The Shade spearmen guarding the sliding entrance doors stood at the top of the ornate yet weathered porch. They nodded to the messenger, then bowed to the king as he approached the stairs. Once he and the others started walking up, the guards pulled back the doors. The inside of the base was a large, spacious room. While the front was mostly composed of wood and paper screens, the back wall was all timber. Daylight still managed to fill the entire room. Two spiral staircases the led to the ceiling were on either side. Against the back wall was a large, carved table. The device that was in place on the center of the table was composed of an enormous metal block that was plated with lacquered boards and crowned with a large, glass sphere with a steel cap. Inside the bottom half of the sphere was what looked like metallic sand.

Sumiko and Jun'ichi took a standing spot by the left staircase. Vez, Liam, Turnie, and Ulices stopped and stood in the center. There were no chairs in the room save for the one by the table. This was not an area for comfortable rest. The messenger brought the gull over to the table. He transferred it to his other hand as he reached down to pull out something from under the table. It was a big iron birdcage with a rectangular hinged door. The gull was spacing out, not even noticing its captor place the cage on the table next to the device. It did squawk again when he slipped it through the doorway. The messenger then took what appeared to be a tiny elongated helmet, along with two red cables, out of the cage. The helmet looked like it was meant for the gull.

The messenger undid the miniature clasp on the helmet, allowing it to open from down the middle. He then reached into the cage again and gently enclosed it around the gull's head and locking the clasp back in. The gull had made no attempt to escape. The messenger then closed the cage and went to work on straightening out the cables, but not before putting on the leather gloves that were next to the device. He laid the cables out on the table in the space between the cage and the device. The gull paced around a little in its prison. A faint tap was heard. It was pecking the inside of its helmet. The air slits were on the helmet's nose, and too small to see from any distance. The messenger opened the cage again and reached in. He made the gull face the left side wall as he plugged the needlelike ends of both cables into the little holes in the helmet's back. The gull flinched a little as the ends went in. The other ends of the cables, which were bigger, were then plugged into the corresponding holes on the device's left side. The messenger pressed the wide false panel on the front. It flapped down to reveal an intricate control set, all composed of brass knobs and switches.

"What is this?" Liam whispered to the king.

"Shh," said Turnie. The messenger checked to make sure the cage was closed again and that the gull was still in place. He then flicked up the biggest switch on the panel. A small hiss sounded. The gull jolted in the cage, its wings flinging up and stiffening. This was followed by a low hum that came from the device. Liam's eyes widened when he saw the gull seize up. He then heard a familiar rattling. The same rattling from the Shades' new guns. That familiar noise was now sounding from the sphere. It was the sand inside, now beginning to shift around on its own! The messenger sat down and began to play with some of the knobs. Muffled chirps were now sounding from the gull, still rigid. As the messenger tinkered with knobs, the metal sand began to break off and float in different spots of its container. The floating clusters started making shapes and lining up in a vertical fashion. Those shapes started to form characters. Danuc characters.

"Hmm... yes, it's coming in." The others watched the message form. Liam was still looking at the convulsing gull. He then felt a hard tap on the back of his shoulder, then looked up at Turnie behind him. Her eyes ordered him to look at the device. Liam turned back forward and watched the messenger continue to fiddle with the knobs. With each little, almost random turn and tweak, another character came into place. All the while the messenger spoke under his breath. He was uttering his language. The sand formed six vertical lines of characters inside the globe. It was then that the messenger spoke aloud in his native tongue.

"Voyage to Uaine in progress, your Majesty. Route is steady. Bringing new equipment. Will be there in two days' time. Victory will be at hand. Sincerely, Lord Zharve."

Turnie had translated the message in her head after the soldier spoke it. Her fluency was above average, but she still delivered the translation in a stiffened manner. The room was silent, save for further static and rattles from the machine. Turnie repeated the message, then the messenger proceeded to shut off the device. The charge ceased and the metal sand fell back to the sphere's bottom. The gull went limp inside the cage, falling on its metal-clad face. The messenger then got out of his chair, unplugged the cables from the device, and then took the gull out of the cage, pulling out the ends plugged into its helmet. There was blood on those ends.

"Standard disposal procedure, watch messenger," said Vez.

"Yes, your Majesty."

21

"Wake up!" The sharp command did not stir the injured soldier to attention on its first or second utterance. Only on the third when the officer upped his volume just a little did she do what he ordered. This woman was a cavalry rider from Reeth's battalion, the only one to escape from the hopeless battle the day before. The march was simple, once word of the enemy's presence near Hornwhite was known. And when the time came for her and the others to charge, they did so with zero hesitation. The Shades' regenerated gunfire was where it all went wrong. It took seconds for the enemy to reload. No need to fumble for a new crystal. Their new guns just refilled the red in the one they had loaded. Even with taking notice of that, this soldier pressed on her charge, hoping to ride down anyone coming out of those nests at the bottom of the hill.

The laser rounds had been very close when they were aimed in her path. About half of them whizzed past her head, just daring to singe her hair or her temple. She had trust in Ivar, her horse, to press on and dodge the enemy fire so that they could both bring them down. All of the Earths' cavalry horses were well cared for and well trained to face the harrowing noise and motion of war. They both headed for the nest that the cannon hit before the charge.

And then one FearSting got behind them. It was all so fast, so she didn't see it descend in the air above her. She did feel Ivar's violent shuffle when his backside was pierced. The reins had almost come out of her hands. She managed to grip them back. And then Ivar started bucking and swaying his head around. The sting got him in just the right spot to take instant effect. As she attempted to steady him again (futile as it was), more of the vermillion hornets came into her view. It had to be Ivar's shrieks that brought them around; they couldn't sense his dose of fear, could they? It all went so fast.

She noticed Staff Sergeant Rufus Alon standing professionally by the bedside. Arms behind his back, legs together, feet forward. She sat up and swung her feet out of the covers. Feeling a slight dizzy, she took time to get to her feet but gave salute without delay.

"Sir!"

"You're needed to report, soldier!" said Alon. "The top Laochs are here and waiting, and they want to know what happened out there!"

"Yes, sir."

***

Cliar Base's infirmary was on the ground floor, on the northwest side of the main building. Alon's office and quarters were on the second floor. He was taking this survivor up a back stairway to get there. At a steady pace, too. Blunt as he was and as his job as a drill instructor required him to be, he still acknowledged that a recovering soldier had to take easy steps when a soldier just came back and shaken from the fight. They walked up two flights to the door to the second-floor hall. The infirmary staff had provided her with plain black slippers to go with the patient fatigues she had been dressed in yesterday. No bare feet on the cold, varnished stairs for her to worry about.

Alon's quarters were small and sparce. Standard army cot, basic desk, one wooden chair. When they both entered, the rider was surprised to find an ornate leather couch placed in the center of the room in lopsided fashion. This was more surprising to her than the occupants on it. Two important

186

looking Earths were lounging on either side. The shorter one of the two sat on the right. He was about the same height as Alon, maybe even an inch taller. He wore a standard uniform but no hat, and he had a pistol and ammo sash on his person. A dark brown cape was clasped to his shoulders. His skin was sun-touched and his crew cut was half sandy and half blonde. So were his set of muttonchops. The most striking feature was his eyes; they were the rare orchid. The other one was the biggest in the room. His hair and beard were darker than his companion's cape. He wore green at the top half and black at the bottom, and his own cape was a shining gold. It was fastened with an epaulet on one shoulder and a metal clasp, styled in a boar's head, on the other. The green he wore was not a uniform but a thick sweater of sorts with a stylish collar. A large gold and red embroidery were well stitched on the right side of his chest.

ΓΣ

Both of them were looking rather bored.

"I hope we did not keep you waiting long, sirs," said Alon. "This one has been through much."

"Apparently," said the orchid-eyed, sounding annoyed. Alon turned to the servicewoman. "This is…"

"Solus GreenSun and Quinley, top Laochs of our nation, protectors of Fort Lightwing, and leaders of the Fifteen," said the bearded. His voice was deep and strong. "But you probably already knew that. Everyone knows."

Still alarmed by the couch, she shook her head a little before bringing herself to attention and saluting.

"It is an honor to be in your presence, sirs," she uttered. Solus GreenSun adjusted himself on the couch but remained seated. He fixed a tassel on his epaulet before speaking again.

"Your name, soldier?"

"Serviceman Taran Ballins, Cliar 1st Cavalry, sir," she answered.

"Report." Alon's eyes widened. That was to be his command. Taran cleared her throat and started from the beginning. She told of the march, discovery of the encroachment, and the mount-up, and kept it all brief and to the point. After a pause granted to her by both listeners, she went into covering the attack.

"The cannons hit one of the nests, and then the general ordered us to charge. I was in the second line. We all headed down that hill, elevation descent training forefront in our minds." Quinley nodded a "No doubt."

"The Shade troops opened fire with their guns. They had no cannons of their own. Our infantry was hiding in the foliage on the hill but returning fire. The hornets attacked from the air. We enacted our dodge maneuvers, keeping steady so our horses took no injury. I imagine some were hit by the rapid fire. I did not stop to look.

"Uh-huh," said Solus.

"If no one briefed you beforehand, sirs, these guns were a new model of sorts. Some kind of round piece on the bottom that allows for the crystal to regain its red. If we had succeeded, perhaps we could have retrieved one as proof."

"Hm, yes."

"I just kept moving forward, heading for the nest in my path. We were looking to encircle. Then they reloaded, and that threw everyone else off guard. I kept moving, not thinking once to stop. And then Ivar got stung from behind.

"Ivar? Your horse, I presume?"

"Yes, sir. He was screaming and shifting and trying to buck me off. I tried, no, worked my best to steady him. Near success."

"Near?" Quinley punctuated. He was even less impressed.

"Yes, sir. Near. Would have managed had it not been for him showing up. Him and his reinforcements.

"Him? The Rí, you mean?"

"Yes. I only got a glance at him, because I was still steadying Ivar… sir! But he was up there. On his flight thingy. I thought that was just rumor."

"And the reinforcements?"

"Pink ones, sir. The SlaveStings. And there were enemy troops riding them?"

"Really?" asked Solus. They've managed that now?"

"Yes, sir."

"What happened next?" Taran stiffened.

"Uh… it's kind of a blur after that, sir. I…"

"Just try. Take your time."

"Well, Ivar calmed a little. For that moment. Then those hornets buzzed up again, and that riled him all over and he took off. The wrong way, too. I kept on the reins. I don't use a bow so it's not like I couldn't handle them. Anyway, Ivar was running again, the wrong way, and he was aiming for the hill. I tried to make him stop, but then he started swaying as he ran, and before I knew it, he wasn't going straight anymore. Shifting left to right in terror. And fast. Faster than he should be."

"That fear venom's more potent than we thought," muttered Quinley. Solus looked at him and shook his head. Not now.

"Ivar ran up the hill. When he did, I was afraid he'd take friendly fire. But he ran up away from our infantry. He just kept running and running, through the woods he went. I just lost all control. He wasn't trying to buck me off now, but he was brushing against trees and who know what else as he ran. I got hit with a branch or two. Again, all so fast. Ivar ran out to the other side of the woods, where we entered." She paused. "And then… he tripped. Broke both his front legs. I got flung off."

"So, how did you get back here?"

"I was knocked out. Don't know how long. When I came to, I was beyond dizzy, and I'm sure my head was bruised or bleeding somewhere. I just shuffled back to where we had made camp, all in that daze. Those we left behind saw me and took me back to base. Sergeant got me in the infirmary at once, as you can see from this." She pointed to the stained wrappings around her head.

"If your horse flung you forward when he tripped, you could have easily broken your neck," said Solus. "It's practically a miracle you're alive."

"Yes. Thank you, sir."

"That is, unless you weren't flung at all." Taran jumped at that.

"What?! No, sir, I had been flung forward. Like you mentioned, it could've killed me."

"No, I said you could have broken your neck. There are chances that one can survive a broken neck. Slim, but chances nonetheless." Solus turned away to the center cushion of the couch. Placed between him and Quinley were his thick black gloves and his large green helmet. The helmet was cylindrical but a dull cone at the top, and the face opening was keyhole shaped. He only picked up the gloves and began to put them back on.

"From what I see, you did take a hit to the head. But not the way you're saying you did. You didn't get injured in the heat of the moment from an obviously unwinnable battle. You got hurt because you are not a real soldier. You're a coward." Those words shocked both Taran and Alon. Solus put a foot down gently on the floor, beginning to stand.

"Sir, I did my best. It was chaos out there…" THUNK! Solus' other foot stomped the floor and made her wince. He was adjusting his left glove as he walked towards her.

"Soldier… if you can still call yourself that… I don't tolerate cowards. Or liars…"

22

Xanthe had managed to get in a little sleep that previous night, but it was on and off. When dawn finally came, she had had one eye open and was still on her side in a stiff, near-fetal position. She had felt herself tremble when those guards came in after her talk with Lieutenant Birrsova. One immediately checked her cell, lantern in hand, and she had shut her eyes. Her mouth was pursed closed to keep him from seeing her gritted teeth. He only stared at her for about half a minute before joining the other guard in going up to the other floors.

The two guards had returned once sunlight had entered the dungeon. They stepped inside in formal movement, followed by six normal troops and Colonel Blare. As the troops came into position, one on the end began ringing a large bell. Its noise echoed into the rafters.

"All prisoners wake up! Wake up and stand to attention!" Xanthe had managed to sit up, despite feeling stiff from tensing the way she had for those hours. She did not stand up right away, but she saw Birrsova already standing to attention. His eyes looked over to her for a second and he told her to get up with a slight jut of his head. The ringing went on for a few more minutes. Xanthe couldn't hear anything from the others on the ground floor or upstairs, but the troops seemed to hear them alright, as they held their guns pointed in the direction of the staircases. They held that position as the ringing slowly died down. The colonel signaled the spearmen to check the upper floors.

Xanthe stood at attention just as they set off upstairs. No one else had bothered to look in her cell. She heard the footsteps of the guards on the floor above. They weren't dashing now. She then heard cell doors being unlocked and opened. One by one on the second floor. In her cell she couldn't see the guards move on to the next one. They were likely retrieving General Reeth. More footsteps sounded on the third and onto the second, and soon those on the second were coming down. Grocer and Ochtó were in the lead, with Gert following behind, and they descended the right-side stair. Gert was nursing the bruises he received last night for his disruption. Behind him were two other Earths, both female. Birrsova's comrades.

Irelan and Reoite, in separate cells on either side behind the stairs were roused by two of the troops. Reoite was on his feet but still felt queasy. The guards returned from the fourth floor; free arms locked with Reeth's as they brought him down. He was making it hard for them, letting his feet hang and drag. When they reached the bottom of the stairs, the guard who had the keys unhooked his arm from the defiant prisoner and went about unlocking the ground floor cells. The soldier in the back assisted Reoite out of his cell and brought him to the front of the room. Irelan stepped out on her own. Xanthe and Birrsova were let out last. All ten prisoners were slowly formed into two lines of five, with Reeth and Xanthe positioned far and diagonal to each other. One guard kept close to Reeth while the other stood behind Gert. Colonel Blare then came forward.

"Good morning," he said in a professional but uninviting tone. No one replied. He moved his eyes over all of them, half-expecting an answer. When none came, he continued. "With ten of you now, we have enough prisoners of war to take on small labor around here. You three will be able to be outside now, and your seven new cellmates will be joining you." He made an abrupt pause to make sure they were all listening. "However," he continued, his tone tightening, "none of you are to be left alone. You will all be supervised by either me or those present. Your duties will be given after breakfast, starting today. When they are assigned, you and those whom you share duties with will immediately follow a guard or guards to your work area. If your duty requires handling discarded food or waste, you must bathe right after. None of you are to speak unless spoken to. And…" He paused again to move his eyes on Gert, then to Reeth. "Any intentional disobedience will be answered to without hesitation. Now, let's have you all change into your new uniforms before you go eat."

Blare signaled one of the troops behind him to come forward. This Shade, a female, carried a stack of folded cloth suits. The suits were all one-piece and buttoned, and they were wine-colored.

"The women will each take one first and go to the back behind the stairs. There, you will strip and put on your uniforms. You will then give us your old uniforms, including your belts. You keep your boots." When Gert and Ochtó heard him say "strip", they suddenly perked up. They made no bother to hide their wry, lewd grins.

"As for the men, they will wait here as the women change, facing me and my troops. Any one who even dares to look behind will be punished. When the women are done, the rest of you will go to the back and do the same. And the women will face us during that interval." Gert and Ochtó scowled. Xanthe glanced at the other three women. Irelan was frowning and looking at the floor. The other two just kept looking straight at the colonel.

"You four may go change now."

"Yes, sir," said the two. Blare looked over towards Xanthe and cleared his throat. She jumped and came to attention once more.

"Y-yes, sir." He then looked at Irelan. She raised her head up before he could "ahem".

"Yes, sir," she said in a low voice.

195

***

The overall changing had taken a little more than seven minutes. Neither group made conversation as they did so, not so long as their captors were keeping watch. The two lines were reformed again, everyone in the same place as before. Seemed that everyone there sensed that any deviation in this line order would be objected to. Colonel Blare then ordered the lines to form vertically before they set out. Xanthe and Birrsova were at the front of the columns. The guards formed a loose perimeter around them, with the colonel following a distance behind but keeping a firm eye of his own. They all escorted the prisoners to a smaller building that was up and behind the dungeon. This was the prisoner mess hall. It was at least a clean space. A Danuc from the kitchen staff was stirring a large copper pot of gruel over the fire pit in the center of the room. Smoke went out through the open skylight above. The columns were brought over to one of the two rough-carved tables inside. One of these tables had attached benches, while the other had ten bowls and ten spoons stacked on one end. The bowls were dark iron, while the spoons were well-treated wood. Each prisoner was to move two by two to get their wares. Xanthe and Birrsova went first and presented themselves to the cook. This Danuc was more heavyset. His apron was stained and his face was shaggier than normal for his species. He ladled a fair helping from the pot and turned it into Xanthe's bowl, then did the same for Birrsova in a second.

Both of them took a seat and looked at their meal. The gruel at least smelled decent, and it appeared to be made from rice. Xanthe noticed that the visible grains were of two different kinds. Coarse brown grains that were known to Earths, and smaller, thin white grains, which had to be from Danuc homeland. Xanthe scooped up half a spoonful and tasted it. Plain but with a hint of sweetness. That must have been either the white rice or a seasoning.

196

"Not bad right?" whispered Birrsova. He sat across from her.

"Uh, yeah. I guess." Xanthe took another bite. Full spoonful this time. The other prisoners were slowly making their way to the table. Birrsova glanced at them as they sat down and began eating. His one comrade, a tall girl with short black hair, sat next to Xanthe. Unlike the others, she seated herself as if they were eating in the mess hall of a camp or base. Totally routine.

Their meal was interrupted by the sound of a bowl clacking onto the floor. They all looked to the fire pit and saw that Reeth had yet to sit down. He and Birrsova's other comrade (a short, wispy girl) were the last standing in line. Reeth had tossed his gruel bowl onto the floor with disrespectful intent, scowling at the cook.

"Keep your slop, you damn furdo," he said in low, clear tone. The Earths had their own slur for the Danucs as well. The cook frowned in offense as expected.

"Ooh, you shouldn't have done that," said the girl, sounding like a petulant young sister. Before Reeth could answer her, the guard behind him came up and struck him on the back with the butt of his gun. Reeth's knees buckled but he did not fall. Instead, he swung up and around towards the guard. Two more slung their guns and ran over to restrain him before he could attempt any kind of hit. Blare came forward and stopped just as the soldiers got Reeth to his knees. He then smacked Reeth across the mouth with the back of his hand. Reeth's mouth was instantly bloody and his mustache disheveled.

"You should be grateful that you're being fed at all," he said sternly. He then looked to the guards. "Take him back to his cell. A morning hungry might teach him some manners." The guards nodded and hoisted Reeth up. As they took him away, he spluttered something but couldn't make anything close to words. Blare then turned back to the other prisoners.

"Go back to your breakfast," he ordered. He pointed at Gert. "Except you. You're cleaning this up first."

***

When they finished, the prisoners were taken to a horse and cart waiting outside. The colonel told them that for now, they'd be tending the stables for the castle workhorses. "You do a good job, and you'll be transferred to the stables in NightPeace. Tend the cavalry horses." He restrained from saying that they'll be needed sooner than you think; better to keep these prisoners in the dark on this march for now. Xanthe and her peers felt a little surprised; they'd heard that Vez had a cavalry unit but assumed it was too small to use.

The cart ride was also in silence. The men and women sat on opposite sides of each other this time, and Xanthe was right between the tall and the wisp. Irelan was sitting on the back end, still withdrawn from the others. Birrsova was sitting close to the horse, diagonal from Xanthe's position. One soldier was leading the horse while the rest formed that perimeter again. The mess hall led to a road that started downhill and went into a winding stretch that would take them to the stables. The trip took them about twenty minutes. The stables themselves were made of basic stone and wood; nothing fancy but nothing dilapidated either. There were ten berths, and less than half of them were occupied. The cart stopped feet away. Another soldier stepped toward the back to unhitch the rear door and signal them to step down. Irelan looked up him, seeming defiant. She complied after two seconds of glaring.

After Irelan stepped down, the rest of them exited the cart in a mixed order, with Xanthe and the other two women leaving as a group after Grocer and Ochtó. Birrsova assisted Reoite, leaving Gert to step down last. This time they all formed a loose cluster instead of a military line. The guards seemed to allow it. Colonel Blare directed them to the open chest of shovels and two bales of fresh hay sitting on a tarpaulin on the stable's side.

"Obviously because of that little outburst, your first job today will be a full group task. We'll be taking those horses out for the day. You'll be cleaning out their berths and replacing the hay. Work together to get it finished. Should take less than an hour. Waste goes in that depository over there." He pointed to another wooden chest near the other side. This one had a closed, slanted lid, and it was locked shut.

"Three of my men will be overseeing your work. I'll inspect your work in two hours. Clear?" Some of the prisoners looked at him and nodded, others gave a faint "yes, sir." He didn't expect them to give him a proper, disciplined answer.

23

Vez had taken another bath before heading to dinner. Instead of his normal armor, he had the servants dress him in a long robe that was seafoam green with an elegant golden trim. A gift from his queen early in the war. *This is what my people will see me in once I reclaim Uaine,* he thought. He made sure that his blades were detached from his arm before putting the robe on. Other than that, its sleeves were wide enough to accommodate his prosthetic.

Dinner tonight was modest. Chicken coated in breadcrumbs and herbs, held together with a mild spice paste. Accompanying that was a light salad, day-old naan (no yogurt), and plenty of that hot tea. Crosta had requested some of the ale that was taken from an enemy camp a while back; Vez allowed him one pint, as council matters were to be discussed as they ate. Since the king was unarmed, Kavanchi was standing guard by his side tonight. They would take their own meal later. Smazeph held off on displaying any flirtations to her husband. No lipstick either. She seemed preoccupied with whatever occurred during her duties today. Turnie was wearing a loose, casual gown of earthen red. The one dinner outfit that she was actually comfortable with. She had two others of the kind in her room. Vez let everyone eat for about over twelve minutes before asking about any business.

"Anyone care to make the first report?" Hurch raised his hand first. Fite was in the middle of chewing a forkful of her chicken but saw him bring his hand up. She sat up straight, knowing that she would have to contribute to this.

"With the queen's permission, Ginearal Fite and I wish to disclose the results of the demonstration of the war machines." Vez looked to his wife. He noticed her ears give a twitch, so he knew that she heard the request. She looked at

201

Hurch and nodded with sincerity. Her eyes roved to Fite for a second and acknowledged she was also prepared.

"The demonstration was a success, my king. The laser turrets are effective and reload well, and the main gun's range and shelling will guarantee strong hits on the battlefield. Fuel will not be of an issue for this march, as long as we only take a maximum of five units on it. We visited the barracks after other duties this afternoon to select men for the crews." Hurch looked to the queen again, keeping a neutral face. That didn't matter. She knew what had to be reported next. She merely shut her eyes for a second instead of nodding. "However, your Majesty, a troubling snag had come up afterwards."

"Is this about Assistant Chief Engineer San?" asked the king. Hurch and Fite became startled.

"My king, how did you come by this knowledge... if I may ask?"

"One of the officers in Cuan informed me you were both escorting him to the jail in the village hall. This was after my business at the watchtower. Her Highness has informed me of further detail." This was why Hurch sought the queen's permission. Corroboration. Fite tensed her jaw. Her brother clearly could not allow himself to withhold anything from *her*!

"We were not informed that you were present in Cuan, my king."

"You were carrying on with your duties. It's not practical to let you know *every* time his Majesty is present so that you just drop everything on hand to bow to him," said Smazeph. Her tone was factual. Fite's jaw tightened. She heard the trace of belittling.

"Of course, my queen," Hurch answered. Smazeph then signaled him to hold any further statements.

"Chief Engineer Aka has been firmly instructed to rectify this gross error. The overlooked elements will be added to the machines before the march on Cliar. For now, they will be only put on five. The rest will be assembled when Lord Zharve arrives, which as you have learned, my king, will be sooner than you think." The seated Ginearals (except Turnie) all looked in surprise to Vez. He anticipated that.

"I apologize for not announcing this sooner, but as our council is in session I am still doing so at the appropriate time. I had informed her Highness first, and Gineral Mave knows as well. Lord Zharve sent a message to the watchtower that he is enroute to us. In two days. The day before the march."

"With all do respect, my king, how is that possible?" asked Runke. "Even with a fast enough ship, the Danuc homeland is still far across the sea."

"Lord Zharve did not say," answered Turnie, looking to Vez for permission to speak before looking to Runke. Vez's eyes approved. "He did say that he is bringing new equipment. No specifics there, either."

"It can be surmised that his lordship has, through his own ingenuity, devised a means to reach Uaine in much less time than his previous visits. When the war was still young." The queen wouldn't have expected anything less from her cousin. "If the enemy is patrolling, he will take them by surprise. Perhaps he will even have a way to counter them. We can only wait and see." All of the Ginearals but the dwarves knew everything about the watchtower's device. They knew it existed but were the only ones not allowed to witness it; the queen had urged Vez that this was best because they might not be so willing to follow him if they knew how it worked. Even worse if the Tiarnabhac learned of it. A Gavi cared little for common birds, and Fite and Hurch were loyal to Vez no matter what, so they could be trusted to see the process.

The queen then addressed Turnie. "Ginearal Mave, his Majesty witnessed your training spar with your new protégé, but he did not mention how it went. Would you care to detail that for us?"

***

Liam was steadily dining in Turnie's quarters. After fighting to his own defense in the sand he found himself feeling pretty hungry. Turnie made sure he bathed first as well as have his nose looked over. It hurt and he had another bleed just as they got back to the Cloch. He had cloth in his nose after bathing. His uniform was being washed and would be returned to him along with his new glasses. He was now wearing plain but comfortable homespun garments as he ate his dinner. He was eating what the king and his council were having, but packed in a convenient portion size in a special reusable box of varnished wood.

He was enjoying his meal well enough and finished it in about half an hour. But as he ate, he began wondering what Turnie's real angle with training him was. She told him she wouldn't be harsh, and yet she almost killed him in that spar. She had really wanted him to activate that field. He looked at his hand for a moment. Why couldn't a wart on his finger be just that? A wart, not a source of extraordinary power. He passed his empty dinner box to the slave standing by the couch. Turnie had given her instruction to return it to the kitchen, and she'd go through the passageway as always. When she left, Liam decided to put his feet up and lay back on the couch. He was alone now, so he just looked around the room. His eyes fixed on Turnie's bed. In a few hours or so he'd be sleeping alongside her there, if not earlier. He began to think what that was going to be like. At least he'd be resting somewhere safe.

Liam looked closer and saw something he didn't see the first time he came into this room. A large box under the bed. It appeared wooden just like the meal box but bigger. He slowly got up from the couch and walked over to the bed, crouching down when he got there and pulled the box out. It had a latch but no lock. The latch was somewhat tight but he lifted it up. Then he opened the lid. Inside was the skull of a bull with a broken left horn laying on a black velvet cushion. At first it didn't seem significant, but then Liam looked closer and noticed the skull was more human-sized, not a bull's normal head size at all. It was large enough in its own right.

"Put that back!" Liam hadn't heard Turnie enter through the other door. He swung around to see her standing with her personal key in hand. Her dressed in that dinner gown while keeping her wild hair looked unusual to him. He said nothing in return but obeyed and latched up the box, then slid it back under.

"It is unwise and impolite to look into other's belongings without asking," she said firmly. "Surely they taught you that."

"Yes, ma'am," he answered as he stood up and to attention.

"At ease." He relaxed and she went to close and lock the door.

"Ginearal, do you wish to know more about me now? Things about me to share with the king?" Turnie sighed.

"There will be time for that soon, but not now. The march is near, and with Lord Zharve to arrive just before then, any time that would be for you sharing your life's story will have to be reserved for preparations. That includes reinforcing your training, power or no power."

"And if my power isn't ready for the battle?"

"That's entirely up to you, young man." Liam nodded understanding and stepped away from the bed, returning to the couch.

"Ginearal, it's not my business but, that skull is from before you became a Laoch, yes? Every Earth has heard your origins."

"Wise of you to know that. But unlike my spear, I do not see that skull as a symbol of the heroism I once had. Not anymore. It's now just a reminder of what inspired the enemy to make me their weapon. Rest on that couch for now while I change, then get yourself to bed."

24

The day before the march came. All inhabitants of both NightPeace and Cuan had been just as active the day before in preparation. The five tanks had been given the needed additions and the crews had gone through crash-training. Hornets from all seven of the swarms were flying about in assistance. Vez and his council had been out and about inspecting everything, and more security was put on the dungeon and the prisoners' work area so they would not get an idea of what was happening.

Turnie and Liam still trained, but only for about half the day, and not with the king watching. Shades under the command of one Ginearal or another, as well as Turnie's own, witnessed their drills when they had no other duties at the moment. None of them were disruptive. Even Fite, Hurch, and the queen saw them at one point as they were walking about the castle grounds.

The warships that were docked in Cuan were now out patrolling the coastline. This was per another message from Lord Zharve to the watchtower. It was positions and monitor lengths for the warships to secure his arrival. The mixed crews of Danucs and Shades were alerted first of course, then the police soldiers, who in turn passed word to their brethren in NightPeace. And those naval positions were relayed to queen and council immediately. The message had also given strict instruction for the ships not to deviate from those positions or the lengths unless there was a chance of enemy attack. The currents and tide would challenge that possibility as well as the crews' orders.

It was late midday when something in the sea air began to change. A shift in the wind slowly garnered attention from the shore's inhabitants, soldier and citizen alike. The ships kept on their back-and-forth course. It was then that faint sparks began to form out in the ocean's open space. No one noticed it right away, even with the air shift. That watchman was the first to notice, up in his post at the top of the tower and through the lens that pointed to the sea. He saw the sparks get bigger and more frequent. That was the signal for him to blow the horn; this time it was three high pips, then a medium blast, and one low note, all done three times. All in Cuan looked to the sea. The patrol ships seemed to stop in that moment even though they kept going. The sparks, which were quite a distance from them, increased in number and frequency, until at last there was an enormous white-gold flash.

Those manning the vessels along the patrolling line became momentarily concerned when two more warships appeared. Both of them were facing toward land. More sparks came, and with it more massive flashes, left and right behind the new ships and in a precise order: six more warships, eight noticeably smaller ships that almost seemed like fishing boats, and furthest in the rear, two massive cargo ships. Last to come was a warship that was slightly bigger than the others, and this was decorated with noticeable ornamentation. It was no doubt Lord Zharve's personal.

The watchman saw the whole fleet materialize through his lens, and once it looked assembled, he sounded another line of notes from his conch. Two pips, then a triumphant heralding blare. The people of Cuan did not need to have the signal repeated. All soldiers, citizens, and dockhands were now scrambling in an orderly fashion. The patrolling ships began turning out of their line to join the outer layer of the fleet.

Half an hour later, Smazeph, Fite, and Hurch were present on the dock, escorted by six troops, and two each of

FearSting and FeverSting. Other hornets were assisting the dockhands in clearing space. Smazeph had her hair tied back, the ponytail held tight by a jeweled band with two long gold pins that passed each other as the ships had done. The fleet had greatly shifted its formation as they waited. The cargo vessels were anchored far away, both port sides facing the shore. The patrollers had switched places with two from the fleet, and those were escorting the flagship to the docks. The rest were assuming a blockade ring formation. It was all now becoming more careful and strategic.

The three ships came in after another hour had passed, figures on both sides double, even triple checking the tide. The escort ships were moored first, then the flagship came in next to the second one. The queen and the Ginearals kept their place, feet away from the bows. One by one the sails on the ships were being furled up. Soon after that, the dockhands brought forth a gangplank to the flagship. They were halted by the hands aboard, as they were ready with their own. It was dark and well-treated, very unlike the weathered, element-exposed one the dockhands were carrying. They abandoned that one to a side and readied themselves to receive the pristine one. In another minute it was secured into place.

Ten Danuc warriors descended the gangplank. They were all wearing full suits of armor combining metal and lacquered wood. Each one carried two single-edge swords on their person, plus a holstered revolver. They all formed a straight line of ten on one side of the pier, facing the ship. Smazeph stood just feet away from the closest one. She looked to the ship and saw her cousin disembark. Two more of his guard flanked him. Lord Zharve was an imposing figure with darker brown fur and bronze-blonde hair that was tied in a ponytail. His native garbs consisted of a pale rose shirt-coat with gold-trimmed collar and hems, a sleeveless drape of thicker cloth (colored teal), a steel gray robe skirt, and a purple sash belt. His raised wooden sandals matched the vest. The armor and underclothes of his guard matched his top dress. He stepped carefully onto the dock, then turned to face Smazeph. She gave a smile and walked forward, joined by two troopers. They stopped halfway down the guard line. Smazeph looked Zharve in the eye for a second, then assumed a deep bow, eyes closed.

"Welcome, dear cousin," she greeted with conviction. He returned the bow but did not smile himself; not to be unfriendly, just professional.

"I thank you for your welcome, cousin," he replied. "And for coming out to meet me." Both of them came back to eye level. "I take it his Majesty is busy on this eve?"

"Yes, but you will be able to speak with him at dinner, where we all shall finalize tomorrow's plan." Smazeph glanced at one of Zharve's hands. The nails on both of them were painted the same color as his sash.

"Honoring his Majesty with those purple claws, yes?"

"Of course. My hands are what builds the tools to his eventual victory. Why wouldn't I show evidence of that? I cannot honor him by painting my feet." Lord Zharve directed Smazeph's attention to his feet. Those nails were not purple. "That would be disrespectful."

"Indeed. Regardless, I am thrilled you've presented your loyalty with such a small token. Perhaps your top employees should do the same from here on in."

Zharve became surprised. "And why is that?"

"Your Assistant Chief Engineer nearly botched our assembled machine line with an oversight on features. Thankfully, your blueprints allow for adjustment. San is being held in jail up the way if you wish to reprimand him."

"I shall, but after I see his Majesty. Time is precious now and I must get things in my fleet arranged before dark."

Smazeph nodded and ordered the troops next to her to inform the king. They headed off immediately.

"Let us away to the Cloch, shall we?"

***

The guard fell into two lines of five, following behind their master and the queen. The four Shade troops formed two and two in front, while Fite and Hurch led the way. Their hornets took flight and hovered above their respective Ginearals. Citizens and other soldiers watched the procession but carried on their work. Now was not the time to break into yesterday's fanfare. Zharve kept looking ahead. His guards would mind his surroundings.

Fite looked back for a quick glance at Zharve just after they started walking. She was fast enough to do so without catching Smazeph's eye. As much as she disliked the queen, she did not mind Zharve. Without him and his resources, she, her brother, and Vez would still be enslaved by the Earths or even dead. He did not look like he changed much after two years, though his mustache looked a little longer. In minutes they left Cuan and took the path to the castle.

"Mind your step, your lordship," said Fite. "The ground can be uneven."

"Thank you, Ginearal," he answered. "Will his Majesty be long?"

"Doubtful, your lordship," replied Hurch. "His Majesty is quite active, and he does not keep his supporters waiting."

"If he's active, I take it he's been putting that flight platform to good use."

"Two days ago, he put on an incredible show on the battlefield, putting a stop to an enemy force that came upon our recent encroachment. Your design has guaranteed him victory, your lordship."

"Good to know." They soon ascended the hill and reached the cobblestone path to the main door. Ginearals Mave and Kavanchi were present, along with a line of Shade troops, just as there were upon the king's return the other day. Zharve noticed the skinny Earth standing beside Ginearal Mave. His eyebrows raised in surprise. And hovering above the greeting line, flanked by SlaveStings and standing on the aforementioned platform, was King Vez.

"Welcome back, dear Lord Zharve," he said. "Your timing is impeccable."

25

"I'll say it again, your Majesty. You've been busy."
Zharve and his retinue had followed the king's company to the
throne room, where the rest of his council were waiting. A
modest afternoon tea spread had been prepared. The remaining
Ginearals were standing until everyone had come in, then Vez
instructed everyone to take a seat. He was now sitting amongst
them instead of on the dais. Kavanchi stood in their guarding
place. Zharve's guards meant to take position by his chair, but
he signaled them to join their brothers on the lines on both
sides of the room instead. There was no danger here.

Lord Zharve was seated on the end of the table, next to
the king and queen. Turnie and Liam were seated diagonally
from him on the opposite end. Before they went inside, Turnie
had presented Liam to their guest, and he obediently greeted
him in proper fashion; something that was no doubt instructed
to him beforehand. The servants all stood far away from the
table. Some were cupbearers, while others would retrieve
depleted dishes when the time came. Vez took a slice of
buttered herb bread from the nearby plate before he answered.
His mask was removed before he sat down.

"A lot of good fortune came our way from defending
the encroachment." He took a bite of the bread, then signaled
his queen to pass over the plate of fruit that was to her left. He
put down the bread slice and added two slices of melon and
three blackberries to his own plate. "We march past it
tomorrow and we'll likely see that the damage has been
repaired. That is, except for some of the trees in the area."

"Will the broken trees be an interference?"

"Not likely, your lordship," said Hurch. "Ginearal Fite
and I were in charge of the encroachment. Our men will no

213

doubt clear any trees in the path that could be either obstacle or danger." Zharve nodded to him.

"And… this one over here," he said, pointing to Liam. "Will his power help us?"

"He just came into it, your lordship," said Turnie. She turned to the private and looked unblinking at him. "But he follows orders well. We shall see out in the field if he can bring it out when commanded to." Liam looked at her, then at Zharve. He bowed his head again.

"I will be aware and ready, your lordship," he said with the faintest hesitation.

"See that you are. For now, you should eat. Someone please pass a morsel over to him." Crosta, who was sitting on Liam's right, did so and passed the sliced horse cheese over. Liam speared two large pieces with the serving fork. He then went to cut it with his own fork. Crosta gripped his shoulder and shook his head.

"Use your hands," he whispered with a friendly smile. Liam nodded and obeyed.

"Speaking of power, your lordship," said Aamjunta. "Any reports of Danucs having the Wart yet?"

"Ginearal! Out of line!"

"It's been two years, my queen. Surely that's bound to have happened by now."

"And if it has, it is not for open discussion!"

"It is alright, cousin. The Ginearal is entitled to his curiosity. I'm sorry to say, Ginearal, that that is still an impossibility. And as her Highness as stated, that is not something to talk about in the open, even within the confines of a council-filled throne room." Aamjunta growled out the side of his mouth and downed his drink. The hot liquid didn't make him wince.

"Orderly, more tea!" The orderly came forward and poured it for him. How his scaly hand held that delicate cup without cracking it was impressive. Vez frowned at that abrupt command but said nothing.

"Anyway, to the greater business. Namely, your lordship's fleet. And those two cargo ships."

"Yes, your Majesty. I take it that there were many who witnessed how my fleet arrived?"

"I noticed a hint of a flash, but I believe my queen saw the actual display, yes?"

"Absolutely, my king. It was a sight to behold. You would have loved it."

"Do tell, Lord Zharve, how is it possible?"

"Well, I cannot give specifics yet, your Majesty. Not because it is considered classified but more so that it would take an extensive amount of time to explain, and we do not have that time with the march coming. I can, however, tell you that it is the greatest technological accomplishment since the watchtower's comm unit." Runke and Crosta exchanged looks, having not been allowed to see that device. Liam looked away, having had seen it. Vez continued to the greater business.

"There is room to spare in Cuan for at least two more of your warships, but your cargo vessels seem too big. Unless of course you decide to moor them on the beach beyond the village, which I would not recommend. The tide is not sincere there.

"I am aware, your Majesty. Instead, we must coordinate unloading those using both my fleet and those of Cuan's citizenry. We will need the cooperation of both your police soldiers and the fisherman, as well as delicate precision and timing."

"It can be done, your lordship, but is it possible to do so after the march?"

"Not likely, your Majesty. Every one of my sailors has been measuring the tides for the next few days as we speak. There are vital supplies and equipment to unload to further your campaign. It will have to be done as you seek to take Cliar."

"Then we will do so. And we will have this all prepared before dawn."

***

The afternoon passed slowly, but Vez, Zharve, and the council used all of it to set everything in place. The fare of their tea fueled their productivity. Many of them gave their voice in putting it together. Only the guards, servants, and Liam were silent. Turnie did not speak much either, but she did nod understanding on every part that would involve her. The only real problem was that Crosta and Aamjunta had not completely solved the issues with their swarms. Aamjunta could not resist repeating his comment that Crosta's green hornets did nothing, even going so far as to call them NullStings. Smazeph reminded them of the presence of their honored guest before either one came to blows. In the end it was decided that Crosta would take a dozen of his back to his homeland to deliver a message in advance to the Tiarnabhac. He was to head out before everyone else. Aamjunta would accompany them with two dozen StarveStings and was to leave them to the king's control when they linked up with the forces at the encroachment.

It was nighttime now. Lord Zharve had returned to his ship. The queen would provide him with a proper place of rest tomorrow. The Ginearals all had their own preparations to do, and no doubt they completed them without delay. Vez and Smazeph retired to their room. They had a small meal brought into them from the kitchen and ate with little conversation.

Nin was bearing the pitcher again, but the queen had not asked for other servants to be present. Instead, she instructed those three to cater to Zharve. Nin watched the king as he rested his eyes on the bed. The queen was in the washroom. He was already out of his suit and wearing plain green sleeping garments. His right arm was not removed yet, which was why the shirt was half-on him. Nin worried that he would doze off and turn the wrong way, risking cutting himself with his retracted blades. His left eye opened and roved in her direction. She jumped back a little. He only gave a faint smile, as if he sensed what she was thinking.

"It's alright, Nin," he said.

"Uh… yes, of course, my king." Smazeph finally emerged from the washroom. She had elected to put on a nightgown whose blue was way lighter than the shade of any dress she had ever worn. It untied and opened in the back. She stared at her husband with a calm but indifferent look.

"Nin, put down that pitcher and remove the king's arm."

"Yes, my queen." Nin promptly did as commanded. After his arm was placed in its safe spot, Vez went about attempting to drape the shirt fully on him.

"Remove that, husband," said Smazeph. An unusual bit of strength was in this order that surprised even him. The queen then unlaced her gown and let it drop to the floor, her naked, furry body once again unveiled to both king and

217

servant. Vez sat on the bed with his legs crossed. He slanted a smile.

"To my knees, yes?" he asked. She nodded. He uncrossed his legs and knelt on the mattress.

"Stand-to-kneel feast, my king. I know you enjoy it just as well as the laying seat."

"That I do."

"And you shall watch, Nin," Smazeph said further, not looking at the pitcher-bearer. "Consider it your reward for adhering to your duties." Nin gulped.

"T-thank you, my queen." Smazeph slowly assailed the bed and stood in its center, legs firm and spread. She and the king locked eyes from their drastic differing positions. As Vez stared, his mouth slowly opened and his lip began to tremble. Smazeph reached out and caressed his head with an open palm.

"When you take Cliar, I shall kneel and feast on you, as you've always wished," she whispered. Nin heard her regardless. Vez only nodded before his queen guided his face closer to her thighs.

26

Dawn had seemed to come and go. It was now early mid-morning. No one had wasted a second in readying to head out. The battalion caravan was now just leaving the farmlands on the road. All on foot who looked back saw that the farmers' pennants were still up. They would stay that way for the rest of the morning.

Vez was resting his eyes in a carriage that was plain but sturdy on the outside, yet well furnished on the inside. Fite and Hurch sat on the opposite of him. Kavanchi was on mobile guard outside, moving in pace with the carriage, their armored feet clanking light and faint. Five of Zharve's guard were assisting them in covering all defense points. Another cart was following behind, carrying the king's flight platform, which was concealed under a tarp.

The rest of the battalion was composed of three hundred infantry, forty cavalry, twenty each of FearStings, FeverStings, and SlaveStings (half of those had riders, including Turnie and Liam), and the five upgraded machines, plus the supply and tent wagons. It was too risky to bring Turnie's litter. In a few hours they would rendezvous with the forces at the encroachment. Runke and a number of InvisiStings had gone ahead, an hour after Crosta set out for the dwarven homeland. They all traveled in cool but faintly damp air. The sun was emerging in and out from persistent clouds.

Sitting next to the king was Aamjunta's orderly, and he was protecting the box that contained Vez's mask. Vez had obviously grown tired of his Ginearal's abusive commanding, but instead of flat out confronting him about it that morning, he gave a firm offer for the orderly to join him in the march as personal keeper of his most valuable tool.

"All of my soldiers must grow through change, Ginearal," he argued. Aamjunta snarled at this, but did not want the king to see disobedience. He conceded. The orderly, Ral, was surprised but grateful. Now in this hour he only just watched the king sit still and quiet, eyes still closed. Every now and again, a smile peeked on Vez's face. Hurch saw one and broke the silence.

"You're in good spirits this morning, my king." Vez's Shade eyelids slowly opened, his gold and black orbs looking straight at Hurch with calm response.

"And why shouldn't I be? This is what we prepared for in three short days, and now we go to claim victory for our kingdom!"

"Yes, but you seem like something else besides the march has got you in more spirits than needed."

"You could say that."

"I hope you do not find me overstepping but, is it something the queen told you before we left? You both seemed more affectionate than normal earlier." Fite only looked away as her brother spoke.

"As a commander of my forces, you would be overstepping. But as my friend, a much greater station than any military rank, you are not. I will allow your curiosity, Hurch. Yes, the queen did tell me something. Last night. She said that when I take Cliar, she will do that one thing I have often asked of her." Hurch beamed.

"You smile because you envision it, yes? Those blue-painted lips finally gracing your royal manhood?"

"Indeed. That future vision will guide me to victory better than any of our gods." Fite exhaled a rude sigh. The king looked at her in surprise. She looked back and acknowledged her error, but did not falter to apology.

"Why do you dislike her so much, Fite?" he asked, all serious again.

"I do not trust her, my king. I never trusted her. You do remember that she and her cousin originally offered their services, and the Swarms, to the Earths?"

"Yes, and she was wise enough to realize that the Earths were not deserving, once she saw our oppression. She saw that we were robbed of our land. She encouraged us to fight back and escape our bondage. If not for her, none of us would be sitting her now!" Fite sat up and looked straight at him.

"And what will happen when we take back this continent and there is nothing left? Nothing left that we can use to pay back the ever-growing debt for their service and provisions?!"

"Our continent will be free, Fite. And whatever debt will be paid. Maybe even removed altogether. Today is the first step to that. Now put this jealousy or dislike or whatever it is you have towards my wife out of your head and out of your duty! I will discuss it no further!"

"… Yes, my king." Fite bowed her head, then resumed looking out the window to the sights. She could not see them well because the window was small, and Kavanchi was marching in the way.

You are a fool to accept anything she promises you, dear friend, she thought.

27

More than an hour later, the caravan reached the encroachment and stopped. Vez ordered Ral to present him his mask, then had Fite and Hurch step out first to call their hornets from the nests. As the king put on the mask, the siblings stepped out of the carriage to look upon the state of the outpost. Tents had been brought to the site the previous day, serving as hospital for those recovering from the attack. The flaps were closed, so they could not see the state of the wounded. The nest that took a cannon blast was nearly repaired. It was amazing how the hornets could fix their dwellings with short time and resources. The replacement pulp was made from bark peeled from the surrounding trees, instead of felling the whole thing.

The soldiers who were unhurt were carrying on with duties. Those that were near the carriage stopped and stood to attention as the Ginearals emerged into view. They in turn stood to attention, face to face on opposite sides of the carriage door. Vez, mask on, emerged and stepped down. Above the carriage were six of Kavanchi's hornets, the grey ones. Kavanchi gave them a look. A silent order to stand by. They hovered in place above the carriage.

Vez walked slow and straight, passing the lines between him. He glanced at the soldiers bowing their heads and gave a quick nod of satisfaction as he walked. He raised his right arm up as he left the lines and brought it to his chest. The blue inlay in the stone fixed into his gauntlet began to shine more, as did those in his crown and the ornament of his mask. They became brighter as he came closer to the nest. Both kinds of red hornets began emerging from it when he was close enough.

"Fite! Hurch! Join me!"

"Yes, your Majesty," they said together. They left their places in the lines and walked down to where he stood, taking position behind and on either side of him. The badges on the hats began to shimmer. Bright but not as bright as their king's accessories. Vez looked the emerging hornets in their eyes. He did not tense his gaze, yet the shimmers increased all around. No further words were spoken by him, but the hornets started tilting their heads here and there as if they were listening to him.

A minute and a half passed before the hornets crawled and hovered out of the nest, clearly commanded to do so. One FearSting came up to Fite, while one FeverSting came up to Hurch. Vez lowered his head after this, then turned back to the troop lines still standing by his carriage.

"You two on the ends, ask the lieutenant in charge of the supply train if those saddles I asked for were packed." Vez had requested the day before to bring two of the cavalry saddles taken from the enemy. The troops saluted and went off down the caravan line.

"We're going to ride on ours?" asked Hurch.

"Yes. Turnie and Runke have accomplished this. Now is the time for you both to do the same. I needed you both present to indicate this to your swarms. They will not object."

"And we're taking this time to practice riding."

"No. We'll do so on the way. I will ask Turnie to keep close to us so you can learn from her just before the battle starts. We will depart in two hours. Gather and recount your flanks while we're here. We leave when Turnie returns from scouting. Not before." As soon as he mentioned this, seven SlaveStings took to the sky and flew above and over all three of them.

***

Turnie and Liam had two jobs on this scouting flight: Look for signs of the enemy approaching and see if Crosta was making his way back (should he deliver his message to his lord sooner than later). They were not to look for Runke because that would give away whatever position she settled on. The scouting party kept close to the tree line, flying over the path the enemy had taken. The severed tops of the trees provided zero obstruction to their flight path.

Liam was sitting in the front of the saddle, with Turnie closely pressed behind him. He had to admit to himself that being this close to her and up in the air was not so bad. She was warm against him, and that combined with the cool leather of her corset made it comfortable against the cooler air up here. Turnie's chest was pressing against the back of Liam's head. They were both leaning forward so he wouldn't sink into her softness. He also made sure to be looking everywhere below them. This was not only to spot the enemy but to prevent him from falling asleep in the saddle if he stayed looking down in one direction. If that did happen, Turnie would nudge him as a superior would in this situation.

She was holding onto the reins, as her arms were long enough to reach around him to hold them properly. The breeze was whistling past them as they flew. They wouldn't be able to speak over the sound of their mount's beating wings. Turnie's spear was held tight by the hornet's legs. Liam's rifle was in the saddle bag. It was his Earth service rifle; Turnie said he was not yet ready for the laser ones. He had his bayonet in its sheath and a pistol in its holster. The belt was taken from a fallen Earth, not one of the prisoners. Liam did not mind.

They left the tree line and flew over the green plains, keeping north. There was no road or path to be seen. When

225

Turnie looked left, Liam looked right. Then, they switched direction of sight after a minute. This went on for some time, to a point where one of the other scouts in Turnie's sight had signaled to look ahead. She permitted him to do so. Liam was feeling a small discomfort in his stomach, but it was not the same queasiness that signaled his power. His focus on what was below lessened the ache to almost nothing.

It was neither of them, or the scout who went ahead who first sighted enemy riders. It was their hornet who spotted them! It gave a short but loud buzz note to bring their attention. They both looked down and right; four Earths on horseback were riding south. Turnie looked back to two of the flyers behind her and signaled them to get in formation, then she leaned in and whispered in Liam's ear.

"Get on my back. Now." Liam nodded and carefully began to swing around. Turnie let go of the reins so her hands were free to assist him. He kept his eyes on maneuvering around her. Her hands guided his legs in the rotation. Liam wrapped all his limbs around her torso, his arms crossing under her breasts. Now his arms were granted warmth. His face was right above her implant.

"All set?" she asked.

"Yes, ma'am," he answered, a bit louder than he should have. Turnie pressed her right foot on the hornet. It started to lean back but kept its course. The spear was coming more into view as the hornet's legs shifted the shaft up to Turnie's view. She grabbed the spear immediately. The hornet straightened down again while Turnie began standing up in the saddle. She winced as Liam tightened on her.

"Eh… careful!"

"Sorry." Turnie looked down in the direction of the riders. Now they had stopped and were looking up. Turnie smirked at their delay in action. She tapped her foot on top of

226

her mount's thorax, and he answered that with a slight dip forward.

Turnie did not jump. She did not have to jump. Gravity took over after the tilt.

28

Turnie's long arms allowed her to get the spear into an attack position, even with Liam latched onto her. She managed to get it up over her head and in both hands. The spearhead faced west. She kept it held up as she and Liam plummeted into the rolling green. With the speed that they were falling at, he could not bring himself to close his eyes. He did somehow manage to take a quick look behind him. Their mount and three hornets with riders were following behind them but sliding fast away from his view. The remaining three had turned back. It was obvious a silent message had been passed along the chain to alert the battalion. Liam looked forward again and fixed his hold on Turnie as they came closer and closer on top of the enemy horsemen.

Turnie swung her lower body up as they reached the ground, sticking her bare feet out. Her legs bent a little in midair. The change in position made her spiky red mane flap a bit in Liam's face. Now he closed his eyes. In seconds he felt his chin bump something hard, making his eyes open wide. He had hit his chin on her implant, but not hard enough to break any teeth. It still hurt, though. Turnie's feet made contact with the left flank of the closest horse. She springboarded off at as soon as it let out its frightened neigh. All parts of her were free of the horses bucking range just as its hind legs went up. Turnie spiraled in the air about two times before her next command to Liam came out.

"Let go!" she shouted. Despite the lingering throb of pain in his chin, Liam unlatched himself from her and made his own body twirl once in the air. Nowhere near as graceful as her rotations. He eyed the ground below him and thought fast, going into a tuck so that he wouldn't land on his head. Liam then tumbled sideways onto the grass like a misshapen ball, his

229

shoulder making contact. Still in the tuck, he rolled off the slight slope he was on and braked himself with the sides of his feet. Once he stopped, his arms slowly unraveled from the pseudo-fetal position, followed by his legs. He checked to make sure his glasses were still in one piece and on him.

"Get up! Cover me!" Liam heard the command well and got to his feet, drawing both pistol and bayonet as he dashed in the direction of the Ginearal's voice. She came into view, assuming a strong fighting stance. The horse that she had kicked to cushion the landing was still frantic but being calmed by his rider. The rider's one half-swinging leg suggested that he had almost been thrown off. The other riders were keeping their distance and facing Turnie and Liam as they waited for their comrade to get his horse under control. Liam noticed the crossed saber badges on their kepis. They were cavalry scouts alright.

Liam came up to Turnie's right side. She glanced back at him and nodded, then ordered eyes forward with a tilt of her head. He cocked his revolver but did not point it. They watched as the scout leader's horse settled down.

"It's the Wheel, sir!" called the rider to his right.

"Eh... I know it's her!" he snapped. The rank patch on the front of his uniform was a single star on an otherwise blank square. A 2nd lieutenant.

"Hm... looks like she swayed one of ours to be a corcra!" sneered one of the two on the lieutenant's left. He drew his own pistol. "Can I shoot hi...AGH!!" The scout didn't get to finish his request because Turnie struck back without hesitation. She had lunged fast and slammed the butt of her spear into his horse's eye. It screamed and reared back, colliding into the other horse behind it.

BANG! In the moment of confusion, Liam fired his pistol at that rider, getting him right in the shoulder. The crack of his shot scared the panicked horse even more. It swung violently and threw the rider off before he could even get his hand over where he was shot. He landed on his head, inches from the lieutenant.

"Traitor!" the far-off cavalryman shouted. He drew his saber and charged towards Liam. Liam fired off two more rounds at him, missing both times. Turnie ran in and grabbed at the charging rider. She yanked him out of the saddle and threw him hard onto the ground. The horse was still coming at Liam. He fired another shot and hit it in the foreleg. It buckled over and landed flat on its face. Turnie then stomped on the fallen rider's chest, making him let go of the saber. She took it with a free hand and slit his throat.

"They're getting away!" Liam shouted. Turnie looked up and saw the lieutenant and his remaining fellow scout withdrawing fast. She stuck her spear in the ground right next to the trooper as he lay gargling on his streaming blood. Turnie's hand that held the saber flexed on the grip a little as she assumed a new stance on the edge of the slope. She wound the sword hand back, wheel energy forming around her knuckle. Somehow it was not even melting the saber's guard. A modest wheel formed around the gripping fist. Turnie made a strong finesse swing and launched the wheel. It flew fast toward the lieutenant. A faint *zzzank* sounded as the wheel scalped him. His body slumped to the left while his feet stayed in the stirrups, preventing him from dangling.

"How did you do that?" Liam asked. Turnie looked at him and smiled.

"I can concentrate the wheel to be a smaller size if I hold a sword while charging it. The one benefit of my power that I discovered on my own." She bent down and wiped the blood on the blade on the grass, then she retrieved the belt and scabbard from its owner. He'd stopped gargling seconds ago. Turnie sheathed the saber and handed it to Liam.

"You can thank me later. You're not a cavalryman yet, but you'll need anything for the fight ahead." She retrieved her spear. The hornets landed right behind Liam.

"Get your rifle out before we mount up," she ordered. "You'll need that too."

***

The battalion was emerging from the forest just as the scouting party returned. Vez's carriage plus ten cavalry, Zharve's guards, and Kavanchi had taken the lead. Fite and Hurch were on their hornet mounts, complete with saddles, that the king had set for them, flying above the tree line. Boots and hooves could be heard coming from the woods. Vez himself emerged from the carriage just in time to see Turnie and Liam dismount. Liam was unsheathing his bayonet and fastening it to his rifle. Vez signaled Kavanchi and a swordsman to follow him.

"Report," the king ordered, all business.

"We flew about six miles before we encountered cavalry scouts. Four of them. Two of our riders assisted the private and me, we took down three of them, including the leader. He went down when he was fleeing."

Vez nodded, then saw the saber on Liam's belt. "And that?"

"Took it off the scout that charged him. Private brought down his horse. We had no time to bring it back."

"Good. That would just give them a trail. Any sign of Crosta?"

"No, my king. And no indication of how many are heading our way."

"Then we get in formation and mobilize immediately. Crosta's in the field, we signal him to regroup. Get your units all together. I'll need you by me in the air. We get the machines over that hill and in place on the other side. Fite and Hurch will scout ahead, check the oncoming forces, then we fire the first salvo." Turnie nodded understanding. Vez looked at Liam.

"You've gotten the first taste of battle. Now you should be ready to try out your power."

"Y-yes, your Majesty."

***

An hour and a half passed before the battalion was all set. The five machines were all in place on stable ground. Vez was on his platform on the hilltop, alongside the cavalry and Turnie's swarm. All infantry were by the tanks. A third of the soldiers from the encroachment had joined them. The machines' commanders were standing by on their respective footplates. They were all carefully spaced to have paths for the cavalry when they charged. All they had to do now was wait for the siblings and maybe Crosta to return. Once they came back, the march would resume.

Vez had the platform in standing throne mode, the points up and spreading out. He did give an order to put it on top of the carriage but the guards advised him against that. The said it would be impractical as well as a good way to ruin the carriage. Vez understood but still thought that would have been neat. He and everyone around him was looking right at the horizon, anticipating a likelihood that the enemy could just come right down onto them when they least expected. They were ready. This would not be anything like what happened at the encroachment.

At last, the siblings returned. All eight of their accompanying hornets with them. Fite nodded to Hurch and he nodded back, then flew ahead to Vez.

"They've set up on flat land eight miles from here, my king. Barrier fence and everything. A dozen and a half cannon in place. The infantry and cavalry numbers appear to match our own, maybe a bit bigger by quick glance. We could not get an accurate number without flying into their range."

"Understandable. Any Laochs?"

"One. It's Quinley, my king."

"The Portalmaster…damn! That means GreenSun can't be too far behind. We'll have to keep a sharp eye out for him."

"What do you suggest we do, your Majesty?" Vez pondered for the briefest of moments, then answered.

"We continue this march slowly. Make them anxious. Infantry and half the cavalry first. Latter half follows the machines. Your lieutenants have their pocket watches. Those in the rear are to wait for ten minutes before moving out. The machines are to follow. You and Fite pass the word around immediately."

"Very well, my king. What about you?"

"Me, the guard, and Turnie's flank will follow after the tanks cover some distance. I shall fly low until the time is right. Infantry attacks after the first shot from the machines. Cavalry sweeps in when there's sufficient damage to their artillery. Hit and run, as well as countering their sweeps. And again, keep an absolute sharp eye out for Solus."

"Yes, your Majesty."

"Now let's get to it!"

29

Quinley was standing on a flat rock, far behind the troop lines and on a small rise in the flat ground. Two dozen cavalry riders were off to his right. All the necessary infantrymen had taken their firing positions behind the barrier fence. Cannons were in position and ready to load. All that was left was for the enemy to come. There were two lieutenants and a sergeant keeping watch through mounted spyglasses over the barrier. Three was sufficient, as those tools were expensive.

This force had been waiting for over an hour, and it was likely they would wait much longer. They had no idea what the enemy's numbers were, and it was obvious they were outgunned. It was only Quinley's presence that reinforced the soldiers' patriotic determination and kept anyone from turning tail.

Quinley turned around to look behind him, making sure his superior partner wasn't nearby. Solus would fly in at just the right time, even if his pride compelled him to show up earlier. He looked forward again and kept his eyes on the hillside in the distance. If anyone on the line was shaking and nervous, he was too focused to chastise them for it.

The acting colonel for this unit was by the fence, on his horse and separate from the cavalry. He was looking through his own field glasses. Quinley had specifically instructed him to watch the sky after the decimated scouting party had returned. If what the one lucid survivor had said was true, then Turnie Mave would be attacking from above. Even before she turned traitor, Quinley had hated Mave from the start. She was an Earth, true, but was the tribal, savage kind of Earth from the south of the Old Continent. To him it was amazing that her kind still thrived out there. When she got the Wart, he thought that was more unsavory than any Shade having it. Solus had liked her well enough, as did a few of the other Laochs. Many of the trainees had idolized her.

A savage is a savage, he thought.

"Portalmaster, sir, do you hear that?" called the colonel. Now Quinley freed his eyes. He listened; a low thunder of buzzing was coming from the other side of the hill.

"Have everyone ready," he ordered.

"Battle stations, everyone!" While the whole of the troops had been in position, those on the ends of the fence and a few artillerymen out of the commanders' lines of sight had been defiantly napping. If the colonel's voice didn't rouse them, the hoofbeats of his now-moving horse did. They all tried to focus and tune out the buzzing.

Rifles cocked and clicked. Cannonballs were being loaded. The cavalry rallied back from the fence and closer to Quinley. They would give their charge leader enough berth to rejoin the line. The hornets were sounding closer.

"Somebody, keep a look on the skies!" Quinley shouted. He had withdrawn his pistol and was loading it as he gave the order. He had to look down as he got the bullets in. Taking them out of the ammo belt around his chest was instinctive. Once the chamber was clicked back in, he returned to his own vigil on that hill. He glanced and saw a few men in front of him looking up at the cloudless blue. Still no hornets coming over the horizon. Quinley looked to his left. Everyone else down the line was alternating their looking positions. Those behind a spyglass kept looking straight. The buzzing got closer but still sounded pretty far away. It was loud enough to mask any marching feet. Quinley then looked down at the grass. The blades were faintly swaying in the breeze. But he felt no breeze, and the swaying was in a circle around the rock where he stood. He shot a fast look to the line and saw more grass swaying from nonexistent breeze. In circles. Fainter than where he stood but still noticeable. A circle above each soldier.

"UP! LOOK UP, YOU FOOLS!"

Only about two or three across the entire line replied to his order in time. Many others found themselves getting distracted by something large and invisible biting them on a shoulder. One of the spyglass lieutenants was turned away by the scream of the soldier next to him, and the next thing he saw was his comrade's arm looking severed but still in place. Blood was seeping around the area. The lieutenant went for his pistol, only to be stopped by something jolting him stiff. His kepi crumpled, a hole piercing through it by something on top of him. He started bleeding out his eyes and then fell down as whatever fixed him in place was yanked out of his head. A bloody point was floating in mid-air. Seconds later, the handle and wielder attached to it materialized. Ginearal Runke, followed by her InvisiSting mount, came into view. Other InvisiStings followed. Some above the line. Some right by the fence.

Forty hornets came into view, right on top of all of them! The one above Quinley appeared after many of the others. Quinley had no time to point and shoot at it. Instead, he flung a hand back and activated his power. A round portal of smoky gray appeared behind him. The smoke dissipated and showed more plains, many feet behind him and away from the descending enemy. He wasted no further second and leaped into the gateway. His brown cape whipped and fluttered as he took flight low and backwards through the portal. The bluish-clear hornet followed him, mandibles agape.

SSSSKUSHH! Safely on the other side of the portal, Quinley held out an arm and closed his fist. The pursuing hornet was severed in half by the portal as it closed fast. Quinley had only transported a few feet away from his command position, and now he was hovering low above the battle lines. Pandemonium was fast ensuing along the fence. The soldiers were taking aim in all directions, trying to hit the dwarf's swarm. Bullets were fired here and there. Other soldiers were thrusting bayonets. The hornets were good at dodging. Only about two or three were shot or pricked, and the hits were hardly fatal. The soldiers were in such a panic they couldn't aim just right. The InvisiStings that dodged a bullet dove in and gave their opponents a good chomp on an arm or a leg. One hornet managed to clamp its mandibles right on the soldier's head through his ears, hoisting him up with limbs flailing.

They're only biting, not stinging. Quinley searched around the field for Runke, still hovering. Sharp whinnies brought his gaze back to the cavalry's position. The horses were going crazy and their riders were struggling to settle them down. Quinley furrowed his brow and called out to the cavalrymen.

"Get those horses under control right now! Over that hill! See what we're dealing with! Cut down any who are close! On the double!" His orders were met with a variety of "Yes, sir" that was different in volume, tone, and timing. The colonel was not visible, so the next highest officer there was taking charge and relaying the Laoch's commands. Quinley watched him get things sorted out. As soon as the riders began to depart for the hill, Quinley turned his focus back on finding the Ginearal. He glided over the field as he roved his eyes. The hornets were too busy with his troops to deal with him. This was his chance to fight back. He aimed at a passing hornet or two as he scanned if they seemed close, but he did not fire. Not yet. He soon spotted Runke somewhere up the left side of the fence. She was spurring her mount away from some lucky aims in all this chaos. Rifles were cracking more here.

"There you are," he muttered under breath. He cast another portal, a smaller one, in the large space of open air between him and her. Her face was magnified in the frame of the smoky circle. Quinley took aim without hesitation and fired a warning shot. The bullet zipped very close to Runke's shoulder. She felt it graze past and saw the tiny portal right in front of her, the enemy pointing his gun at her and cocking another round. Runke gave her mount a hard kick on the side, prompting it to fly up. Quinley fired again just as it was going up. The bullet missed its mark and found home in the upper back of an artilleryman. Quinley stifled a curse by biting his lip. There was a bigger risk for friendly fire here.

He closed the old portal and took flight again. He saw Runke's hornet flying well far and above him. Another mini-portal was cast, but Quinley took care not to hold his hand out in front so quick this time. It would've given him away. He flung out both arms out this time, aiming and firing into the new portal. As he did that, his free hand cast another portal a couple of feet left of the first one. Runke started to fly straight and away. The bullet missed again. She and Quinley started to fly parallel now. He fired again into the second portal. She dodged this one too. A third portal was cast. The pistol was cocked and aimed again.

He might've said "You can't dodge me forever, dwarf!", but Quinley was too professional for such a cliched quip. All he focused on was portal, aim, fire. This went on three more times, and each time Runke dodged the shot. Quinley clenched his free hand again and closed the mini-portals. He had one shot left but felt it was time to reload. He started flying backwards and away, positioning himself to take out the new rounds. Runke saw the portals close, then saw her foe drifting away. She frowned. No way was he getting another chance.

Runke gave her mount a gentler kick, signaling it to fly higher, and added some pressure to suggest going faster. The hornet obeyed. As it flew up, it locked eyes on Quinley. He just got five new rounds in the chamber. Still in midair, he was steadying himself again to resume portal-and-shoot. Runke brandished her axe, arm up and at the ready to strike. She spurred her hornet to charge, and it started to do so. This caught Quinley off guard for a moment. He cast another portal, but this time it was bigger and would redirect Runke to go the other way. The hornet was picking up speed and Runke was starting to rein it in before it could reach the gate. Just as it was close, the hornet suddenly braked in midair and inches from the portal. Runke tugged the reins to push it onward. It wouldn't budge, and this started to make her frustrated. She stood up a little and loomed over its head, attempting to look it in its eyes. Then she noticed the shimmer wash across those compact cells.

It was no secret what that shimmer meant, not to any of the Ginearals. Whether the enemy knew or not was hard to say. Quinley noticed the shimmer but his face did not react to it. Runke relaxed her hold on the reins and let the hornet change its course. It took off back to the fence. The other InvisiStings were already flying over the boundary. Runke kept her axe on hand just in case someone thought to take a shot at her.

Quinley watched her go, ignoring that his gate was still open. Then he looked down at the battle line. All across the fence were troops attempting to nurse the bites they took. The lieutenant that Runke had brained was being carried off by two artillerymen. Quinley heard the sound of hoof beats and looked up. The cavalry had returned. It seemed that all were present. He looked back and saw his portal, then promptly closed it. He then flew back to the fence. But as he was coming closer, he heard a new noise coming from the hill. It was the sound of enemy troops marching.

***

A good distance away from the enemy's position, the infantry was getting into place to ascend the hill. They stayed still and in formation as the InvisiStings flew over their heads. The air was full of hornet wings. Air and ground cavalry were forming behind them. Fite and Hurch had their swarms ready to go. Their hornets all had shimmers rippling through their eyes. The sibling Ginearals soon saw Runke approach. She

nodded to them, and they to her. They let her pass. More wings were starting to sound behind them. It was not easy to hear the increase. This had to be Turnie's flank.

More sounds soon followed and managed to pierce just a little through the buzzing; hoofbeats and some large things that rumbled on the ground. The hornets that Fite and Hurch were on turned around. Their eyes had been shimmering too, but now they turned at just the right time.

The rest of the battalion had arrived, all getting ready to storm the hill. The siblings' hornets took off toward the assembly. Vez and his platform came into sight. His mask's ornament was giving off a glow that was visible even in this daylight. Fite and Hurch steadied their mounts as they came close to the king. Once they were in earshot, he spoke to both of them.

"Tell the crews to prepare to fire."

30

PAHOW! PAHOW! PAHOW! PAHOW! PAHOW!

Less than ten minutes later, the enemy's position became a firestorm. Five massive explosions hit the enemy's battle line, blowing apart the fence at integral points. One hit landed right where a cannon was placed, and to make matters worse, it was just as the artillerymen there were preparing to fire. The blast ignited both the powder inside the cannon and the lit torch that soldier was holding ready to light the fuse. He was incinerated, while his comrades were blown apart by both flame and shrapnel. Other soldiers along the line had been caught in the hits as well. The first shell hit three cavalry troops; they and their horses were in pieces and those close to them were instantly burned. Various shouts attempted to sound over roaring flames.

"RETURN FIRE! RETURN FIRE!"

"REGROUP! RECOVER!"

"Commander! COMMANDER QUINLEY!"

"AAAAAAAGHHHHH!"

There was nothing but cacophony and smoke filling the area. The troops tried to reform their firing lines and keep away from the impact spots to no avail. Cavalrymen retreated from the fence, looking for their Laoch commander through all this chaos. They moved less than halfway from that position before stopping to a noise they managed to catch on the wind. In truth, it was two noises combined they could faintly hear. Buzzing wings and marching feet.

"Reform! Reform and face!" The horseman at the front of the column took initiative (with all this around them it was hard to tell if he was the one in command). He drew his saber as he shouted and directed the other riders to an unspoiled space. The cavalry dashed there right away. Infantrymen that could still move and fight joined them.

"Has anyone seen the commander?"

"He has to be somewhere!"

"Any artillery still present?"

"Can't tell, sir!"

POW! No sooner was that answer given that something big fired. But it wasn't the enemy. It was a cannon on the line. The smoke and fire made it impossible to see the hill but they all heard the impact. That should have taken some of them out. The marching and buzzing could still be heard. POW! Another cannon fired. Least they still had some.

As the enemy's motion sounded closer, infantry and cavalry got ready. Rifles aimed, pistols and sabers drawn. Two thirds of the cavalry were present. The riflemen formed a haphazard perimeter around them. If the riders charged, they'd have to clear the way fast.

The enemy's steady marching began to change to running. Hope for another cannon fire to slow them down was forming. The smoke along the line began to clear. The Earths looked forward, only to be met with a horrible sight. Shades and hornets were pouring down the hill towards the fence. The wine-coats' automatic laser rifles were being held at the ready as they ran, as did the ones atop SlaveStings. Riderless Fears and Fevers were mixed in. In this moment, the pinks and reds seemed to be as if they were all one swarm. Those cavalrymen more to the left tried to see if the cannons were being readied again. The smoke dissipated to reveal a soldier about to load another ball. A Shade saw him and took aim. Three red shots

244

to the back made the Earth drop the ball before he could bring it to the muzzle.

"Open fire the second they cross that fence!" Soon enough about half a dozen Shades were reaching out a hand to vault the fence, while the riders on pinks were rising over the others in the swarm. The Earth riflemen aimed and fired as they climbed. Only two were hit. Six, then nine more Shades made it over the fence. Recovering quick, they resumed running and took aim at the clustered soldiers. A barrage of red lasers came straight at the Earths. The first few shots only scorched the grass, but as the Shades kept running, a few of them met a green-belly and knocked him down. The cavalry horses started to rear again. A few of the riders were smart and began moving them back before they could panic. The riflemen still standing began returning fire. Their shots rang out without hesitation. At least one or two neared their marks. One Shade was grazed, another hit. They began clustering together while moving somewhat zigzag to avoid the shots. As they ran, they took aim again; their reload time was much too fast.

Another cavalryman saw Shades on horseback coming up over the ridge. He wheeled his horse to the one giving the orders and got his attention with a "sir" (still couldn't check rank in the heat of the moment). The other horseman looked at him, and he directed his attention to the ridge. The Shade cavalry was on the move.

"Cover us!" The Earth riders set off to the right. Some infantry followed them, hoping to get a shot off. The rest were occupied with the foot troops. They were coming closer fast. In seconds bayonets would have to be used. The Earths who still had shots fired them without hesitation. All but one to a Shade's foot missed. Some Shades in the front slung their rifles right away, preparing to use fists. Others kept theirs out and were ready to shoot again. The Earths held their rifles like spears and charged. Two Shades in the front took aim and fired as both forces neared collision. The shots floored their targets to the ground. They were instantly trampled by those behind them. An Earth reached an unarmed Shade and struck him with the butt of his rifle. The Shade was stunned but proceeded to reply with a hard elbow to the stomach. Another Shade made the first move and socked the Earth who came upon him. The punch was strong enough to knock him off his feet.

All of the Shade cavalry had their own laser rifles, but they also carried normal revolvers. As they rode down the hill, they started drawing them. The Earth cavalry began to do the same. Someone from both sides fired off the first shot, and more followed. Two more daring Earths had their hands off their reins so they could rapid-fire, which was not a regulation combat maneuver. One hand on the trigger, the other swiping the hammer. The faster succession managed to wing a Shade on the fringe of the line. Effective but reckless.

The leading Earth had raised his saber, ready to use it. The Shade who led his own force had no saber of his own. He did carry a large dirk and a bayonet, the latter a trophy from a fallen foe. He drew the dirk as his challenger came closer. It had the better blade to match the saber. Their fellow riders split into two groups and went around them to deal with each other. With more space to fight, the two horsemen ran towards each other. The Earth moved his horse a little to his left and swung the saber. Its sleek curved blade met the dirk's thick straight one with a clang. The Shade had put enough strength into his counter to block the saber but not break it. They both wound their blades back and swung them again. They kept at this a few times, both looking for an opening. The Shade spotted a chance and went to thrust at the Earth's torso. The Earth slapped the saber's flat on the oncoming dirk, disrupting the thrust. The Shade made a quick response and moved the dirk up and diagonal. He slashed at the Earth's sword hand. The Earth recoiled and dropped the saber. With that distraction, the Shade lifted his leg out of the stirrup and kicked his opponent's horse hard in the neck. The horse screamed and reared away while the Shade moved his own horse away from those rising hooves as quick as he could. The Earth rider, still nursing his cut hand, began frantically searching for his dropped weapon. Too late he found himself being tilted back fast. He thought he caught the glint of his saber out of the corner his eye and proceeded to force himself out of the saddle.

That Earth leaped off his horse and dove to the ground shoulder-first like a wrestler. The landing on his elbow was hard and painful. It did overthrow the sting from the dirk cut. He spotted the saber nearby and grabbed it with his still-bleeding hand. Getting to his feet, he saw his opponent dismount. He had now drawn the bayonet, holding downward in his other hand. They both began to circle each other as they attempted to move closer. One misstep from one meant the other could make a good strike, and the Earth had a better reach. His grip on the saber was weak from the cut, but he tried to maintain it. He stared his opponent in the eye to look for an opening. He bit his lip in frustration at this; Earths just hated that sclera.

In his mind, he was opting to feign a lunge. But before he could even execute it, the sound of the hornets came into the area. Under all the buzzing there were other noises coming from the hill. Rumbling. And hissing. The Earth cavalryman took his eyes off his opponent for just a second. He saw the five tanks rolling up. And above them were three Ginearals on hornets and the king on his platform. Hornet walls of red and pink were behind them. Soldiers on both sides were halting their scuffles. The green-bellies started to unconsciously lower their weapons. A sign that this battle was turning out of their favor. Those who looked closer noticed an Earth in burgundy sitting in front of the Wheel on her mount, pointing his rifle in their direction.

Vez glided forward, over his tanks and descending the hillside. Quinley flew down from the opposite direction, emerging from smoke and dust. The saber and dirk combatants were feet away from him at a diagonal point. His boots returned to the ground before Vez's platform faced inches from his feet. The wings bent down just a little as Vez became almost level with the enemy commander.

"Your soldiers have been fighting valiantly, Portalmaster," said Vez. There was true courtesy in his voice.

"Spare me the flattery, you scum," Quinley replied. "This battle is hardly fair."

"I don't believe war is meant to be fair. It wasn't fair for us in the time when our ammunition was less than yours. But now I think the field is as even as it can get."

"Like any corcra's opinion about war matters. You can style yourself any way you like. It doesn't matter. You're still just filth in the end." Quinley eyed Turnie Mave for a moment and pointed with unwarranted contempt. "Same goes for her and her inferior, savage heritage."

"Your insults are unbecoming. And they do not phase either of us."

"But *my* presence on this battlefield can faze you!" That booming voice made the king, Laoch, and Ginearals all look up. High above them all, with the sun reflecting off his golden cape, was Solus GreenSun. His helmeted face was darkened by shadow. He looked to Quinley and gave a nod. Quinley rose up to his position, pistol holstered. Vez looked to the Ginearals and signaled him to follow. He adjusted his feet and the platform went up. The mounted hornets followed carefully behind. Vez kept his eyes on the two Laochs, but made a quick glance to those behind him. Fite and Hurch had their weapons sheathed but a hand on them. Liam had lowered his rifle and was leaning back as Turnie whispered caution to him. All of the soldiers below and the swarms had their eyes on their leaders. The height of this battle was on them.

Solus and Quinley floated side by side, well apart from each other. As soon as Vez came into their line of sight, Solus moved forward with the king following his lead. The Ginearals and Liam watched him close, eyes on the tail of his platform. The Laoch and the king were face to face right away.

"Your side has fought well, GreenSun. But if they keep fighting, they will be wiped out in the end."

"And what about if I just use my power to its fullest and incinerate you all right now?" asked Solus. His tone was aloof and dangerous.

"You wouldn't allow yourself to do that. Your people see you…" He paused to indicate Quinley. "…and your compatriots, as their saviors. I'm certain they would question why the greatest of them would sacrifice all his forces to bring down the enemy, just because he was unable to face the Hornet Rí in a one-to-one fight. But what do I know? I'm just a corcra, right?"

Solus grimaced a second, then resumed his pompous smile. "What do you suggest, *your Majesty*?"

"Me and you. Up here for all to witness. To the death." He looked at his support. "No interference." His gaze then went back to Quinley. "From either side. I take you down, your troops retreat and let us continue our march to Cliar Base. They can even make a show of it and fight back as they run."

"And if I manage to kill you?"

"You'll have the honor of flying over to NightPeace and dropping my corpse in the center of the village for all to see."

"Vez, no!" shouted Fite. She started to urge her hornet forward but her brother stopped her. He shook his head. Turnie and Liam were still looking at the king, their own eyes wide. Vez gave a wordless command to Fite. Relax. Solus stopped smiling and thought for a moment, finger to his chin. He looked up at Vez when he returned looking at him.

"Very well. I accept your terms. Just one more thing before we start this. Lose the stupid mask. I want to see your whole face enter death." Now Vez was taken aback, but he tried his hardest to make sure Solus did not notice this. Hard to do when his eyes gave him away. He took a deep breath and sighed.

"Very well," he echoed. The king reached behind his head and removed his mask without delay. He turned away and flew over to Turnie and Liam, then passed it to the latter.

"Guard this with your life," he ordered without a sound. Liam could read his lips well enough. Vez returned to his position before GreenSun. The Ginearals urged their mounts further back. Quinley floated back to open more space as well. Vez looked at Solus without a blink. They began to circle as they faced each other down, both wondering who would make the first move.

Vez kept his arms open but at his side, and he started to cross the fingers of his left with a hair's breadth. Small green sparks, too tiny for Solus to notice, started forming about the digits. Solus was raising his shoulders and his hands were open. His cape seemed to shimmer the same way Vez's mask did. In seconds Vez had formed his left-hand prong. The green sparks became more visible and they continued to circle. About halfway through the next rotation, Vez made the first move. He thrust out his arm and fired a long bolt straight at Solus. Solus immediately shifted to his right and dodged it. The bolt cracked and burst in that space. Solus proceeded to counterattack right away, winding back his right arm. A small solar fireball formed in his open palm. He hurled it just as it took shape. Vez shifted his feet on the platform. The wings reversed, pointing in GreenSun's direction. The machine backed away as fast as possible. Vez made a tilt and flew himself off to his left. The ball exploded closer than he would've liked it to; he felt its heat but it did not manage to burn him. He'd have to keep a good distance from here on in.

Solus proceeded to hurl more fireballs when Vez regained his flight balance. And with each one of those projectiles, Vez shifted his legs to move the platform with zero hesitation. The Ginearals could feel the heat of those small blasts too, even though they were a further distance from them. After six or so more fireballs, Vez shot another green bolt. He made sure to fly forward a little so it had more chance of reaching. It came apart inches from Solus' torso. He was looking right at it when it did so, his head down. From Vez's current distance, it was impossible to see if he was actually thrown off guard. Solus raised his head. He was sneering now.

"That all you can do? A single lousy bolt?!" Vez did not frown or clench his teeth. He gave a disarming yet politer smile.

"Oh, I've got more." Vez waved both his arms off to the sides and then clapped them together. His left hand was still pronged and crackling. He then slowly brought his hands apart. A row of five strings of his lighting formed and stretched between them. Now he could see Solus looking alarmed. The Ginearals began to look hopeful upon seeing the electric cat's cradle between the king's hands. Liam saw up close that Turnie was smiling. He didn't know that this smile was her becoming thrilled of all the power training that she had joined Vez in during the infancy of the war. It was now about to pay off.

Vez charged fast at Solus, his new lightning strings out and curved up. At the speed and angle he was going, he was looking to wrap it around the Laoch's head. If he wanted to do so more effectively, he'd have to find some way to kick Solus' helmet off. Solus appeared to anticipate that possibility, because he started to back away just as Vez was halfway towards him. He charged up another fireball in each hand, still reversing, then hurled the smaller fireballs. Vez saw them launched and braked himself, then cast his lighting like a net. It reached the fireballs with no delay. Vez clapped his hands again, his fingers now uncrossed. The lightning wrapped around the hot orbs, merging them into a single ball. The green then overlapped the solar orange. Discharges followed. The ball bulged from a muffled bang inside, then it formed into a small implosion and fizzled in on itself. Everyone above and below stared with disbelief. Solus stared at the dissipation spot, mouth agape. He looked at Vez and saw a smile across his short black beard.

"It would seem my power truly is on your level," Vez remarked. The Shade soldiers below began to cheer. Solus put an ugly look on his face at these sounds and words. He turned back and looked down at his own soldiers.

"Someone! Give me a blade!" Fite heard this and started to move for protest, but Vez halted her.

"He's within his right, Ginearal. Please come here and hand me one of yours." Fite thought for a moment and realized this was an unspoken term to this trial; a weapon was alright as long as it was asked for, not concealed. She urged her hornet to the king and unsheathed one of her sabers, then passed it to him. Quinley had flown down and retrieved a saber from a cavalryman. He came back up and handed it to Solus. Vez assumed a fencing position with legs straight and left arm behind his back, sword arm up. Solus kept his limbs spread wide, holding his own saber more like a cutlass.

They didn't circle each other this time. Now they were opting to flying slow to each other and crossing blades at just the right moment. Keeping their different poses, they inched closer to each other. The platform's jets were steady now. Vez urged it just a little more, so little that Solus couldn't detect it, and with a quick swing he made the first move. A silent en garde.

Solus met his light strike with a down-hand parry, then put just enough arm strength into swiping away. Vez brought his sword back then swung again. Solus parried upward this time. *Interesting. The man of sun and muscle can fight with finesse.* They parted again, then Solus attempted a lunge. Vez swatted it back. He returned with a light overhand. Cling. Block. Thrust again. Block. Swing. Parry. Both Rí and Laoch had strong footwork up in the air, even though one's standing ground seemed limited and the other had no ground at all. The back and forth crossing of the sabers was making them circle, and they were both unconscious of that. More and more of the soldiers below had their weapons down and their arms relaxed, watching the duel unfold. The Ginearals and Liam were the most fixated. Liam was holding onto the king's mask tight but he kept his eyes on the fight. Fite was focused, unblinking, looking for an opening that Vez could take. She wouldn't be able to indicate it to him.

As Vez continued to manage his footwork, he found himself rocking the platform slightly. Left and right like a pendulum. He wanted to look down and make sure that his feet were steady but knew that would cost him. He glanced closely at Solus' face; Solus seemed to be fighting calm, but the look on his face suggested fatigue. *No surprise. This is not his style of fighting after all. Can't let him relax. He relaxes enough he'll get a second wind to use his powers.* He blocked another swing, then clenched his right fist in a split second.

SHING! His double arm blades swung out and clamped the sabers, locking Solus' wrist in place.

"What're you…?" The jets came into Solus' earshot. The blades retracted. And the next thing Solus saw was the edge of the platform's base coming up toward his chin. A direct hit flung him backward, knocking his helmet off. It plummeted down to the field. Quinley formed a portal in the fall path and another above him. The helmet fell through one and came out the other. He caught it in both his hands. During this break, Vez reversed fast toward his Ginearals. Fite took the hint and met him to reclaim her sword. He then flew back forward towards Solus, who was making a recover. He was breathing heavy, and his lower lip was bloody. His crew cut was slick with sweat. He moved his mouth around a bit and then spit out a tooth. His eyes stared hard at Vez.

"Now we end this without any further hesitation! That is, if you've still got some energy in you," the king mocked. He presented his arm blades again. Solus growled and shot forward. Vez made a hopping motion but still kept his feet on the platform. The whole glider shifted up and arced, then it dived gracefully into Solus' fight path. He formed his prong again and charged up the lightning, then thrust out his arms, left on top of right.

"PRONG CANNON!" Vez shouted the words with little thought but total intent. The green bolts surged from his fingers to down the blades. Their metal amplified the lightning, and it fired down from the cutting edges to form a single chain bolt. It shot down fast and struck Solus on the right shoulder, knocking him off course. He staggered and flailed to regain balance. Once he settled, he caught a whiff of something burning. He looked down and saw that his embroidered symbol was singed.

"YEAGGGGGH!!!" He charged again, palms out and fireballs forming. "I'M GOING TO VAPORIZE YOU OFF THE FACE OF THIS LAND!" he bellowed. Vez made no reply. He just took aim and fired again. Another thick green bolt streaked toward Solus. He saw it and barrel-rolled away.

It cracked loud within his earshot. Solus chucked his left-hand fireball. Vez dodged it. Solus threw the right-hand one. Vez dodged it. Return fire with another prong blast. Solus spiraled fast towards him. He got in close before Vez could ready the Prong Cannon again. Vez unwrapped his arms and retracted his blades. He brought up his right leg in an immediate swing. His toe blades grazed across Solus' cheek, making him flinch.

"ENOUGH!" Solus raised his hand fast as he yelled and conjured a quick fireball. He flung it down hard.

WABOOOM! The platform exploded into pieces. Gasps sounded from below. Solus shot out of the smoke in the wrong direction. Wrong for Vez that is. Away from the Ginearals, who all took their reins and followed fast. Quinley saw them and flew after them, drawing his pistol once more.

"You will stop now and let this happen!"

"Think again!" Turnie wasn't having any of this. She swatted at Quinley with her spear, one handed. He retreated. Fite and Hurch kept course after Solus. The GreenSun had Vez by the throat and throwing punches with his free hand. They were only hitting Vez's wrist as he struggled to pry his iron grip. The world around both of them was rushing fast. In seconds it seemed to Vez that he was succeeding in freeing himself from Solus. But then he soon realized that his foe was letting go on his own volition. Why? He looked up and saw that pompous sneer again on Solus' bruised and cut face.

"The Rí dies today," he whispered with enough breath in his voice to sound confident. And before Vez could answer this, Solus shoved him into the open air. The next thing Vez saw was surging golden light all around him. It didn't look like the solar power but he felt it burn. Not his body, but his mind. He was frozen with panic and confusion. The light overwhelmed his eyes to the point where it was all he could see. He shut his eyes, seeing only red now instead of gold. Then it all went black, and he saw and heard no more.

EPILOGUE

Vez slowly opened his eyes. It may have been minutes or hours since he decided to do so. All that time he was waiting for the inevitable crash of his body to the ground. A crash that would likely kill him. But it never came. After the golden flash there was only silence. Silence and dark. Only noiseless floating.

With his eyes opened he found that he was no longer in the air; he was lying down. On something soft. A mattress. But this mattress was different from his own in his chamber back at the castle. It was even softer. Regardless, did the Ginearals come to his rescue in the heat of the moment?

He looked up at the ceiling. Instead of wood and stone he was looking at white plaster. This alarmed him. He became even more startled as he noticed that he felt lighter. He sat up and noticed that his armor was gone. In fact, his suit, his crown, even his prosthetics were gone! He brought his arms into view, then jumped back at what he saw. His hands were no longer clad in metal. They were flesh once more. But they were all wrong. The skin was not purple. It was white.

That was enough to make him scramble to his feet. He found himself sitting up on a bed that was very close to a wall (also plaster). He looked at his arms again. They were skinnier than before. His whole body felt leaner than it should have. He looked at his legs; they were skinny and white too. He brought up his hands to his ears and made himself jump once more. His ears did not feel sharp and pointed. They were smooth and round.

Vez spotted a mirror on the other side of the room, attached to the door. He stumbled to his feet and ran to it. The reflection that he faced was not his own. At first glance, he thought he was looking at an Earth. A skinny one like Liam. But this one had shorter hair. Yellow blonde. The eyes had white sclera and hazel irises. A little bloodshot. The face was somewhat gaunt but not a deathly sallow, with a pimply jawline. He had no beard but did have uneven stubble. The clothing he now wore was light. A gray t-shirt with a strange red and blue figure emblazoned on it. The figure had a mask on, with big white eyes. The shorts that Vez was wearing now were a darker gray, and they had two kinds of pockets. Small, open slit ones on the top, bigger ones with fastened flaps on the bottom. He was wearing plain white socks.

Now Vez surveyed the room, trying to subside any panic all the while. This room was smaller, enclosed. It was definitely not his apartment in the Last Cloch. There were shelves full of books he did not recognize. There was a desk to his right. It was cluttered with papers and writing implements. The implements themselves were not quills. He found himself breathing fast and heavy and proceeded to calm himself down. A challenge to do so. This room could be a prison for all he knew. He reached for the desk and felt around it. It was real, not an illusion. Suddenly, a knock on the door sounded.

"Adam!" said a muffled voice. It was male. He didn't recognize it. The knock came again.

"Adam, are you awake?" the voice asked, calmer. Vez had no idea what to do next. This name was unfamiliar to him. He soon realized that this Adam was the person in the mirror. The person that he was now. There would be no point protesting this. Whoever was on the other side would think him mad if he did so. His strategic mindset, the mindset of an effective king, was snapping back into action. He took a deep breath and went for the door, opening it without delay but not so fast. Standing in the doorway was a young man who was taller than him. He too looked like an Earth with rounded ears. He had a clean-shaven face and his black hair was formed into a faint, triangular wedge. He was wearing a pale-yellow dress shirt and gray pants. Those almost matched his own shorts.

"I didn't just wake you up, did I? You really shouldn't nap more than an hour. It'll disorient you for the rest of the day."

"Uh, yes… I shall keep that in mind." The young man shrugged a little.

"Did you actually sleep through that whole argument?" the stranger asked.

"Y-yes. I did manage that."

"Well, I'll say that's impressive. We never had a heavy fight with them before, but those two could scream if they wanted to."

"Eh, you mean…?"

"The Riel sisters, Adam. Kait and Cail. Our housemates. They just stormed out of the house when I put the kibosh on they're gaming. You were right to not get involved. Got better things to do anyway."

"Yes. I do have such." The young man gave an inquisitive look.

"You're talking funny there, Adam. I haven't heard you this articulate except on camera." Vez's eyes widened. *What is a camera? No, no. Can't ask him that. Must not look suspicious.*

"I… guess I was more out of it than I thought. The sudden awakening must have tussled my mind a bit. Unintended improvement is all." *Stupid fool, don't say that!*

"Well, how about we go down to the kitchen and get some water? You look thirsty."

"That… would be good." Vez jumped at the sound of a faint buzzing. *My swarms! They have found me! They are near!* He then saw the stranger remove a strange rectangular device from his pocket. His heart sank when he noticed that the buzzing was coming from that. The young man looked at the glowing face of the device and frowned.

"Real mature, Cailey," he muttered under his breath.

"Hey, Oliver! Is Adam up?" called a distant voice. A young woman. Another stranger. Oliver looked up from his phone.

"Yeah, he's up! We're coming down!" Oliver turned back to Adam. "Let's get that water, then maybe we can figure out what to do with Kait and Cail.

"That sounds reasonable. Lead on." Oliver gave him a different shaped look of inquiry, then began walking away with his eyes back on the message device. Vez clenched and unclenched his fists. He could feel internal panic rising in his head.

I must get out of here as soon as I can! I must get my body back to the way it was! He looked at his hands again. At least one thing of his being was still there; the wart on the base of his left pinky finger.

APPENDIX

The Kingdom of the Shades

King, Queen, and Council

- ❖ VEZ, King of the Shade Elves, the Hornet Rí
- ❖ SMAZEPH, Vez's wife and queen, a Danuc
- ❖ FITE, Ginearal that commands the Eaglaceal, a Shade
- ❖ HURCH, Ginearal that commands the Fiabhraceal, Fite's brother
- ❖ KAVANCHI, Ginearal that commands the Spandaceal, personal bodyguard of the king, a silent, full armored Gavi; called "The Croc in Pangolin's Armor"
- ❖ AAMJUNTA, Ginearal that commands the Faigceal, a decadently dressed warrior Gavi
- ❖ RUNKE, Ginearal that commands the Dofheiceal, a dwarf
- ❖ CROSTA, Ginearal that commands the Mioscaceal, a dwarf horseman
- ❖ TURNIE MAVE, Ginearal that commands the Sclabceal, an Earth Elf, former Laoch; known as "The Spinning Wheel", "The Wheel", "The Slaver", "The Brawn", "Red Mane", "The Traitor"

The Seven Swarms of the Tíorafaoi (Tyrant Hornets)

- The Eaglaceal, known as FearStings (Color: Vermillion)
- The Fiabhraceal, known as FeverStings (Color: Red)
- The Spandaceal, known as SlugStings (Color: Grey)
- The Faigceal, known as StarveStings (Color: Tan)
- The Dofheiceal, known as InvisiStings (Color: Clear)
- The Mioscaceal, sting power unknown (Color: Chartreuse)
- The Sclabceal, known as SlaveStings (Color: Pink)

Servants and Soldiers

- LORD ZHARVE, head of the Deshomino Yokei Arms Company, Smazeph's cousin
- AKA, Chief Engineer of Deshomino Yokei
- SAN, Deputy Chief Engineer of Deshomino Yokei
- SUMIKO, a Danuc servant
- JUN'ICHI, a Danuc servant
- AYA, a Danuc servant
- NIN, a Danuc servant
- BLARE, a Shade colonel, warden of the dungeon
- ULICES, a Shade lieutenant
- RAL, a Shade private, Aamjunta's orderly
- DR. CHIKA REN, Danuc medical officer

The Nation of the Earths

Cliar Base

- ❖ GENERAL ORTHUR REETH
- ❖ SGT. XANTHE TOLL
- ❖ PRIVATE BUí IRELAN
- ❖ PRIVATE GERT NORL
- ❖ PRIVATE SKYLARK REOITE
- ❖ PRIVATE MASON OCHTó
- ❖ PRIVATE ABRAM GROCER
- ❖ PRIVATE LIAM PAIRC

Fort Twoships

- ❖ 1ST LIEUTENANT LIAM BIRRSOVA
- ❖ PRIVATE LEIGH GILES
- ❖ PRIVATE BAY PEREGRINE

The Laochs

- ❖ SOLUS GREENSUN, leader of the Laochs and supreme commander of Fort Lightwing
- ❖ QUINLEY, Laoch of Fort Lightwing, known as the Portalmaster

AFTERWORD

Hello, dear readers! And welcome to the beginning of a new story that follows the world of "VR Nana" from a much different angle!

This was a most unexpected project, and like a lot of what I put into "VR Nana," it was influenced by a number of things. The biggest thing was how the character of Vez and his whole deal came to be. A year or two ago I was revisiting a personal favorite movie (one where a certain team of elemental warriors battle an army of spiders commanded by a king and queen). The one villain (the king) appeared menacing but in the end was a total fizzle (especially compared to the queen). A thought came into my head about what if you had such a king that was truly fearsome and competent, and instead of spiders he commands hornets. He also has a formidable entourage/war council, much like a certain undead light novel protagonist.

Originally, I wanted to give this series one of those long goofy titles (working title was "The High-Falutin' Hornet King Becomes a College Geek!"), but it just didn't fit. It would have also defeated the point of surprise for this character's journey if it was spelled out for everyone on the front cover! And to make it a real "surprise" companion, it was best to save the point of connection to "VR Nana" until the very end, as well as use a completely different structure and length for the story. Delving into a high fantasy style seemed to be the right course. Technology and motivations were elements I focused on to make this really stand out. That's why I thought it'd be kind of neat to have the Earths and Shades fight with Civil War-style weapons and uniforms. Instead of blue and gray we have green and burgundy. The history of this world and the continent of Uaine has been touched on. It'll be interesting to continue that and the overall worldbuilding with future volumes, while also building the intertwinement to "VR Nana."

As always, I dedicate this work to Nana Johnston, who always supported my creativity. Big thanks again to my Dad for his support and his editing, and to my Mom, my Aunt Anna, and my cousin Mike for their continued support. Lastly, thank you to those who've followed the "VR Nana" series so far and started this series, as well as anyone new who've started here. If you are new, "I'd recommend diving into "VR Nana".

Hope to see you around for the next volumes!

THANK YOU FOR YOUR PURCHASE!

WE HOPE YOU ENJOYED THE BOOK, AND
WILL LOOK FORWARD TO THE RELEASE OF

Hornet Rí

Volume 2

BE SURE TO ALSO CHECK OUT THE ORIGINAL
ONGOING SERIES

VR Nana